THE ANIMAL RIGHTS MOVEMENT

OTHER BOOKS IN THE
AMERICAN SOCIAL MOVEMENTS SERIES:

American Environmentalism
The Antinuclear Movement
The Antislavery Movement
The Civil Rights Movement
The Feminist Movement
The Sexual Revolution
The White Separatist Movement

AMERICAN
SOCIAL
MOVEMENTS

THE ANIMAL RIGHTS MOVEMENT

Kelly Wand, *Book Editor*

Daniel Leone, *President*
Bonnie Szumski, *Publisher*
Scott Barbour, *Managing Editor*
David Haugen, *Series Editor*

GREENHAVEN
PRESS®

™

GALE

San Diego • Detroit • New York • San Francisco • Cleveland
New Haven, Conn. • Waterville, Maine • London • Munich

LIBRARY OF CONGRESS CATALOGING-IN-PUBLICATION DATA

The animal rights movement / Kelly Wand, book editor.
    p. cm. — (American social movements)
  Includes bibliographical references and index.
  ISBN 0-7377-1046-2 (lib. bdg. : alk. paper) —
  ISBN 0-7377-1045-4 (pbk. : alk. paper)
    1. Animal rights movement—United States. I. Wand, Kelly. II. Series.
  HV4764 .A654 2003
  179.3—dc21
                                                                2002021476

CONTENTS

Chapter 1 • THE GROWTH OF THE MOVEMENT

by Keith Thomas
Until the twilight of the eighteenth century, the exploitation of nature was seen as the means by which
civilization had progressed. But with the rise of science came more critical consideration of humans'
integrated relationship with the environment.

by Rod Preece and Lorna Chamberlain
With the publication of his *Origin of Species*, Charles
Darwin changed the political climate of the budding animal rights movement for better and worse.
His research into the kinships between humans and
other animals led to increased empathy in some
quarters but resentment and religious indignation in
others.

by Craig Buettinger
Antivivisection societies, composed primarily of
Christian women, flourished in the 1890s. Their
Victorian idealism and approaches, however, were
no match for a highly organized and state-sponsored
biomedical establishment.

by James M. Jasper and Dorothy Nelkin
Numerous animal activist groups splintered off in
the 1950s and 1960s; their efforts produced the

movement's first real legislative results in the nation's history. Rifts began to develop, however, between "welfare" moderates and "rights" radicals over vegetarianism and the handling of stray cats and dogs.

Chapter 2 • LEADERS OF THE MOVEMENT

Chapter 3 • PHILOSOPHIES AND CRITICISMS

Chapter 4 • LANDMARK CASES

FOREWORD

Historians Gary T. Marx and Douglas McAdam define a social movement as "organized efforts to promote or resist change in society that rely, at least in part, on noninstitutionalized forms of political action." Examining American social movements broadens and vitalizes the study of history by allowing students to observe the efforts of ordinary individuals and groups to oppose the established values of their era, often in unconventional ways. The civil rights movement of the twentieth century, for example, began as an effort to challenge legalized racial segregation and garner social and political rights for African Americans. Several grassroots organizations— groups of ordinary citizens committed to social activism— came together to organize boycotts, sit-ins, voter registration drives, and demonstrations to counteract racial discrimination. Initially, the movement faced massive opposition from white citizens, who had long been accustomed to the social standards that required the separation of the races in almost all areas of life. But the movement's consistent use of an innovative form of protest—nonviolent direct action—eventually aroused the public conscience, which in turn paved the way for major legislative victories such as the Civil Rights Act of 1964 and the Voting Rights Act of 1965. Examining the civil rights movement reveals how ordinary people can use nonstandard political strategies to change society.

Investigating the style, tactics, personalities, and ideologies of American social movements also encourages students to learn about aspects of history and culture that may receive scant attention in textbooks. As scholar Eric Foner notes, American history "has been constructed not only in congressional debates and political treatises, but also on plantations and picket lines, in parlors and bedrooms. Frederick Douglass, Eugene V. Debs, and Margaret Sanger . . . are its architects as well as Thomas Jefferson and Abraham Lincoln." While not all

American social movements garner popular support or lead to epoch-changing legislation, they each offer their own unique insight into a young democracy's political dialogue.

Each book in Greenhaven's American Social Movements series allows readers to follow the general progression of a particular social movement—examining its historical roots and beginnings in earlier chapters and relatively recent and contemporary information (or even the movement's demise) in later chapters. With the incorporation of both primary and secondary sources, as well as writings by both supporters and critics of the movement, each anthology provides an engaging panoramic view of its subject. Selections include a variety of readings, such as book excerpts, newspaper articles, speeches, manifestos, literary essays, interviews, and personal narratives. The editors of each volume aim to include the voices of movement leaders and participants as well as the opinions of historians, social analysts, and individuals who have been affected by the movement. This comprehensive approach gives students the opportunity to view these movements both as participants have experienced them and as historians and critics have interpreted them.

Every volume in the American Social Movements series includes an introductory essay that presents a broad historical overview of the movement in question. The annotated table of contents and comprehensive index help readers quickly locate material of interest. Each selection is preceded by an introductory paragraph that summarizes the article's content and provides historical context when necessary. Several other research aids are also present, including brief excerpts of supplementary material, a chronology of major events pertaining to the movement, and an accessible bibliography.

The Greenhaven Press American Social Movements series offers readers an informative introduction to some of the most fascinating groups and ideas in American history. The contents of each anthology provide a valuable resource for general readers as well as for enthusiasts of American political science, history, and culture.

A Brief History of Animal Rights in America

Human concern for animals dates back many centuries. Compassion for other creatures is mentioned in texts as ancient as the Old Testament,[1] and recorded vegetarianism dates as far back as the Greek philosopher Pythagoras during the sixth century B.C. Even as late as the 1800s, European families shared living quarters with animals, with companion pets and horses often better fed than servants. But the first anti-cruelty statute on record was penned on American soil; in 1641 a Puritan minister in the Massachusetts Bay Colony, Nathanial Ward, drafted a document of ninety-six laws called the "Body of Liberties," which included the injunction that "no man shall exercise any tyranny or cruelty toward any brute creature which are usually kept for man's use."[2] Though this statute was invoked several times for mistreated oxen, the new continent was still mostly untamed wilderness, and concern for beasts of burden was rarely taken up by farmers in need of plowed fields.

The first serious organized efforts to improve humane treatment of animals did not begin until the late eighteenth century, among the English intelligentsia. In 1780 British philosopher Jeremy Bentham wrote his now famous inquiry, "The question is not can [animals] reason? Nor can they talk? But can they *suffer*?" Bentham, who often compared the status of animals with the plight of black slaves, spoke of a future when "the rest of animal creation may acquire those rights which never could have been withholden from them but by the hand of tyranny."[3] In 1809 Lord Thomas Erskine proposed the first recorded effort at animal welfare legislation: a bill prohibiting "bullbaiting," an age-old British mainstay that involved tethering a bull to a stake and taunting it to death with mastiff dogs and sharp sticks. Though the bill was killed repeatedly in the House of Commons, its mere existence suggested changing attitudes in the public sentiment.

What caused this sudden concern for "dumb brutes" to become suddenly acceptable? A variety of sociological forces contributed to this expansion of moral horizons, not all of which were altruistic. Pressure to eliminate cruel sports such as cockfighting and bullbaiting stemmed at least partly from a desire to mold less bloodthirsty citizens out of the workforce. Science and philosophy were also converging. Long-held philosophical assumptions such as dualism, the idea that the mind (or "immaterial soul") and body are separate substances and that only humans possess the former, were giving way to Darwin's evidence of genetic linkage between humans and their animal cousins.

But most of all, as would be the case again a century and a half later, the concept of rights for the oppressed was already in the air. It seems hardly coincidental that the evolution of the animal rights movement paralleled that of women's suffrage and the abolishment of slavery, nor that activists in one movement subscribed to them all.

MARTIN'S ACT AND THE BEGINNING OF SOCIAL CHANGE

The early 1800s showed isolated signs of rising concern for animal welfare in both England and the United States. The Reverend William Metcalfe established a vegetarian church in Philadelphia in 1817. In 1822 another English nobleman, Richard "Humanity Dick" Martin, drafted "An Act to Prevent the Cruel and Improper Treatment of Cattle," which would "punish people who wantonly and cruelly beat or ill-treated a horse, mare, gelding, mule, ass, ox, cow, heifer, steer, sheep, or other cattle by a fine of not more than five pounds or less than ten shillings, or imprisonment not exceeding three months."[4] This bill, unlike Erskine's, took no issue with established British forms of recreation; it was passed and was amended in 1835 to encompass stoning and beating cattle as well as dog- and cockfighting. A similar act was passed in Massachusetts the following year. Though such events hardly qualified as a formal movement in any sense of the word, the mistreatment of animals had inarguably become a popular object of debate.

Historian James Turner credits this steady upsurge to the shift of population to the cities, which left people feeling adrift from their rural past, and animals symbolized that lost past. The corrosive side effects of early industrialization—smokestacks, slums, all forms of physical misery—were so shocking to those who made the transition that it produced displaced (some would say enhanced) compassion in many forms: the drive for universal public education, child labor laws, penal reform, education of the deaf and blind, the founding of hospitals, housing for the poor, and animal rights legislation.

Even so, nearly forty years elapsed between the formation of England's first humanitarian organization, the Society for the Prevention of Cruelty to Animals (rechristened the RSPCA—the R indicating *Royal*—in 1840 following the endorsement of Queen Victoria), and the founding of its American counterpart.

HENRY BERGH AND THE FOUNDING OF THE ASPCA

The founder of the first anticruelty society in the United States was Henry Bergh, the son of an affluent shipbuilder. President Abraham Lincoln had appointed him secretary of legation in St. Petersburg, a post he left in 1864 when the Russian climate, and perhaps the tedium of his duties, proved too much for him to stomach. While in Russia, he witnessed accounts of animal cruelty that left an indelible impression on him, among them peasants' abusiveness toward horses, an animal for which Bergh held special sympathy. Whatever the scope of his encounters, it was enough to encourage him to visit the RSPCA headquarters in London on his return trip home. Bergh was greatly moved by the institution's methods, drive, and mere existence and it fostered in him hopes of founding a similar institution in his home country. Returning to New York, Bergh sought and, in April 1866, secured an official charter for the American Society for the Prevention of Cruelty to Animals (ASPCA). Its short-term goal was to "improve the lives of farm and work animals in New York City" and eventually to "alleviate pain, fear, and suffering in all animals."[5] More than fifty of New York City's dignitaries and elite citizens signed this document, among them millionaire John Jacob Astor Jr. and journalist Horace Greeley. Bergh became the group's leader, figurehead, and chief enforcer as well as a visible celebrity for his cause in Victorian-era New York City.

In the face of frequent ridicule and occasional death threats, Bergh and the embryonic ASPCA were responsible for convincing the New York State legislature in person and in writing to pass the nation's first citywide anticruelty laws. They also successfully demanded the placement of drinking fountains for horses throughout the city and housed the first pet ambulances to ferry wounded horses to medical facilities. Moreover, the ASPCA was in charge of actually enforcing the laws for which they had lobbied. Bergh himself saw to the prosecution of criminal offenses and was unintimidated by threats of reprisal from the powerful opponents with which he was constantly butting heads, including circuses and meat distributors. The first such arrest was that of a butcher for tying the legs of calves and piling them into an overcrowded cart; his punishment was a ten-dollar fine and a day in jail. Bergh and the ASPCA's efforts produced hundreds more convictions in the months and years to come, including indictments for cockfighting and for the protracted whipping of livestock.

The example set by Bergh inspired others. In 1868 a Boston attorney, George T. Angell, horrified by a forty-mile horse race that claimed the lives of both of the competing animals, founded the Massachusetts Society for the Prevention of Cruelty to Animals. Other individuals, including Emily Appleton and Caroline Earle White of Philadelphia, also held meetings with Bergh and, heartened by his manner, went on to found similar, more religious-based societies for animal welfare, which in the passing months came like Bergh's to boast members of distinguished social prominence. Despite their similar acronyms, each of the groups operated separately and sometimes differed in their aims and methods. Angell's views were more moderate than Bergh's, favoring humane education over the acts of civil disobedience and political lobbying Bergh employed.

More and more groups followed, the majority of them adopting Angell's passive techniques. The largest of these was the American Humane Association (AHA), founded in Washington, D.C., in 1877. The AHA's goals were much broader than those of its predecessors, equally promoting the welfare of children as well as animals and making the passage of child labor laws one of its main priorities. By the turn of the century, humane organizations with paying memberships throughout the United States numbered in the hundreds.

UPHILL BATTLES OF THE FIRST ANTIVIVISECTIONISTS

Experimentation on animals had proliferated throughout Europe as late as the 1830s, including dissections of live cats and dogs for French and English medical students. Such practices drew so many squeamish detractors, especially among the English students themselves, that in 1862 the RSPCA successfully lobbied for the use of anesthesia during "painful experiments involving the use of animals."[6]

In America during the same decade, vivisection was less common, partly because American science had yet to catch up with the European scene. Bergh and Angell opposed animal experimentation in all forms and had tried in vain to help get legislation passed curtailing the mass roundup of dogs for experimental use. (One group of medical practitioners in Philadelphia had tried in 1871 to acquire dogs from the Pennsylvania chapter of the SPCA but was rebuffed.) In 1882 Caroline Earle White founded the nation's first institution dedicated to lobbying for the regulation of animal use in sci-

entific research, the American Antivivisection Society (AAVS).
The medical establishment, spearheaded by the thirty-five-
year-old American Medical Association (AMA), responded by
launching a countercampaign in 1884 insisting that experimentation on animals was the most useful way of acquiring
medical knowledge and assiduously thwarted every reform
proposed by White's group to regulate the sale, transportation,
and use of animals for medical research, ensuring the defeat of
any bill before it reached Capitol Hill. With nothing left to
lose, the AAVS grew increasingly hawkish in its rhetoric and
began crusading for total abolition, but it met with little public or political support. It was difficult to argue against the usefulness of animals in research coming so closely on the heels
of French researcher Louis Pasteur's "germ theory" of disease,
which had led to vaccines for anthrax and rabies, all derived
from studies of deliberately infected animals.

The antivivisectionists kept trying anyway. In 1894 Angell
and the MSPCA managed to help get a law passed prohibiting the exhibition of vivisection practices in Massachusetts
public schools. Two years later they managed to persuade
Michigan representative James McMillan to propose a bill to
regulate vivisection in the District of Columbia, but the AMA

Louis Pasteur developed life-saving vaccines by using animals in his research.

and a cartel of scientists and physicians helped shoot it down in the House.

Things came to a head in 1908 when the defenders of animal research rallied to form their own propaganda organization, the Council on Defense of Medical Research. The council's policies on both the political and educational fronts were consistently effective, even as the antivivisectionists, already reeling from the deaths of their motivational leaders Bergh and Angell, foundered. Widening rifts within the antivivisectionist movement itself did not help either. Some, like the AAVS, still favored strict abolition, others advocated a more gradual campaign. A few even tried to repudiate Pasteur's germ theory, claiming it was a pseudoscientific excuse to inflict fresh torments on animal subjects for financial gain. Neurologist Charles Loomis Dana counterattacked with his theory of "zoophilpsychosis," a form of mental illness he claimed afflicted women in particular because of their mental and physical inferiority and which took the form of heightened concern for animals.

If anything, the early antivivisectionist movement only helped to consolidate the medical establishment against what it saw as sentimentalized interference with crucial research. To this day, those attempting to discredit the animal rights movement often adopt the nearly century-old argument that animal rights lobbyists are by definition misanthropic, respecting the lives of animals over people, although, as mentioned, most activist organizations included children under their umbrella and tended to be equally reactionary to oppression in any of its forms. The final nail in the antivisectionist coffin was the formal excommunication issued by the more mainstream animal welfare groups. In 1900 the AHA and other groups convened and officially withdrew all support for the antivivisection cause. Even the ASPCA, following Bergh's death in 1888, took pains to unlimber itself of its own founder's principles and concentrate instead on the less contested issue of cat and dog overpopulation.

With the outbreak and aftermath of World War I, whatever

national attention the movement had thus far enjoyed was dwarfed by what were seen as larger, indisputably human concerns. A token antivivisection measure placed on the 1920 California ballot was thrown out by a two-to-one margin. Another bill intended to prohibit the use of dogs in research in Washington, D.C., never made it as far as the Senate.

THE PRICE OF FREEDOM

Wars, especially ones popular on the home front, tend to be disruptive for social reforms. The first generation to be born and raised in modern cities had come into power, and America's focus during the early twentieth century shifted toward mass industrialization and urbanization, whatever the cost. The years from 1920 to the 1950s were a period of stasis for the movement. Institutionalized animal research swelled, along with fatter government funding. The field of scientific research had been given a blank check for its significant contributions in winning both world wars. Studying the effects of radioactivity and new poisonous gases required a constant influx of living mammal specimens.

Agribusiness thrived too, more than ever. Meat was now the second-largest industry in the United States, second only to that of automobiles. The advent of modern "factory farming" led to enormous increases in the breeding, confinement, and slaughter of animals for food, which came with attendant overcrowding and disease problems. New technologies were designed to combat the results of these new stresses, such as chicken debeaking machines, feather pluckers, and chemical additives meant to provide faster weight gain in livestock.

The public remained ignorant of such innovations, and humane societies not only took little interest but actively cooperated in the selling of pound animals to research laboratories throughout the 1950s. The only marks of progress for animal rights in this decade were the 1958 passage of the Humane Slaughter Act proposed by Senator Hubert Humphrey, which required meatpackers to anesthetize or "stun" all food-producing animals prior to slaughter, and the Wild Horses Act of 1959, which banned the "capture, branding, harassment, or killing" of wild horses and burros.

"Animal Rights" vs. "Animal Welfare"

If the increased clamor from animal rights activists during the 1960s came to be drowned out by myriad other causes or seen simply as a fringe offshoot of the environmental movement, it was at least a substantial upgrade from the apathy of the preceding decades. Seemingly overnight, a number of new organizations sprang up, fiercer and more systematic than their forbears. These fledgling groups were quick to distinguish themselves as being concerned with "animal rights," which refers to the abolition of animal exploitation of any type by humans. They rejected the cause of "animal welfare," the mere regulation of such exploitation, espoused by the venerable and better-funded humane organizations. Relations between "rights" groups and "welfarists" ranged from the tart to the vitriolic, with both camps claiming that the other did animals more harm than good. The new grassroots groups argued that the welfare organizations diverted badly needed funds to their own salaries; the latter charged that the guerrilla tactics of the former hurt the image of the movement as a whole. Friction between the two camps persists to this day.

Ironically, welfarist groups proved a fertile breeding ground for rights recruits. In 1954 American Humane Association member Helen Jones, disaffected with what she saw as the AHA's overly conservative stances on many issues, left to found her own organization, the Humane Society of the United States (HSUS). The HSUS claims to be the largest animal protection organization in the world with a staff of more than two hundred and a constituency of over 3 million. Its charter is to "prevent suffering and abuse to animals," and it pursues this objective through education, investigation, litigation, and legislation. The HSUS is not opposed to "legitimate and appropriate"[7] utilization of animals for meat, leather, and wool, though they oppose the use of fur. In 1957 Jones defected from her own HSUS to establish the more radical International Society for

Animal Rights. Its goal is to end the use of all animals in research by sponsoring seminars, organizing demonstrations, drafting legislation, and promoting development of animal rights law.

One of the most effective groups to emerge from the 1960s was Fund for Animals (FFA), founded by author Cleveland Amory in 1967. The agenda of FFA, whose motto is "We Speak For Those Who Can't," rather uniquely straddled that of welfare and rights, concentrating on the protection of wildlife, though its broader goal is to eradicate cruelty to animals. The group successfully lobbied for the passage of the Marine Mammal Protection Act in 1972, the federal Endangered Species Act the following year, and, in 1979, established the Black Beauty Ranch, a two-hundred-acre stretch of Texas farmland initially purchased to provide sanctuary for 577 feral burros the U.S. Park Service had planned on shooting in the Grand Canyon. Since then the Black Beauty Ranch has served as refuge for thousands of animals rescued by the fund.

The 1960s also saw articles detailing animal abuses attaining national exposure in mainstream periodicals. In 1965 a Pennsylvania family, the Lakavages, learned after the disappearance of their dalmatian, Pepper, of an animal dealer's arrest for overloading his truck with dogs. This trail led to an uncooperative dealer in New York, who refused to help them find their dog even when New York representative Joseph Resnick intervened on their behalf. Finally, the news surfaced that Pepper had already been sold, "used up," and cremated at a New York hospital. This incident and others similar to it were reported in both *Reader's Digest* and *Life* magazine (an article in the latter was entitled "Concentration Camp for Dogs"). Resnick was able to pass his Laboratory Animal Welfare Act in 1966, which, though conservative in tone (it dealt solely with the licensing of animal dealers and improving conditions for their living cargo), at least signaled a time of reform was at hand.

SUCCESS AT STOPPING VIOLENCE

The concept of rights for animals, which seemed such a natural extension of the civil rights and antiwar movements, was also becoming a hot topic across college campuses. In 1971 Richard Ryder, the new head of the RSPCA, first coined the term *speciesism*, the notion that it was unethical to assume human priorities superceded the lives and wants of other creatures. Then, in 1975, Peter Singer's book *Animal Liberation* was published. Widely considered the bible of the animal rights movement, the volume continues thirty years later to be a key recruiting tool for many of the grassroots animal rights groups. Singer's writing was unsentimental, readable, impassioned, and thorough. Taking the lead from Ryder and Tom Regan (whose first articles on vegetarianism appeared around the same time), Singer graphically detailed the conditions of animals in factory farms and research laboratories and explained why such exploitation was ethically indefensible. He backed up his position with examples of legal double standards, moral analogies, hard statistics, and damning quotes by those he labeled as the oppressors, namely the meat industry and animal researchers.

In the year before the publication of *Animal Liberation*, Singer taught a course on the subject at New York University. Among the attendees was a former merchant seaman, union activist, and high school teacher named Henry Spira. Spira wrote, "Singer described a universe of more than 4 billion animals being killed each year in the USA alone. Their suffering is intense, widespread, expanding, systematic, and socially sanctioned. And the victims are unable to organize in defence of their own interests."[8]

Spira also thought the animal movement was currently "going nowhere":

> The standard strategy of animal welfare groups seemed to be to send out literature saying: "Look how the animals are suffering. Send us money!" And then, next month, the group would use the money to send out to the converted more descriptions of atrocities in order to generate more money to mail more horror stories. Moreover, interest was focussed largely on the 1 per cent of animal suffering most conducive to sentimental fund-raising efforts—that of dogs, cats, seals, horses and primates. Thus the 99 per cent of an-

imal pain suffered by animals in factory farms and in the laboratories, by species who did not make it on the popularity list, was ignored.[9]

Spira planned his first target carefully: the American Museum of Natural History in New York, which was performing federal–tax-funded studies of sex drive aberrations in mutilated cats. After the museum refused Spira's offers to parley, he acquired the reports of the museum's progress under the Freedom of Information Act and wrote a detailed exposé in a Manhattan weekly paper. Then he and a crowd began picketing the museum every weekend for a year, along the way garnering the support of New York congressman Ed Koch. Eventually the museum caved in and the experiments ceased. Spira had succeeded where others had failed: He had not simply protested but had managed to actually stop the abuse. Even other scientists had sided with him, along with Koch and 120 other congressmen. The significance lay not in the number of animals saved but in the prominence and visibility of his target, and in his victory itself.

Spira then went on to stage one successful campaign after another: the repeal of laws that allowed researchers to seize stray dogs and cats from pounds, the abolition of the Draize test (which pharmaceutical companies used to test the toxicity of new products in the eyes of albino rabbits), and the LD50, which measured the fatality of various products in hundreds of animals per test.

PETA AND ALF

Meanwhile, other organizations were materializing, the two most high profile of which were People for the Ethical Treatment of Animals (PETA) and the Animal Liberation Front (ALF). The cofounders of PETA were Alex Pacheco, who at one time had considered a career in the priesthood but became converted to animal rights after touring a slaughterhouse, and Ingrid Newkirk, who had borne witness as a child in India to much animal suffering and later worked for the Washington

Humane Society/SPCA. There she met Pacheco, who had just finished reading *Animal Liberation* and gave her a copy. In 1981 Pacheco found work as a volunteer for Dr. Edward Taub at the Institute for Behavioral Research (IBR) in Silver Spring, Maryland, where his functions included administering pain-response tests on experimental monkeys who had been subjected to a variety of physical mutilations and negligible hygienic conditions. In the following weeks, Pacheco covertly brought numerous people in professional fields by night into the lab as eyewitnesses for any future testimony, and he eventually orchestrated a police raid of the premises. The ensuing court case gained national attention, as did the fact that the IBR had been receiving government funding from the National Institutes of Health. Though Taub was eventually exonerated for most of his crimes and the monkeys were eventually returned to the custody of researchers and "sacrificed," public shock over Pacheco's testimony, verified by so many sources, gave the movement unprecedented credibility and sympathy.

The Animal Liberation Front began in Britain in 1972. Originally christened "Band of Mercy," two students named Ronnie Lee and Cliff Goodman began conducting raids on fox-hunt kennels in England. Raids on other labs followed, as many as ten in 1976. The first ALF action undertaken in the United States was in 1979, when three women and a man disguised in white smocks posed as faculty members at the New York University Medical Center and successfully removed a cat, two guinea pigs, and two dogs from the premises after the facility had closed for the day. Subsequent forays involved the destruction of lab equipment, arson, and other vandalism, but spokespeople for the group, which is shrouded in so much secrecy that members claim not to know each other (initiation into the group consists of orchestrating a raid and attributing it to ALF), state that harming a living thing would violate all of their principles, as opposed to property damage.

ALF is viewed with ambivalence by the other organizations, including PETA, which has actively collaborated with ALF and which has served on occasion as a sort of public relations front. ALF's guerrilla methods obviously erode public sympathy for the movement, but the group's track record of animals freed and its ability to secure key evidence that could not be acquired any other way is impossible to deny. One example of this was *Unnecessary Fuss,* the name of the documentary edited from sixty hours of videotape stolen from the laboratory of Thomas Gennarelli at the University of Pennsylvania on May 28, 1984. Gennarelli had been awarded an annual budget of $1 million in federal grants to study head injuries, money he had spent in the development of a device that could be cemented to the heads of baboons before delivering blows of varying intensity to the skull (the device, in fact, had to be removed by hammer and chisel, nullifying any possible results). A few animal rights groups, including the Fund for Animals, had condemned the experiments and talked with Gennarelli, but thay had been refused inspection of the lab. ALF broke in, took the tapes, and gave them to PETA, which in turn used them to produce *Unnecessary Fuss.* Though the Department of Health and Human Services initially refused to view the tape, PETA persevered, taking its case to Congress and forcing its members to watch the documentary footage. Eventually Gennarelli's funding was cut and the tests dismantled.

During the 1980s other organizations bloomed, including George Cave and Dana Trans-Species, Farm Animal Reform Movement, and the Rutgers Animal Rights Law Clinic, headed by Gary Francione, which focused on the legal end of the movement, including an ongoing project to establish civil rights for great apes. Within twenty years, over fifty thousand animal rights groups existed in the United States with a paying membership.

THE FUTURE OF THE MOVEMENT

The gestalt shift in public consciousness that Peter Singer and Henry Spira labored for has yet to transpire. Americans still enjoy eating meat and find animal testing for science and corporate industry morally acceptable, and the numbers of animals used in agriculture and research grows by the billions every year. Yet animal rights organizations flourish worldwide, new literature continues to be written on the subject, and most colleges feature the issue prominently in their philosophy courses. As Singer once wrote:

Human beings have the power to continue to oppress other species forever. . . . Will our tyranny continue, proving that morality counts for nothing when it clashes with self-interest, as the most cynical of poets and philosophers have always said? Or will we rise to the challenge and prove our capacity for genuine altruism by ending our ruthless exploitation of the species in our power, not because we are forced to do so by rebels, but because we recognize that our position is morally indefensible? The way in which we answer this question depends on the way in which each one of us, individually, answers it.[10]

NOTES

1. Deuteronomy 22:10 reads, "Thou shalt not plow with an ox and an ass together," theoretically for the benefit of the ass's shorter legs. There are numerous other examples, although the text is fairly emphatic about animals' role of servitude to man.

2. Quoted in Lawrence Finsen and Susan Finsen, *The Animal Rights Movement in America: From Compassion to Respect*. New York: Twayne, 1994, p. 42.

3. Jeremy Bentham, *An Introduction to the Principles of Morals and Legislation.* 1823. Reprint, New York: Hafner, 1948, chapter 17, section 1.

4. Quoted in Finsen and Finsen, *The Animal Rights Movement in America*, p. 31.

5. Quoted in Harold D. Guither, *Animal Rights: History and Scope of a Radical Social Movement.* Carbondale: Southern Illinois University Press, 1998, p. 36.

6. Quoted in Peter French, *Antivivisection and Medical Science in Victorian Society.* Princeton, NJ: Princeton University Press, 1975, p. 24.

7. Quoted in Guither, *Animal Rights,* p. 41.

8. Henry Spira, *In Defense of Animals*, ed. Peter Singer. New York: Basil Blackwell, 1985, p. 196.

9. Spira, *In Defense of Animals*, p. 197.

10. Peter Singer, *Animal Liberation.* New York: Avon Books, 1975, p. 247.

THE GROWTH
OF THE
MOVEMENT

AMERICAN
SOCIAL
MOVEMENTS

The First Vegetarians

KEITH THOMAS

Though abstinence from meat-eating can be traced back to such Greek philosophers as Seneca and Pythagoras, vegetarianism did not become a topic of serious debate until the mid–seventeenth century. England, once a nation that preferred its meat undercooked, underwent a philosophical metamorphosis when an increasing number of individuals began questioning man's right to subjugate nature in general and slaughter animals for food in particular. According to author Keith Thomas the first serious raising of such questions, though resulting in little change in the national diet, would have a lasting impact on the way people saw themselves in relation to other creatures. Keith Thomas was educated at Balliol College, Oxford. His other works include *Religion and the Decline of Magic*.

B y the later seventeenth century man's right to kill animals for food was being widely debated. The vegetarian teachings of [the Greek writers] Plutarch and Porphyry were well known to the educated, while Pythagoras's moral objections to meat-eating (based on his belief in the kinship of all animate nature) gained wide currency through successive translations of Ovid's *Metamorphoses*. In his version of 1700, [poet John] Dryden interpolated the ringing lines

> Take not away the life you cannot give:
> For all things have an equal right to live.

Along with these conscientious objections to meat-eating went more practical considerations. Later-seventeenth-century scientists like Walter Charleton, John Ray and John Wallis were much impressed by the suggestion that human anatomy,

Excerpted from *Man and the Natural World: A History of the Modern Sensibility*, by Keith Thomas (New York: Pantheon Books, 1983). Copyright © 1983 by Keith Thomas. Reprinted with permission.

particularly the teeth and intestines, showed that man had not originally been intended to be carnivorous. This argument subsequently provided additional support for the view that meat-eating was 'unnatural'. Many scientific writers also felt, very reasonably, that the heavy meat diet which was every Englishman's ideal was distinctly unhealthy. As one of them put it in 1721, 'It is that dreadful mixture of the souls . . . of so many thousand animals, destroyed to pamper one, that raises that terrible war in the blood which has made it a prey to such distempers as have baffled the skill of the most learned physicians'. A simple diet would keep the blood free of 'noxious juices' and conduce to a longer life. John Evelyn wrote a tract to prove that it was possible 'to live on wholesome vegetables, both long and happily', while the naturalist Edward Bancroft agreed that 'not only humanity, but self-interest, conspire to engage us at least to abridge the quantity of animal food which at present we devour with so much avidity'. In 1780 the philosopher Adam Ferguson was restored to health by following a 'Pythagorean course of diet'. The notion that meat was unhealthy thus became central to much later vegetarian teaching. Beef tea, it would be claimed, had killed more people than had Napoleon; and no vegetarian had bad breath. . . .

'Taking away the lives of animals, in order to convert them into food', thought the philosopher David Hartley in 1748, 'does great violence to the principles of benevolence and compassion. This appears from the frequent hard-heartedness and cruelty found amongst those persons whose occupations engaged them in destroying animal life, as well as from the uneasiness which others feel in beholding the butchery of animals'. 'The trade of a butcher', agreed [economist] Adam Smith, 'is a brutal and an odious business'. In Victorian times the slaughtermen were frequently said by social investigators to be the most demoralized class of all. No wonder that it was widely believe in the early modern period that butchers were ineligible for jury service in capital cases, owing to their cruel inclinations. There seems to have been no legal authority for this notion, but it was held throughout the seventeenth and eighteenth centuries by scores of commentators who should have known better.

By the beginning of the eighteenth century, therefore, all the arguments which were to sustain modern vegetarianism were in circulation: not only did the slaughter of animals have a brutalizing effect upon the human character, but the consumption of meat was bad for health; it was physiologically unnatural; it made men cruel and ferocious; and it inflicted untold suffering upon man's fellow-creatures. By the end of the century these arguments had been supplemented by an economic one: stock-breeding was a wasteful form of agriculture compared with arable farming, which produced far more food per acre. . . .

The early vegetarians thus made little appeal to the masses. Their inspiration was often literary, many claiming to have been converted by reading the arguments of Pythagoras or Plutarch. They wrote at a time when meat was still a precious luxury for many people and consequently a matter of status. In attacking roast beef they were hurling themselves against a cherished national symbol as well as against the weight of medical opinion, which continued to insist that some flesh intake was necessary to human health. Their cause was also hindered by its association with unfashionable dissenting groups. It is true that many kinds of religion were represented among the early vegetarians: Thomas Forster (1789–1860) was a Catholic, Lewis Gompertz a Jew; and Joseph Ritson was an atheist. But heterodox sects like the Quakers, the Bible Christians, the Swedenborgians and the Behmenists (later Theosophists) were disproportionately prominent. Inevitably the 'Pythagoreans' tended to be regarded as cranks and eccentrics by their contemporaries.

Nevertheless, they offered a notable challenge to conventional practice, and one to which official thought no longer had a ready answer. . . . By the end of the eighteenth century [the] claim that animals were made only for man's use was still being advanced, but it no longer carried general assent. Very soon, it would disappear almost altogether.

THE DEBATE INTENSIFIES

Undaunted, many utilitarian thinkers continued to argue that to kill animals for human food was wholly consistent with benevolence and virtue, so long as the beasts were carefully looked after during their lifetime and slaughtered with the minimum of cruelty. Animals, they urged, could not anticipate their deaths and they felt no terror. If beasts were not killed for food, maintained [writer and philosopher] John Lawrence in 1798, they would overstock the earth; so 'in numberless cases' it was 'an act of mercy to take their lives'. Moreover, as the Nonconformist Philip Doddridge pointed out, many people subsisted by breeding and selling cattle; what would happen to their livings if the custom of eating flesh were suddenly laid aside?

But it was no longer enough to say that cows and sheep would never have been bred in the first place if they were not to be slaughtered, for, as [critic and lexicographer] Dr Johnson observed in 1776, 'the question is whether animals who endure such sufferings of various kinds, for the service and entertainment of man, would accept of existence upon the terms on which they have it'. In the eighteenth century defenders of meat-eating found themselves increasingly forced back upon the mandate of the Old Testament. The right to slaughter for food, remarked [Scottish philosopher] Francis Hutcheson, was 'so opposite to the natural compassion of the human heart that one cannot think an express grant of it by revelation was superfluous'. Without the explicit authority of scripture, thought [theologian] William Paley, man's right to kill beasts for meat would be difficult if not impossible to justify. Ever since the 1680s, when [author] Thomas Tryon questioned the legitimacy of meat-eating, it had been biblical precedent upon which the defenders of the status quo had based their case. But in a secular world arguments founded on scripture alone would prove increasingly unimpressive. As Hutcheson shrewdly observed, if there was force to the humanitarian argument against meat-eating, then any grant by revelation of the right to slaughter would appear that much more incredible.

All that remained was the [Thomas] Hobbesian view, justifying the human species in doing anything it felt necessary for its survival. The rights which brutes had over us, declared [Dutch philosopher Baruch] Spinoza, we had over them. The objection to killing animals was 'based upon an empty superstition and womanish tenderness, rather than upon sound reason'. Civilization would be impossible if humanity acted justly towards nature; man could not survive without being a predator. This was the argument which overcame [author and statesman] Lord Chesterfield's scruples about meat-eating. 'Upon serious reflection I became convinced of its legality, from the general order of nature, who has instituted the universal preying upon the weaker as one of her first principles'. 'Philosophy', remarked David Hartley, 'has of late discovered such numberless orders of small animals in parts of diet formerly esteemed to be void of life, and such an extension of life into the vegetable kingdom, that we seem under the perpetual necessity, either of destroying the lives of some of the creatures, or of perishing ourselves'. The whole of nature, agreed [naturalist] Erasmus Darwin, was 'one great slaughter-house'. Anyway, man was a superior species and his interests should come first.

OUT OF SIGHT, OUT OF MIND

The brutal realism of this view conflicted sharply with the principles of benevolence and good nature to which it was now customary to pay lip-service. As a contemporary wrote of Joseph Ritson, 'to follow his plan of abstinence were absurd, and nearly impossible; yet it is surely a disagreeable necessity which drives us to form part of a system where . . . the powerful exist by preying on the weak'. John Tweddell (1769–99), a Cambridge classical scholar who gave up eating flesh on conscientious grounds, declared himself 'persuaded we have no other right, than the right of the strongest, to sacrifice to our monstrous appetites the bodies of living things, of whose qualities and relations we are ignorant'. No wonder the vegetarians were so confident that future ages would come to share their view of meat-eating as a hideous barbarity.

Meanwhile they were contemptuous of the sentimentalists, able to eat, yet unable to kill, particularly when previously acquainted with the animal concerned. As [physician and satirist Bernard de] Mandeville observed in 1714, there were now many meat-eaters who would themselves have been reluctant to wring a chicken's neck. When the second Duke of Montagu was talking to a visitor at Boughton, a flock of sheep went past. 'The duke admired the prettiness, the simplicity, the innocence of the animals', but confessed that 'when by chance he saw 'em killing one, he turned away his head and could not bear to look'. This was the humbug denounced by the poet Nathaniel Bloomfield:

Well might he who eats the flesh of lambs
. . .
Boast his humanity, and say 'My hand
Ne'er slew a lamb;' and censure as a crime
The butcher's cruel, necessary trade.

In 1756 [clergyman and naturalist] Gilbert White planted four lime trees at Selborne between his house and the butcher's yard opposite, 'to hide the sight of blood and filth'. His action symbolized a growing effort, not to abolish slaughter-houses, but to hide them from the public gaze. Dr Johnson, who had 'a kind of horror of butchering', said 'he was afraid there were slaughter-houses in more streets of London than one supposes'. Even in Elizabethan England there were people who were too 'squeamish' to see animals killed. By 1714 Mandeville could write of the growing aversion to animal slaughter that 'in this behaviour methinks there appears something like a consciousness of guilt'. In the past it had been customary to serve pigs, calves, hares and rabbits at the table with their heads attached, but around the end of the eighteenth century there seems to have been a growing tendency to conceal the slaughtered creature's more recognizable features. 'Animals that are made use of as food', wrote [critic and essayist] William Hazlitt in 1826, 'should either be so small as to be imperceptible, or else we should . . . not leave the form standing to reproach us with our gluttony and cruelty. I hate to see a rabbit trussed, or a hare brought to the table in the form which it occupied while living'. Killing animals for food was now an activity about which an increasing number of people felt furtive or uneasy. The concealment of slaughter-houses from the public eye had become a necessary device to avoid too blatant a clash between material facts and private sensibilities.

The Influence of Darwin on Animal Rights

ROD PREECE AND LORNA CHAMBERLAIN

Charles Darwin's works, including *The Origin of Species*, proved a mixed blessing to the budding animal-rights movement, according to Rod Preece and Lorna Chamberlain. Though he asserted genetic linkage between man and other mammals, especially primates, his "survival of the fittest" doctrine only further supported the notions of man's superiority and entitlement. Rod Preece is a professor of political science at Wilfrid Laurier University and author of *Animals and Nature: Cultural Myths, Cultural Realities*. Lorna Chamberlain is the executive director of the London Humane Society.

In 1859 Charles Darwin published his *Origin of Species*. By common consent among most animal supporters it was the book which presaged a revolution in human thinking about our relationship to other animals. For example, Michael W. Fox tells us with perhaps some exaggeration that, "As the concept of human superiority is, as Charles Darwin emphasized, logically and ethically untenable, then the only grounds for contending that it is humankind's right to exploit animals are based on custom and utility." Even more significant for our understanding of our biological and evolutionary relationship to other animals were Darwin's *Descent of Man* (1871) and *The Expression of Emotions in Man and Animals* (1872).

Important as Charles Darwin's writing was, it should be understood both that his theories were not quite so novel as

Excerpted from *Animal Welfare and Human Values,* by Rod Preece and Lorna Chamberlain (Waterloo, Canada: Wilfrid Laurier University Press, 1993). Copyright © 1993 by Wilfrid Laurier University Press. Reprinted with permission.

is sometimes imagined and that some of the consequences of Darwin's ideas were in some respects quite detrimental to the animal realm. Moreover, Darwin did not escape the limitations of prevailing scientism quite as completely as his admirers suggest.

Charles Darwin's grandfather, Erasmus Darwin, published his *Zoonomia* in parts from 1794–96. In it he explained organic life according to evolutionary principles, and it was on the basis of these findings that Charles Darwin began collecting his natural history data during his five years as naturalist aboard the *Beagle*. Evolutionary concepts can be found among a number of classical Greek authors including Thales, Empedocles, Anaximander—who deemed humans to be descended from fish—and Aristotle but from Roman times until the middle of the eighteenth century the Christian belief in the special creation of human and each other species held predominant sway. The great Swedish botanist and taxonomist Carolus Linnaeus, in his late–eighteenth-century writings, showed a clear indication of his acceptance of the idea of the mutability of species; and at around the same time the French naturalist Comte du Buffon was noting that use and/or disuse influenced the retention or obsolescence of vertebrate organs. It was, however, Buffon's naturalist associate Jean Lamarck who first developed a thoroughgoing evolutionary theory of the origin of species in his 1801 work, *Système des animaux sans vertèbres*. Unfortunately for the reception of the evolutionary theory it was associated with a theory of acquired characteristics being passed on to the offspring. With the effective repudiation of the environmentalist part of the thesis by the famed French naturalist Baron Cuvier the significance of the evolutionary aspects of the theory were lost. Nonetheless, in his preface to his novel *Père Goriot* of 1842, Honoré de Balzac noted that the teachings of Leibnitz, Buffon, Needham and Bonnet, if not evolutionary, all led to the same conclusion, "There is but one animal. The Creator used one and the same principle for all organized beings." It is a matter of no small significance that such matters pervaded the literary as well as the scientific mind and that they were present prior to the acceptance of evolutionary theory.

THE UTILITARIAN PERSPECTIVE

Immediately prior to Charles Darwin's announcement of his discoveries, A.R. Wallace submitted an almost identical theory based on his studies of comparative biology in Brazil and the West Indies. Both Wallace and Darwin acknowledged the importance for their ideas of Malthus, the noted population theorist, and Charles Lyell, the Scottish geologist who relied on the findings of James Hutton concerning the geological development of the earth. What distinguished Darwinism was the dynamic process of natural selection. In short, Darwinism was a doctrine with a long evolutionary history of its own—and it was predicated on the kind of scientific methods associated with [philosophers René] Descartes and [Thomas] Hobbes which had proved so unkind to the animal world. The irony was that Darwinism was, or at least was interpreted as, a direct affront to the cherished Christian beliefs of most of those directly involved in the work of the societies protecting the interests of animals. Almost all the publications and pamphlets put out by the early S.P.C.A.'s and Humane Societies—and they were legion—have a very strong evangelical Christian bent. And Darwinism was viewed as incompatible with Christian thinking and morality. Ironically, it was those who repudiated Darwin's elevation of the status of animals who, in practice, did most to protect the interests of animals.

Certainly, though, Darwin indicated a very real concern for the interests of animals, not merely by showing how similar in every respect, including that of the possession of a moral sense, humans were at least to the primates, but also by castigating, for example, the cruelty of the trade in fur. However, the means by which he indicated the similarity between human and beast was by relying on traditional Hobbesian and utilitarian analyses of behaviour in which our moral sense is derived from utility—from enlightened self-interest rather than any altruism or compassion. Nonetheless, he does quote [English philosopher] Herbert Spencer to the effect that through our "experiences of utility, consolidated through all past generations of the human race" we have come to acquire "certain faculties of moral intuition which have no apparent basis in the individual experiences of utility." This is, of course, itself quasi-utilitarian and directly Lamarckian [of the organic evolution theories of Jean de Lamarck]; and contrary to our current understanding of heredity. Nonetheless, it did allow Darwin to transcend the very real limitations to a genuine awareness of the rights of others implied by contemporary scientific suppositions about the understanding of behaviour— i.e., all behaviour involves a self-interested maximization of pleasure and a minimization of pain. Indeed, in Darwin's own altruistic concern for the animal realm he demonstrated the inadequacy of the philosophical method on which he relied.

If Darwin himself transcended in some degree the limitations to utilitarian scientific methods his disciples did not. Darwin wrote of the evolution of all life from a common ancestral origin by the process of adaptation to environmental conditions. The Darwinists wrote of the competition among beings for scarce resources with the resultant survival of the fittest (and, of course, humans, especially male white Anglo-Saxon humans, were the fittest!). Darwin gave humans and animals a greater affinity. The Darwinists—more properly, the Social Darwinists—made humans (especially certain types of humans) once again the pinnacle of nature, deserving of far greater consideration than all other sentient beings.

SURVIVAL OF THE FITTEST

It is customary to comment that Darwin is without responsibility for the views of his Social Darwinist disciples. Unfortunately, that is not quite true. Not only did Darwin retain a close intellectual association with Herbert Spencer, who coined the phrase "survival of the fittest"—which Darwin himself adopted in later editions of his work—with its aggressive anti-egalitarian implications, but racist overtones were to be found in Darwin's writings directly. Thus, for example, we read in his

Animals Are Machines

French philosopher Rene Descartes (1596–1650) elucidates his conviction that all nonhuman creatures are comparative to clockwork mechanisms fueled by chemicals. This "Cartesian" worldview, as it came to be known, provided grounds for clinical indifference to animal suffering for more than a century.

We can also recognize the difference between man and animals. For it is a very remarkable thing that there are no men, not even the insane, so dull and stupid that they cannot put words together in a manner to convey their thoughts. On the contrary, there is no other animal, however perfect and fortunately situated it may be, that can do the same. And this is not because they lack the organs, for we see that magpies and parrots can pronounce words as well as we can, and nevertheless cannot speak as we do, that is, in showing that they think what they are saying. On the other hand, even those men born deaf and dumb, lacking the organs which others make use of in speaking, and at least as badly off as the animals in this respect, usually invent for themselves some signs by which they make themselves understood by those who are with them enough to learn their language. And this proves not merely that animals have less reason than men, but that they have none at all, for we see that very little is needed in order to talk. . . .

It proves, on the contrary, that they are not rational, and that nature makes them behave as they do according to the disposition of their organs; just as a clock, composed only of wheels and springs, can count the hours and measure the time more accurately than we can with all our intelligence.

Rene Descartes, *Discourse on Method*. New York: The Bobbs-Merrill Company, 1956, pp. 36–38.

discussion of the various races that their "mental characteristics are . . . very distinct; chiefly as it would appear in their emotional, but partly in their intellectual faculties." Nonetheless, Darwin was also responsible for creating the intellectual climate in which humans would come to recognize their responsibilities to animals, not as was customary as a consequence of human benevolence to creatures different in kind but because such beings were in all relevant respects similar to ourselves. The idea of a community of sentient beings with common interests can be derived directly from Darwin's writings.

Unfortunately, the immediate political implications of Darwinism were less palatable. Darwin was appalled to read in a newspaper that he had proved that might was right and therefore that "every cheating tradesman" was right! It was this 'Darwinian' consciousness that inspired [English critic] Thomas Carlyle to write his infamous article on 'The Nigger Question' in which he eulogized "the law of force and cunning," hero-worship and the natural domination of the inferior by the superior. Further, in a private letter, Canon of the Anglican Church and Christian socialist Charles Kingsley expostulated: "Sacrifice of human life? Prove that it is *human* life. It is beast-life. These Dyaks [Malay people of Borneo] have put on the image of the beast, and they must take the consequence. Physical death is no evil. You Malays and Dyaks of Sarawak, you . . . are the enemies of Christ, the Prince of Peace; you are beasts, all the more dangerous, because you have a semi-human cunning." . . .

THE RESURGENCE OF MECHANISM

If Darwinism immediately failed to produce the benevolent and compassionate treatment of animals consistent with Darwin's findings on the significant continuity between human and other animal biology and psychology, it fared no better in the scientific realm. Of course, the theory of evolution was gradually accepted, but Darwin's treatment of animals as intelligent, complex, thinking and feeling beings (not always consistently with the scientific language he employed, mind you) was replaced by a behaviourist psychology which treated both humans and animals as insensate machines. Descartes and Hobbes still reigned!

Mechanism ruled the studies of animal psychology, largely because it was deemed more 'scientific,' just as such thinking plays a predominant role in some of the social sciences today. In the early years of this century sociologists and anthropologists continued to deny that comparisons with other species could be scientifically relevant, but as they gradually began to accept the more 'scientific' mentality they reduced both human and animal to the level of machines rather than elevating the animal to the sensate level of the human. Intellectual arrogance has played a comic role. If our drives and interests, rather than our ideas and moral sense, play a decisive role in determining our behaviour, social scientists are presumably no more immune than others. And if that is so, the research of social scientists can reflect only their own drives and interests rather than an objective concern to understand reality! Even today such behaviouralism, is not a rarity in the social sciences (including economics and political science) although its former pervasiveness is now spent.

Antivivisection in Late Nineteenth-Century America

CRAIG BUETTINGER

The antivivisection movement, which reached its first apex in America during the late nineteenth century, boasted a predominantly female membership, according to author Craig Buettinger. Its heart of power was the American Anti-Vivisection Society, founded in Philadelphia in 1883, and spreading to a nationwide network of women by the 1890s. Their position, however, lay grounded in a Victorian sense of female responsibility for the advance of Christian values and the molding of young minds, which eventually wound up costing them not only potential male converts but also the support of the more feminist-driven suffrage movement, which favored protests for legislation over mere education. Craig Buettinger is professor of history at Jacksonville University. His other articles include "Anti-Vivisection and the Charge of Zoo-Psychosis in the Early Twentieth Century."

"O sister women, I appeal to you," said the antivivisectionist leader Mary F. Lovell in March 1895, addressing an audience of several hundred at the triennial convention of the National Council of Women (NCW). "Will you, with the chivalry which belongs to good and true womanhood, side with the suffering and the helpless? This wrong will never be righted until women do their part." Caroline E. White, Lovell's colleague from the American Anti-Vivisection Society (AAVS), also spoke. She too knew that the progress of the antivivisection movement depended upon the mobiliza-

Excerpted from "Women and Antivivisection in Late Nineteenth-Century America," by Craig Buettinger, *Journal of Social History*, Summer 1997. Copyright © 1997 by Craig Buettinger. Reprinted with permission.

tion of women, and she echoed Lovell's entreaty. "I appeal to you, the women before me, begging you to help us in this work." The AAVS leader admonished her audience to "Remember your moral accountability."

The antivivisection movement in late nineteenth-century America drew upon a number of social groups for its membership. Clergy who were troubled by the materialism of medical science and physicians whose training predated the laboratory revolution in medicine were well-represented in the crusade. The defining presence, however, especially by the 1890s, was that of hundreds of middle-class women. Antivivisectionists comprised influential contingents inside the nation's anti-cruelty societies (SPCAs) and they had their own organizations, notably the AAVS, founded in Philadelphia in 1883. Opposition to experimentation on animals was on the rise, dismissed by a critic in 1898 as nothing but "a lot of zoöphilist women."

AAVS founders Lovell and White spoke for America's antivivisectionist women. The NCW convention, a gathering of reform-minded women, provided a perfect opportunity to expand the cause. The occasion called upon Lovell and White to explain why action on behalf of animals was particularly a female concern, pitting women against the exclusively male medical research establishment. Their speeches in 1895 were the cause's manifestos. What did Lovell and White say? What made AV an issue in the minds of so many women in late nineteenth-century America, a number to which Lovell and White, in addressing the NCW, hoped to add?

LOVELL, WHITE, AND THE FOUNDING OF THE AAVS

Caroline Earle White was born in 1833; Mary Frances Lovell in 1844. White's Quaker father, Thomas Earle, was a noted Philadelphia abolitionist and the vice-presidential candidate of the Liberty Party in 1840, and "Mrs. White spent her childhood days in an atmosphere of strong antislavery sentiment." She married Richard P. White in 1856, converting to her husband's Catholic faith. Decades later, her husband and her son, both lawyers, wrote the antivivisection bills that she introduced to the Pennsylvania legislature.

When she was a young wife and mother, White resolved to fight against the suffering of the horses and mules that hauled freight down Philadelphia's streets. After the Civil War, as the idea of organized humane activity came to America from Britain, White spurred prominent Philadelphia men to action. She drew up a pledge endorsing a Pennsylvania Society for the Prevention of Cruelty to Animals and went door to door collecting signatures. The men formed the PSPCA in the rooms of the Board of Trade in 1867. Two years later White organized the Women's Branch of the PSPCA (WBPSPCA), an arrangement allowing her to exercise executive authority. She was president of the WBPSPCA until her death in 1916. In Britain and America, the movement to prevent cruelty to animals was parent to the movement to protect children, and White was instrumental in the formation of Philadelphia's Society to Protect Children.

Lovell, London born and Philadelphia raised, was the daughter of engraver Robert Whitechurch. Her marriage in 1864 to George S. Lovell, a wholesale clock dealer, was childless, and Lovell bestowed her attention on her nieces and nephews. She helped White found the WBPSPCA in 1869, becoming its longtime corresponding secretary. Like White, Lovell fought cruelty on several fronts. She joined the Women's Christian Temperance Union in the mid-1870s to combat the problem of cruel drunkards, rising to state and national prominence within that reform organization.

The antivivisection movement in which White and Lovell would play prominent roles began in the 1860s in Britain and America, as humane leaders reacted quickly to the appearance of the first animal experimentation laboratories. In New York, Henry Bergh, head of the American Society for the Prevention of Cruelty to Animals, was an antivivisectionist whose organization opposed experiments along with other forms of cruelty to animals. The ASPCA attempted to include a ban on vivisection in 1867 anticruelty legislation. The antivivisection essays of New York physician Albert Leffingwell served the movement by gleaning examples of experimental cruelty from the medical literature. The crusaders in America drew inspiration from the legislative success of their colleagues in Britain, where Parliament enacted a law regulating animal experimentation in 1876. The leader of British antivivisection was Frances Power Cobbe, head of the Society for the Protection of Animals Liable to Vivisection, more commonly known as the Victoria Street Society. White travelled to Britain and met Cobbe, who inspired her to organize American antivivisection on a separate basis from the generalized anticruelty societies.

The AAVS was formed in 1883 at a meeting called by the Women's Branch of the Pennsylvania SPCA, in the belief that preventing torture in the labs should be the exclusive work of a concerned organization. In founding the new society, the women did not intend it to be exclusively female, and they especially sought the participation of Philadelphia's clergymen and physicians. Men and women held office in the AAVS according to Victorian notions of propriety. The society looked to men to be the president, most of the vice-presidents, and the treasurer, while women served as secretary and corresponding secretary. The twenty-member Executive Committee, comprising the bulk of the society's officers, began with an even balance of men and women.

The AAVS quickly converted, however, into a woman's movement. The minutes of the organization reveal that after the first year few men showed up at the monthly officers' meetings. The president was often the only male present. Male officeholders, citing the press of other business, routinely resigned. A decisive moment in the gender balance of the organization occurred in 1887, when White, following the lead of British antivivisection, proposed the AAVS commit itself to the abolition of animal experiments, not just their regulation. When the society as a whole concurred, with mostly women present to vote, physicians left the society in telling numbers. Albert Leffingwell declined an honorary vice-presidency of the AAVS because it advocated abolition. The composition of the Executive Committee changed rapidly from the moment of the decision for abolition. As men departed, the society appointed women to the vacancies. The even balance of men and women from 1883 to 1886 gave way to seventeen women and three men by 1895. From the declining pool of interested men the society continued to appoint its president, most vice presidents, and treasurer. Male departures did not, however, demoralize the movement; rather the AVs were excited by the cause's potential for becoming a female crusade.

Corresponding Secretary White and Vice-President Lovell piloted the AAVS. When the president missed a monthly meeting, and no other male officer was present (a frequent combination of events), White took the chair. Lovell attended officers' meetings by invitation for over a year before an opening appeared to which she was elected. That the officers desired White's chairmanship and Lovell's presence indicates the central roles the two women played in the life of the society. White and Lovell raised the significant issues and guided the deliberations in the officers' monthly and the members' annual meetings. The two women carried on the debate in the Philadelphia press with the society's opponents, edited the society's *Journal of Zoophily* (established in 1892), and wrote its editorials. When AAVS bills came before the state legislature, White and Lovell went to Harrisburg to testify on their behalf. . . .

DEVELOPING A SENTIMENT

AV and temperance [the movement to ban alcohol—also considered a women's movement] interlocked, but antivivisection women were not as closely connected to the other great women's crusade of the late nineteenth century, women's suffrage. Antivivisectionists talked little about the right to vote or even, more pragmatically, about using the vote for AV ends. For their part, the suffrage organizations of the period were single-issue groups, unlike the "do-everything" Women's Christian Temperance Union (WCTU), and cautious not to become entangled in other women's causes, which they believed were hopeless anyway without the vote. Such caution worked both ways. Crusaders to uplift vivisectors, drunkards, or other reprobates banked on their moral authority as Christians and mothers, and shied away from insisting on women's rights as individuals, which de-emphasized the roles on which that authority rested. Lovell urged her NCW audience to take part "in developing a sentiment" that would culminate in antivivisection laws, never mentioning the vote. . . .

THE CHRISTIAN IDEAL

The AVs of the 1890s proceeded first and foremost as Christian women. They insisted vivisection was unchristian, an appalling case of the nation moving not toward but away from Christian living. The infliction of pain on innocent creatures, contrary to Christian teachings to be merciful, was not simply wrong or immoral as AV men characteristically said, but sinful. Lovell told the NCW that vivisection is the worst form of cruelty, and cruelty the deadliest sin. Vivisection "is opposed to all the teachings of God," added White. "God loves mercy," she said, and "it would be difficult to imagine" anything more at variance with the doctrine of mercy than was vivisection. Hell became a metaphor for the laboratory. The NCW heard Lovell admonish, "We do not need to make this earth a hell to God's innocent creatures.". . .

Antivivisectionists asserted from the outset that the victims of vivisection include not only suffering animals and patients who wait in vain for cures but also the vivisectors themselves. Vivisection, they said, brutalizes the people who perform and observe the experiments. Lovell told the NCW that, "Besides the evil so apparent in this practice of outrageous wrong to the helpless, there is the . . . degradation of the moral character of those who do it, and of those who see it in done . . . in schools and colleges." A "mania for torture" inevitably takes hold of experimenters' souls. White's address called attention to "the demoralizing effect [vivisection] has had upon those who have practiced it, and consequently upon the community at large." The AVs predicted that once researchers became brutalized by experiments on animals, human vivisection would inevitably follow, a prediction which, they claimed, several controversial cases in the 1890s confirmed.

A sense of alarm at the male potential for cruelty ran under the charge of brutalization. Schoolboys who already have callous tendencies and must be shielded from the hardening effect of vivisection in the classroom; medical students for whom cutting up animals has become a kind of intoxication; brutalized scientists who have wholly succumbed to a "mania" for vivisection and are no longer capable of any kindness or mercy: these male characterizations fill the pages of anti-vivisection literature.

The AV women of the 1890s especially lamented the degrading effect of vivisection demonstrations on the moral character of school children and medical students. The fate of the young more than the lost soul of the adult researcher received their attention. To the antivivisectionists, the young, especially males, would descend into callousness and cruelty unless carefully guided to kindness and mercy, a central task of mothers with their sons. Accounts of "unfeeling" boys who buried kittens alive and grew up to be murderers were common AV fare, examples of "the menace to society which exists in the unchecked evil tendencies of many children." The key to bringing up boys was to stop their childish acts of cruelty to animals and instruct them in kindness instead. Doing good deeds to animals "makes us more tender," antivivisectionist Sarah Bolton of Cleveland recorded in her diary. . . .

THE MARCH ON WASHINGTON

Linking antivivisection to motherhood and the moral upbringing of children, women made the 1890s the great age of AV legislation. Soon after its founding in 1883 the AAVS had sent the state legislature a bill inspired by the British law for the regulation of vivisection. The society was unsuccessful, and for years thereafter decided against further legislative efforts on the grounds of public indifference. But in 1893, as antivivisection gained momentum as a cause among women, the

AAVS returned to the legislature, this time with a bill to abolish vivisection demonstrations in the public schools and to mandate the teaching of kindness. White, Lovell, and Leffingwell gave testimony at Harrisburg [Pennsylvania], where the bill passed the Senate but failed in the House.

Following the lead of the AAVS and under the banner of safeguarding the young, antivivisectionists in state after state sponsored bills for abolition in the schools, not without some close calls and successes at passage. The state of Massachusetts enacted a bill in 1894 that prohibited vivisection in the public schools. The law, sponsored by the Massachusetts SPCA, gave a great boost to the AV legislative movement, though in the end Massachusetts was the site of the only complete success. In 1894 fifty women founded the American Association for the Spread of Knowledge of the Extent and Existing Methods of Vivisection to support such legislation in New York. In early 1895 the legislature in Washington state passed a WCTU bill prohibiting vivisection in all schools other than medical colleges, news which Lovell happily presented to the NCW. The governor, however, later vetoed it.

The AV cause of helping mothers raise their sons by abolishing classroom vivisection was so resonant with Victorian culture that the national media, normally supportive of experiments on animals, voiced some support for the new legislation. *Harper's Weekly* endorsed the campaign for abolition in the schools. The magazine found itself forced to agree with the AVs on the "recently presented" issue of demonstrations before young pupils. Echoing the conclusions of the AV women, *Harper's* editorialized that "such grewsome exhibitions will have a most unwholesome effect upon the mind of a child, tending to strengthen rather than to repress its selfish and cruel instincts." The child learns some facts but at "a distinct ethical sacrifice," the magazine concluded.

The high water mark of the AV legislative campaign occurred in Congress. Working through Senator Jacob Gallinger, chair of the Committee on the District, the women of the Washington Humane Society repeatedly introduced legislation to prohibit demonstrations in District of Columbia classrooms as well as subject research in federal laboratories to British-style regulation. The legislation, proposed in 1896, 1897, and 1899, had some promise of success: it twice passed committee, only to be defeated on floor.

Faced with the antivivisection onslaughts, scientists organized to fight the AV women. Welch and Keen orchestrated nationwide medical lobbying efforts that turned back Gallinger's legislation every time. In defending animal experiments, medical scientists asserted the contributions of their research to the war against disease and furthermore declared themselves to be humane men who brooked no unnecessary pain in their labs. The defense also included a strong measure of resentment that women would question the men of science. Nineteenth-century science already classified women as less capable than men of sustained rational thought, as the sex whose emotions were apt to break free from the control of their rational side. Female irrationality now became a vivisectionist theme. AV charges were falsehoods concocted "in the feverish brain of some poor anti or aunty," said the *Philadelphia Medical Journal*. An agitated Harvard physiologist said of the Massachusetts antivivisectionists,

> These well-intentioned women are so short-sighted in cases, or so discriminating in their pity in other cases (they extend it to lower animals but refuse it to man), or so hysterical in maudlin sentimentality (Mrs. Ward) in still other cases, that they refuse to listen to the facts.

The most truculent blast at the antivivisectionists came from New York pharmacologist William J. Robinson in 1897, laying all the blame on the gender of the AVs. "One of the easiest things to manufacture in the United States is—sentiment," said Robinson.

> Be the cause ever so unworthy, an appeal in its behalf, if cunningly worded and pictorially illustrated, will always find a responsive chord in the hearts of many of our good people, who, not overburdened with education and unused

to deep independent thinking, are unable to analyze the merits of a case and take everything they read for pure coin. If we take into consideration the eagerness with which the fair and gentle sex catches at all sorts of fads, we shall easily understand why the antivivisectionists are making headway in this country.

Robinson lamented that unanimous resolutions of medical societies carried less weight with legislators than "half a dozen letters from the wives of their constituents." The AV campaign to boycott physicians who upheld vivisection particularly incensed Robinson, because it could place "a man's practice" at the mercy of "some influential and overofficious lady." AVs were morally blind and mentally perverse, deserving to be silenced. "I used to consider them ill-informed, but well-meaning and kind-hearted people," Robinson concluded, but "I [now] know them to be hard-hearted fanatics (as fanatics are likely to be), deliberate prevaricators, and impudent ignoramuses, who deserve no consideration and are to be handled without gloves."

Blocked in its legislative bids in the 1890s, the antivivisection movement went into decline after 1900. The veneration of "social efficiency" in the Progressive era provided laboratory medicine with an increasingly impregnable place in American life. (Temperance, becoming aligned with the cult of efficiency, would experience increased momentum.) Moreover, the reform interests of American women shifted toward suffrage and professional altruism, de-emphasizing women's moral authority as Christians and mothers. The shift weakened the antivivisectionists, now out of step with feminism's front ranks. In 1919 an AV solicited the support of suffrage leader Carrie Chapman Catt for the ongoing but despairing effort to block vivisection in the classroom. The writer admitted she did not know Catt's views on vivisection, but knew Catt's endorsement "would bring many women to lend their aid also." The reply, that Catt had no time for antivivisection, marked a reversal of fortune from 1895, when the National Council of

Women invited the antivivisectionists to join up.

The AV position of the 1890s was grounded in the Victorian era's strong sense of female responsibility for the advance of Christianity and the molding of the young. Women championed antivivisection because they believed that animal experimentation threatened these sacred trusts. They agreed with Lovell that antivivisection was a cause for good and true women, and accepted White's counsel that women were morally accountable for what transpired in the labs.

Postwar Organizations and Reforms

JAMES M. JASPER AND DOROTHY NELKIN

In the late 1960s, a new breed of animal rights activist with more radical approaches began appearing in increasing numbers, splintering off to form grassroots groups that favored political action and protests over mere humane education and the operation of euthanasia centers. Here authors James M. Jasper and Dorothy Nelkin trace the proliferation of these more combative organizations and how they sometimes butt heads with their more moderate but higher paid compatriots among the older national organizations. James M. Jasper is the author of *The Art of Moral Protest: Culture, Biography, and Creativity in Social Movements*. Dorothy Nelkin is professor of sociology at New York University; her other works include *Selling Science: How the Press Covers Science and Technology*.

After half a century of relative quiescence, animal protection began to make the news again in the 1950s. If we are right in linking animal protection with bourgeois domesticity, its reemergence at this time is understandable. The 1950s saw strong social and political efforts to reinforce domestic family life after the strains of the war years, to spread the image of detached suburban houses with picture-perfect nuclear families cared for by full-time mothers and emotionally enriched by pet dogs.

Several new groups formed in the 1950s, often in response to the fear that the growing market for research animals threatened personal pets. The Animal Welfare Institute was founded in Washington, D.C., in 1951. In 1954, some members of the American Humane Association broke away to form the Humane Society of the United States (HSUS), because, "A great many people throughout the United States were aware of the tremendous need for a strong humane group that would actively endorse and work towards eliminating . . . the more obvious cruelties and injustices imposed on animals." HSUS activities, initially driven by concerns about research, soon extended to a wider range of issues, including trapping, the conditions of animal shelters, the protection of wildlife, slaughterhouses practices, the overbreeding of animals, and the use of animals for entertainment. A third group, Friends of Animals, began operation in New York in 1957. Together, these groups represent the emergence of a new kind of animal welfare movement. While the early humane tradition tried to change individual behavior and attitudes toward animals, these new groups also occasionally sought to change institutional practices.

They also introduced more aggressive tactics. In 1966, HSUS joined the Maryland State Police in a raid on the facilities of a dog dealer who had been collecting strays to supply medical research laboratories. The chief investigator of the state police, a member of HSUS since 1961, had been monitoring the dog auctions supplying animals to labs. He organized the raid and HSUS arranged to have *Life* magazine reporters on the scene. A picture of the facility appeared on the front cover of *Life,* captioned: "Concentration Camp for Dogs." The event brought public attention to the "animal slave trade" in which lost or stolen pets were picked up and sold to dealers who trucked them off to universities or pharmaceutical laboratories. HSUS offered awards for information leading to the arrest and conviction of abusive animal dealers, and hired its own investigators to expose illegal suppliers. Some even posed as dealers themselves to discover abuses first hand.

The new activities had legislative results. The federal Humane Slaughter Act of 1958 required packers to provide anesthesia and to stun animals prior to slaughter. Nineteen Congressional bills were introduced in the early 1960s to control the laboratory use of animals, culminating in the Laboratory Animal Welfare Act of 1966. This, the first federal law dealing with the care and treatment of laboratory animals, required licensing of dealers and registration of laboratories, and set minimum standards (for certain species) for food, water, and sanitary conditions, although it said nothing about research procedures themselves. A 1970 amendment added requirements for the use of appropriate anesthetics and tranquilizers, and extended protection to all warm blooded animals.

In the public hearings prior to the 1966 act, Congress heard testimony from people who had lost pets to laboratories, and from HSUS and other organizations concerned about the growing business of dog dealing. These groups did not propose to abolish the use of animals in research, but wanted research labs to purchase animals only from licensed dealers. They were disturbed by the cruel irony, perhaps the ultimate betrayal of proverbial canine loyalty, that former pets made good research subjects since they were obedient and would not bite humans. These organizations were not, though, opposed to vivisection in general.

Nor did the welfare groups take action against pound seizure laws that required animal shelters to release unclaimed dogs and cats to research institutions. Only in the 1970s, under pressure from the radical flank of the animal protection movement, did more and more welfare societies promote legislation to prohibit the use of pound animals in research. By then, the societies began to take more seriously their goal of assuring domestic animals a humane life and, barring that, a humane death.

THE NEW VANGUARD

Tension within the movement grew with the increasing animal welfare activism of the 1960s. A handful of groups—usually driven by a single forceful personality—went far beyond traditional welfare concerns. These prophets heralding the animal rights crusade were isolated voices decrying not just the unusual cruelty of cockfights, dog dealers, or sadistic pet own-

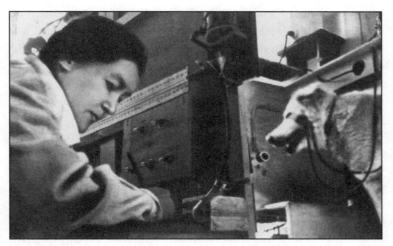

A scientist performs an experiment on a dog, a practice that many pet owners find appalling.

ers, but many practices—the wearing of furs, the eating of meat—that were an accepted part of American life. They were people like Cleveland Amory of the Fund for Animals, Alice Herrington of Friends of Animals, Helen Jones of the International Society for Animal Rights, and Ellen Thurston of the American Fund for Alternatives to Animal Research. Too radical for existing welfare societies, they founded their own groups. They were animal rightists before the term, or even the ideology, had been created. . . .

Thurston's and Amory's activities reflected a growing radicalism among animal welfarists in the 1970s due partly to frustration with the conservatism of the humane tradition and partly to awareness of broader issues like environmental threats or the callous pursuit of profit by private companies. The effort to protect animals in new contexts and the accompanying proliferation of tactics would accelerate over the next decade.

BIG MONEY IN IDEALISM

The animal welfare organizations that had grown steadily through the postwar period became an important inspiration and source of information for the animal rights movement at the end of the 1970s. They gathered and published useful information on laboratory research, trapping, hunting, and other uses of animals. Even more, they inspired a new generation of activists. Compassion for animals, based on romanticized and anthropomorphic sentiments, became an essential ingredient of the emerging rhetoric of animal rights.

The large animal welfare organizations still dominate the animal protection movement in money and members. Indeed, they have gained from the recent interest in animal rights, expanding their membership and increasing their services while continuing their traditional activities: the education of children, the care of stray pets, and the prevention of outright cruelty. They are often defensive about their role. As one activist put it, "I'm tired of other activists assuming that I'm politically unsophisticated, too moderate, or afraid of confrontation, simply because my main emphasis is humane education." HSUS established a legal department and began giving more attention to public relations in the 1970s. To extend its outreach, it held annual conferences and increased the size of its staff. Its membership has grown exponentially to top 1,000,000 in 1991. The Massachusetts SPCA, largest of the many SPCAs, has a professional staff of 350 and assets of over $60 million. The New York-based ASPCA, the direct descendent of [Henry] Bergh's organization, has 300,000 members and assets of $40 million. No fewer than six animal protection groups have assets over $10 million.

Their wealth has in fact made these large societies vulnerable to attacks from a new generation of animal rights activists, who claim that large salaries are being paid without large results for animals. The heads of the large societies earn over $100,000 annually. In 1989, according to *Animals' Agenda,* nine staff members of the Massachusetts SPCA received salaries over $70,000. Yet, critics ask, how many animals have been saved? Because they compete with animal welfare groups for direct mail contributions from the same population, animal rightists insist that they are far more effective. PETA, for instance, points out the high percentage of its contributions that goes "directly" to helping animals rather than to overhead, and boasts of its low staff salaries. In fact, however, its overhead rate is higher than that of HSUS or the Massachusetts SPCA.

THE GREAT DIVIDE

Animal welfare organizations have been rocked by such attacks. Tied to the assumptions and values of their forebears, they accept the instrumental use of animals when essential for human well-being. While they borrow radical language by engaging in "rights talk" and arguing that all life has intrinsic value, the welfare groups are willing to make cost benefit calculations that weigh animal rights against human needs. HSUS asks: "What does it mean to recognize the rights of animals? It means that before we make use of any animal . . . we should weigh our desires and needs against those of the animal—giving equal consideration to each—to see which is of overriding value." And in the spirit of the nineteenth-century compassionate tradition, HSUS remains concerned about the effect of cruelty to animals on the morality of human beings. In 1979, HSUS President John Hoyt called for "sensitivity, commitment, and sacrifice" for the cause of animal welfare reform; "The greatest task facing the humane movement today is the task of assisting man in the recovery of his own humanity. For unless he is able to affirm himself as one with the world he is intent upon destroying, it will matter little that we have acted to protect a few million animals." Tied to their ongoing programs, especially involving strays, welfare groups have retained as their primary goal reforms that will stop unnecessary cruelty.

Animal welfarists still perceive their supporters primarily as pet lovers. Their mailings have a special character designed to appeal to pet owners. They are personalized, addressing people by their first names, praising volunteers for their work, and publishing the names and sometimes the pictures of community volunteers. They provide advice—even special recipes—for the care of pets. They print memorials to pets: "Chablis—in memory of my beautiful friend who always kept my lap warm" and "honorarials" to people: "Thank you Dave and Debby for contributing your services." A group called Volunteer Service for Animals circulates stories about the heroic activities of their volunteers and "special people lists." And they run a "Golden Bone Club" for those who "remember VSA every week of the year."

But membership does not imply participation in decisions, which remain the prerogative of the staff and leadership. Aside from infrequent rallies or marches, members' participation in animal welfare organizations is restricted to letter writing and financial contributions. The limited involvement of members has left these organizations vulnerable, and some of their active constituents found that the new rights groups provided more opportunities for direct grassroots engagement in the struggle for animal protection.

The growing animal rights crusade has affected the rest of the animal protection movement in diverse ways. The radicals have especially influenced the ideologies and attitudes of many staff members, whose devotion to animals made them sympathetic to arguments drawing on sentimental anthropomorphism. Rights arguments merely carry to an extreme many of the sentiments about animals that already motivate welfare society staffers, who often join rights groups too. The older organizations themselves have adopted increasingly strident objections to many uses of animals. They criticize the unnecessary repetition of research involving the use of animals, seek to restrict dissection of animals in science classes, endorse alternatives to animals in substance testing, and campaign for additional inspectors to enforce the Animal Welfare Act. But despite the hyperbole about the horrors of animal research, they do not propose abolishing all use of animals. The literature of the large national groups does not suggest that animals have moral status equivalent to that of humans. Nor have these groups usually encouraged direct political activism by members. Thus rights groups portray the welfare community as stodgy and rigid, and manage to steal away many active and devoted members. The differences between moderate welfarists and radical rightists are highlighted by the persistent problem of what to do with stray animals.

Most humane societies operate shelters where unclaimed animals are killed. The organizations shield donors from this fact by emphasizing their adoption programs, and some shelters claim to be "no-kill" (they send animals elsewhere for the dirty work, or accept only clearly adoptable animals). Yet groups founded on compassion for animals kill (or as they say, "put down") from twelve to twenty million animals a year—roughly the number of animals killed annually by trappers. Animals are treated with compassion before being killed, but the stark contrast between loving care and death makes shelters especially poignant for those who work in them. Says one such worker: "Very often what they get is the best five days of their lives. They are entitled to a stress-free environment, a disease-free environment. They're entitled to be kept warm and dry and played with and to get attention, and they're entitled to a humane and dignified death."

Despite one hundred years of humane education efforts, many people still do not take proper care of their pets, and shelters see the results. The manager of a California shelter complains, "It's very difficult to work at an animal shelter and continue to love people. You have to remind yourself that we're all the same, that people are our brothers too. It's very difficult when you see the kinds of things they do." Pets are part of the family, but many families are destructive: "Man's best friend has become man's biggest victim," says one writer.

The animal protection movement tries to place abandoned animals in good homes, but only one in five is ever claimed or adopted. Members of the animal welfare and animal rights movements themselves adopt large numbers of pets; many activists have five or ten or more animals of their own. Even in densely populated New York City, not only did 72 percent of the animal rights demonstrators interviewed in 1988 have more than one animal, but 31 percent had animals from more than one species. But such efforts are not on a sufficient scale to deal with millions of animals a year. Hence the shelters.

ANIMAL "SANCTUARIES"

Animal rights groups have tried to resolve the dilemma by building, not animal shelters, but "sanctuaries," as protective refuges. Instead of painless death, they provide the means for animals to live out their "natural" lives. Some of the animal sanctuaries are for stray animals, others for retired work or laboratory animals. They are costly and often elegant. The Defenders of Animal Rights, for example, sent out mailings to raise the $500,000 needed to complete a pet sanctuary. For a contribution of $1,000, a donor's name is on a plaque. For $2,000, one's name is on a kennel. Another sanctuary is promoted as "a unique housing development for underprivileged felines." It contains "kitty condos" where cats can nap, with large windows for our "sun worshippers" and for "an entertaining bird's-eye view of the great outdoors." This sanctuary, in the middle of a thirty-five-acre wildlife area, costs about $600,000 a year to run. One California group named DELTA (Dedication and Everlasting Love to Animals) houses 400 abandoned dogs and 200 rescued cats which live in their own three-bedroom home and outdoor recreation area. Homeless humans should be so lucky.

Sanctuaries are not without their critics. There are simply too many dogs and cats, so that most specialize in certain species they know they can care for. But a no-kill shelter in Elmsford, New York, accepts all animals; it has over 400 dogs and cats. Unfortunately, it lacks room for so many, and dogs are kept on short leashes and, according to critics, not given adequate care: "I understand what she's trying to do, but unfortunately you can't save everything. There's a point where your head has to take over your heart, and that's very hard." Both HSUS and the ASPCA oppose no-kill shelters as cruel to many of the animals. . . .

THE BIPARTISAN CRUSADE

The formation of radical groups alongside existing ones is characteristic of many protest movements, attributed by most observers to frustration with the plodding pace of social change. Disillusionment with reformist strategies is expressed in both ideological and tactical innovations. . . .

Compelled by similar moral sentiments, radical and reformist wings of social movements are often capable of sustained cooperation. Yet heightened competition for resources creates conflict, and allied groups may come to trade accusations of "sellout" on the one hand, and "political naïveté" on the other. Moderate organizations in a movement usually control greater resources, because they attract broader support from the rest of society. If unable to tap into these resources, movement radicals develop low-cost tactics (street protests rather than lobbying Congress). Or they heighten their radical rhetoric in hope of obtaining some resources even while they claim to spurn such support as a sign of co-optation. In some cases, radicals gain resources through strategic alliances or by direct takeovers of existing moderate organizations. The animal welfare community has provided these kinds of opportunities to the emerging animal rights movement. . . .

The notion of welfare lies partway between private charity and a full concept of individual rights. The gradual radicalization of the animal protection movement thus followed changing images of animals; from pitiful objects of charity, to innocent beings with interests of their own, and—finally—to autonomous individuals with a right to their own lives.

The Creation of a Mass Movement

LAWRENCE FINSEN AND SUSAN FINSEN

Inspired by the civil rights debates and protest marches of the Vietnam War era as well as the 1975 publication of Peter Singer's book *Animal Liberation*, the animal rights movement attained unprecedented popularity in the early 1980s, according to coauthors Lawrence Finsen and Susan Finsen. A groundswell of new grassroots organizations sprang up seemingly overnight, led by a new breed of pragmatic, politically conscious activists. These groups, such as People for the Ethical Treatment of Animals (PETA) and the Animal Liberation Front (ALF), were distinguished from their statelier predecessors by more combative rhetoric, goals of radical social change, and a greater willingness to work outside the law to achieve their ends. Lawrence Finsen is professor of philosophy at the University of Redlands in California. Susan Finsen is chair of the philosophy department at California State University, San Bernardino. Both are cofounders of a grassroots animal rights group, Californians for the Ethical Treatment of Animals.

Two groups are most widely associated with work for animal rights: the Animal Liberation Front (ALF) and People for the Ethical Treatment of Animals (PETA). These names are widely recognized and identified with the movement by people who know little else about them. PETA was founded by Ingrid Newkirk and Alex Pacheco in 1980. Through a series of carefully focused campaigns, PETA grew to an organization with an annual budget in excess of $7 million and over 300,000 members in less than a decade. Pacheco writes of its founding, "We decided the time was right for a

Excerpted from *The Animal Rights Movement in America: From Compassion to Respect,* by Lawrence Finsen and Susan Finsen (New York: Twayne Publishers, 1994). Copyright © 1994 by Twayne Publishers. Reprinted with permission.

grassroots movement for animal rights. . . . Although we would fight for all the animals, our primary focus would be on those animals largely ignored by traditional humane societies—animals used for experimentation, food and fur."

PETA's offices reflect the dedication and no-nonsense orientation of the organization. The converted warehouse provides cramped quarters for the approximately 90 employees. In sharp contrast to the plush offices of some of the older animal welfare organizations, Pacheco's tiny office is bare-bones and utilitarian. The walls are decorated with PETA posters and photographs of Pacheco and various famous people. . . .

Pacheco had thought at one point that his future lay in the priesthood, primarily as an avenue to work on social issues. A chance visit to a slaughterhouse led him to animal rights. Appalled by what he saw as he entered the slaughterhouse, Pacheco educated himself about animal issues. Ultimately this led to his departure from his studies for the priesthood—disillusioned, as he was, at the lack of sympathy among fellow students and instructors for his growing concerns about animal exploitation. Dedicating himself to a life of activism for animals, he spent the next few years "apprenticing" with those already active in a variety of settings: with the Hunt Saboteurs in Britain, aboard the *Sea Shepherd* in the Atlantic, and learning from activists, especially Nellie Shriver and Constantine Salomone. . . .

PETA's work for animals has been prodigious. To name but a few accomplishments, PETA has exposed cruelty in numerous product testing companies, at Carolina Biological Supply, at a Montana fur farm, and at General Motors, which until recently performed crash tests using animals. PETA's undercover investigations have repeatedly brought to light gross violations of basic law and decency, and in each case the organization has effectively brought pressure and publicity to bear. PETA's effective and thorough research and investigation have become a model for the movement. Their educational and direct action tactics make it highly visible—a library of hard-hitting documentary videos, educational and training materials, a course on activism ("Animal Rights 101"), street theater, and demonstrations—and effective enlistment of celebrities (such as Paul McCartney, the late River Phoenix, Berke Breathed and Kevin Nealan) and direct action keep a steady media spotlight on the organization.

PETA has frequently found evidence from ALF raids on its doorstep and has acted as a media connection for the underground group. In addition, Ingrid Newkirk has recently published a book about the ALF. The perception that PETA is itself involved in illegal ALF activities has led the FBI to investigate PETA's leadership and various staff members. . . .

THE ANIMAL LIBERATION FRONT

It is sometimes said that the Animal Liberation Front (ALF) is not an organization but a state of mind, and if one wishes to "join" the ALF, there is no way to do this other than to raid a laboratory or factory farm and to take credit for this action in the name of the ALF. The ALF is certainly not an *organization* in the usual sense of the word. Yet based on the few published sources (interviews with ALF "members," media accounts of raids, and two recent books—Ingrid Newkirk's *Free the Animals* and Rik Scarce's *Eco-Warriors*) the loosely knit cells of the ALF in the United States do seem to share a number of strategies and philosophies beyond the "state of mind" that leads them to liberate animals. Furthermore, the ALF may not be so open-ended as the state of mind criterion suggests. The ALF raids that have attracted so much attention in recent years do not appear to have been either spontaneous or amateurish. Those involved have managed to escape apprehension for years, and it was only in the fall of 1992 that the FBI arrested and charged some alleged ALF members. The professionalism surrounding the ALF is reputed to include training, experience, and a complete veil of secrecy, such that even ALF spokespersons do not know the identity of ALF activists or about any of their plans in advance of a raid. Nevertheless, even if shared philosophy and strategy were not enough to qualify the ALF as an organization, its profound influence on events in the movement qualifies it for serious examination. . . .

Unquestionably, the direct-action, illegal tactics of the ALF are the most controversial of any in the animal rights movement. There are many who see the ALF as a dangerous terrorist organization with the potential of destroying the movement by discrediting it as violent. There are also many who see the ALF as the most dedicated and important arm of the movement, providing information available through no other means and liberating animals where all other efforts have failed. Others feel deeply ambivalent about the ALF, lauding its successes and at the same time fearing the possible repercussions of the ALF image. Examining the history of liberation groups is highly useful in understanding the sources of these complex and conflicting perspectives.

There have been a number of organizations with broadly liberationist tactics operating in Great Britain, France, Germany, Holland, Canada, and Australia. The first of these was formed from within the Hunt Saboteurs Association in Britain. In 1972 Ronnie Lee and Cliff Goodman, both "Hunt Sabs," decided to embark on a campaign of direct action against vehicles and other property used by the hunt. To do this they formed the Band of Mercy, which began by carrying out raids on fox hunt kennels in the south of England, and in autumn of 1973 the group expanded its campaign to attacking other forms of animal abuse. In November of that year it carried out arson attacks (causing over 45,000 pounds worth of damage) on a laboratory being built for the Hoechst drug company at Milton Keynes. They followed with the successful sinking of a seal hunter's vessel and numerous attacks on lab-animal suppliers. After the arrest of some key members of the Band of Mercy in connection with a raid on Oxford Laboratory Animal Colonies, the activities of the Band of Mercy came to a halt. Nevertheless, the publicity surrounding the imprisonment of members of the Band of Mercy brought out the support of a new group of activists. Together with the remnants of the Band of Mercy, this new group formed the Animal Liberation Front in Britain in June 1976.

The newly formed ALF carried out 10 raids against animal research targets in 1976 and rescued beagles from the Pfizer laboratory in Sandwich. This group restrained itself from damaging property unless it was directly connected with animal abuse; nor did they attack homes of vivisectors. In one raid when a considerable amount of money was discovered, they are reported to have refrained from taking it for fear of being considered common thieves. In 1977, 14 laboratory raids were carried out, and more than 200 animals were taken from laboratory suppliers.

The first U.S. ALF raid occurred in 1977, when the "Undersea Railroad" released two porpoises from a Hawaii research lab. This deed had more of the character of traditional civil disobedience than an ALF action, as it lacked the clandestine nature of other raids to come. Two years later the ALF rescued five animals from the New York University Medical Center. According to the *New York Post* (15 March 1979), three women and a man disguised themselves in white smocks and posed as faculty members. They entered the unlocked laboratory and took a cat, two guinea pigs, and two dogs. In their press statement the spokesperson for the group stated that during months of observation of the laboratory she had seen many animals left bleeding and in pain after experiments. She stated, "We're not against working to save human lives. We're just against the attitude that animals can just be used for any kind of experiment, without regard for the fact that they're alive." The unlocked laboratory, the surprised and confused response of NYU (whose spokesperson stated, "We're sorry that anyone would resort to criminal trespass to draw attention to something that is a matter of public record"), and the moderate statement from the ALF all stand in marked contrast to subsequent ALF raids. . . .

In the United States the ALF appears to have consistently held to a philosophy of nonviolence, while distinguishing between property damage and violence toward living beings. An anonymous interview with a member of the ALF involved in the 4 July 1989 raid of John Orem's Texas Tech laboratory is representative of many statements made by ALF members. In answer to the question, "Would you ever harm a person?" the ALF member states, "No. The ALF will break things, but we will never harm a living being. The vivisectors are terrorists. Every day they cut, shock, burn, poison and drive insane thousands of frightened, helpless, innocent animals. They kill without a thought. Our aim is to slow down and eventually stop their violence."

In destroying laboratory equipment used in animal experimentation, the ALF regards itself as destroying the tools of violence and hoping to divert money that would otherwise be used to exploit animals. As the animal liberator Sarah H. puts it, "Economic sabotage entails the destruction of devices used to torture animals, it raises the cost of animal abuse, and provides irrefutable proof that a raid did, in fact, occur. This proof, in turn, serves to corroborate our documentation in the eyes of the public. And, in the final analysis, is it not a moral act of mercy to destroy an instrument of torture?"

Thus, ALF raids are focused on one or more of three goals: liberating animals, obtaining information (such as videotapes and records of experiments that reveal the exploitation of animals), and destroying equipment used in exploitation of animals and diverting research funds. While some people consider destruction of property a form of violence, a clear distinction should be made between violence to living beings and destruction of property. Thus far, no credible reports have linked any ALF action to violence against people in the United States. As a result, the ALF enjoys broader support from within the animal rights movement in the United States than have similar groups in Great Britain in recent years. . . .

While no U.S. ALF raids to date are known to have physically harmed any individual, there have been ALF actions (such as the arson at the University of California at Davis) in which the methods used placed people in danger. Furthermore, researchers who have been the targets of raids claim both psychological and professional harm. That they have been professionally harmed is obvious: their laboratories have been destroyed, their animals removed and research interrupted, and their reputations damaged. In many raids such information as photographs, videotapes, and documents relevant to establishing those research projects as fraudulent, illegal, and callous were obtained. In the wake of adverse publicity, researchers have received threatening telephone calls and had their homes picketed by outraged activists. Some have abandoned their research. For example, an examination of government-funded research grants reveals animal research at the University of California at Riverside has decreased quite dramatically in the years since the massive ALF raid. This sort of result is, of course, the foreseeable and sought-after end of such raids.

Whether one agrees with the tactics of the ALF, there can be no question that the information brought to light in numerous raids has played an important role in educating all of us about what happens in some laboratories. It has also had a galvanizing effect on the movement. The images of animals removed from laboratories in such raids—of their miserable living conditions and the pain they have endured—serve as powerful symbols for activists, and the ALF's success in removing even a few animals is empowering to those who feel helpless in the face of powerful institutions. Implicated vivisectors provide a personal face for the evils of institutional animal suffering and a concrete target as well.

CHAPTER 2

LEADERS OF
THE MOVEMENT

AMERICAN
SOCIAL
MOVEMENTS

Henry Bergh and the Founding of the ASPCA

GERALD CARSON

Until 1866, animals in America had virtually no protection of any kind. That year the nation's first Animal Protection Act was passed, largely thanks to the efforts of Henry Bergh, a onetime diplomat to Russia who abandoned his career to pursue the cause of what he called "reviving the principle of mercy in the human heart" and went on to found the American Society for the Prevention of Cruelty to Animals. This brief biography of Bergh comes from Gerald Carson's *Men, Beasts, and Gods*. Biographer Gerald Carson's articles have appeared in *American Heritage, Natural History,* and *Smithsonian* magazines. His books include *The Old Country Store, One for a Man, Two for a Horse,* and *The Polite Americans.*

On an unseasonably warm evening in April 1866, a well-tailored gentleman with a drooping mustache and a long, thin face, obviously a member of the "Upper Ten," stood at the intersection of Fifth Avenue and Twenty-third Street in New York City, watching the tangle of traffic where Broadway slants across Fifth Avenue. A wilder individualism than we know today prevailed among the horsecars and omnibuses, the struggling carriages, drays, vans, and butchers' carts. Suddenly the observer stepped off the curb and threaded his way toward a teamster who was giving his horse an unmerciful beating. This dialogue followed, as the pedestrian recounted the incident later:

Excerpted from *Men, Beasts, and Gods: A History of Cruelty and Kindness to Animals,* by Gerald Carson (New York: Charles Scribner's Sons, 1972). Copyright © 1972 by Gerald Carson. Reprinted with permission.

"My friend," said I approaching, "you can't do that any more." The man paused in sheer amazement.

"Can't beat my own horse," he exclaimed, "—the devil I can't." And he fell to again. Again I ordered him to stop and added:

"You are not aware, probably, that you are breaking the law, but you are. I have the new statute in my pocket; and the horse is yours only to treat kindly. I could have you arrested. I only want to inform you what a risk you run." The fellow stared at me with open mouth, and exclaimed:

"Go to hell—you're mad!"

Thus Henry Bergh began, quietly and politely, a twenty-two-year effort to arouse the American conscience to the plight of fellow creatures who cannot protest or explain their predicament. Earlier that same day, the nineteenth of April, the New York State legislature had passed a law punishing an act, or omission of an act, that caused pain to animals "unjustifiably." It was a historic step forward in the nineteenth-century movement toward the protection of animals.

It became one of Bergh's most effective arguments to emphasize the *cost* of cruelty to the more than eighty-five million animals "contributing in one way or another to the daily support and enrichment of the people of this country." Cruel treatment of cows resulted in contaminated butter, cheese, and milk. The horrors of the cattle train endangered the meat supply. And the aphorism that "horses are cheaper than oats" lost its specious appeal when in 1872 two-thirds of all the horses in the city of New York were stricken with a deadly respiratory disease, producing, in Bergh's words, "a panic among the human inhabitants." Thousands walked, and the flow of urban life slowed almost to a standstill.

ROOTS OF THE ASPCA

There were laws to protect animals on the statute books of several states, including New York. But they were narrowly drawn. Machinery for enforcement was lacking. They were largely ineffective. Just a few days before the New York legislature passed the animal protection act of 1866 entitled "An Act better to prevent cruelty to animals," it had also chartered a humane society, a private corporation exercising delegated police powers. The new organization, first of its kind in the Western Hemisphere, was called the American Society for the Prevention of Cruelty to Animals.

The sponsors who signed the petition for the chartering of the ASPCA were representative men of New York, leaders in finance, commerce, the. law, and politics. But the driving force behind the idea was Henry Bergh. He was the founder, president, inspirer, advocate, diplomatist, lecturer, writer, administrator, fund raiser, and tireless propagandist for the protest against the abuse of animals. "To plant, or revive, the principle of mercy, in the human heart," Bergh said, would be "a triumph . . . greater than the building of the Great Pacific Railroad."

The cause became known as "Bergh's war." The ASPCA was the "Bergh Society," its agents "Bergh's men." The tall, muscular figure and long, sad-eyed face of Henry Bergh himself, as he patrolled the streets, appeared in courtrooms, or stopped in at the American Museum to see how P.T. Barnum, the circus impresario, was treating his menagerie, became as familiar to New Yorkers as William Cullen Bryant's magnificent white beard or Horace Greeley's long, flapping duster and high, white hat. . . .

BERGH'S EARLY YEARS

Henry, the youngest of three children of Christian Bergh—a prosperous shipbuilder in New York City whose yard produced sailing vessels of advanced design during the first forty years of the century—was born on August 29, probably in 1813, in a homestead that stood in an orchard of oxheart cherry trees at the northeast corner of Scammel and Water streets. . . .

Bergh entered Columbia College in 1830 with some thought of a career in the law. Meanwhile he lived as a young man of fashion, enjoying the balls and the company of the

town wits. Preferring the plea-
sures of foreign travel to the life
of study, Bergh dropped out of
Columbia, and after tasting Europe, turned his thoughts to
marriage. In 1839 he married
Catherine Matilda Taylor,
daughter of an English architect
practicing in New York. Following Christian Bergh's death in
1843, the shipyard was closed,
and Henry and his wife, childless

Henry Bergh

and well off, traveled and lived for extended periods in Europe. A hint of the future came at Seville, where the Berghs
attended a bullfight and were revolted as eight bulls were
killed and twenty horses eviscerated.

During their visits abroad the Berghs received social attentions at the American legations, at the Elysée Palace during the
presidency of Louis Napoleon, and at the Tuilleries after Bona-
parte assumed the imperial role as Napoleon III. In search of a
calling, Bergh's thoughts turned to literature and diplomacy. . . .
Ignored as a writer, he was, briefly, more fortunate in diplomacy.
In the spring of 1863 President Lincoln named him to succeed
Bayard Taylor as secretary of legation at the court of Czar
Alexander II. In St. Petersburg Bergh served under the color-
ful fire-eater and southern abolitionist, Cassius Marcellus Clay.
Bergh enjoyed his life in Russia, but disillusionment came
when Clay resented his popularity with the Russians and sum-
marily dismissed him. Clay said, in fact, "Go, God damn you!"
Bergh lingered in London for several months while he ma-
neuvered for a new appointment, but it never came.

During his tour of duty in Russia, Bergh had watched the
peasants beat their horses and had, from the legation carriage,
directed his splendidly liveried Vladimir or Alexander to order the droshky drivers to stop it. "At last," he commented,
"I've found a way to utilize my gold lace." Bergh often admitted that previously he had never been particularly interested

in animals. Once when he was calling upon Clara Morris, a leading emotional actress of the period, Bergh drew back when her small dog put a friendly, inquiring paw on his knee. Miss Morris asked him if he objected to her pet because it was small, but Bergh said no—it was because the dog was a dog.

Not as one devoted, then, to the beast world or out of a sentimental flinching at happenings that caused animals pain, but rather because of a kind of abstract concept of justice, Bergh seems to have undertaken his life work. Yet one wonders if that quite covers it. Horses must have been his secret passion. His lectures and reports were filled with affectionate praise of "that generous and faithful servant, the horse," or "that noble creature, the horse." Why else did this gentleman, who looked rather like a blend of Quaker and French count, wear a gold horsehead scarfpin in the folds of his black satin cravat, and recall, in one of those classical allusions of which he was somewhat too fond, how "Darius . . . owed his crown to the neighing of a horse?" "What struck me most forcibly," Bergh declared, "was that mankind derived immense benefits from these creatures, and gave them in return not the least protection."

GROWING SUPPORT FOR THE CAUSE

Before leaving London for home in June of 1865, Bergh met the Earl of Harrowby, president of the Royal Society for the Prevention of Cruelty to Animals, then in its forty-first year. Stimulated by what he learned of the service rendered by the RSPCA, Bergh resolved to found a similar institution in the United States. The advancement of "merciful principles," he assured Lord Harrowby, was the "long cherished dream of my heart." After careful preparatory work, Bergh unveiled his proposal in February 1866 to a small but carefully chosen audience, which included the mayor and later governor of New York, John T. Hoffman, and other figures of importance in the life of the city and state. Noticing in a quick historical survey what happened to animals, and humans, too, in the Roman arena, the tortures inflicted in the Spanish bullring, and the brutalities of modern vivisectionists, Bergh denounced the blood sports still popular in New York, the abuse of the street-car horses, and the barbarities that accompanied the transportation and slaughter of food animals. "This is a matter purely of conscience," Bergh concluded. "It has no perplexing side issues . . . it is a moral question . . . it is a solemn recognition of . . . mercy."

The response was positive. As a result of the meeting and the circulation of a paper outlining the objectives of the proposed society, the ASPCA came into being with Henry Bergh as president. Bergh now had at his disposal an effective law and a private society clothed with public authority. Bergh himself was empowered by the attorney general of the state and the district attorney for the city to represent them in all cases involving the law for the protection of animals. In later years educational activities and relief work became more important than punishing offenders. This gain was due in part to the spread of a social gospel, which included a new attitude toward inferior creatures, and in part to another circumstance: the ASPCA was able to secure convictions in over ninety percent of all cases that reached the courts.

President Bergh hoped that the word "American" in the name of the society would come to stand for a national organization. But the charter, under New York laws, was not appropriate, and the idea of branches outside New York state proved impractical. The ASPCA's influence, however, was national, as other humanitarian societies quickly came into being. Within five years, an astonishingly short time for the diffusion of a new idea, nineteen states and the Dominion of Canada had established societies of similar character.

TIRELESS COMMITMENT IN THE FACE OF RIDICULE

There was plenty of work to be done in New York. Wealthy sportsmen held live pigeon shoots. The gambling fraternity repaired to Kit Burn's Sportsmen's Hall at 273 Water Street, just north of Peck Slip, to see bulldogs fight a black bear. Terriers dispatched wharf rats in a zinc-lined enclosure for the delight of the Bowery boys, and as a special afterpiece, Kit's son-in-law, William Varley, alias Reddy the Blacksmith, pickpocket and thief, would, for the price of a glass of beer, bite a live rat in two.

The president of the ASPCA carried a cane that could be used as a weapon of defense. But usually a lifted finger and a glimpse of his official badge were sufficient to tame his adversaries. Bergh spent long hours in the Court of Special Sessions, where he was formidable in cross-examination, or in climbing the bleak hill to the Capitol in Albany, where he frequently appeared before legislative committees. Meanwhile he carried on the routine business of the society, cajoled the editors of the fifteen daily newspapers then existing in New York, and beat the bushes for money. "My time by day and night," he told a correspondent, "is devoted to the Institution which I have founded." Yet the strenuous life was not without its rewards. Bergh clearly enjoyed the exercise of his very considerable authority and had in his temperament that focus on a single purpose necessary to the accomplishment of any great reform. As one newspaper editor remarked of him, "He who doeth one thing is terrible!"

Bergh was always urbane, but he was also always precise. When he wrote to the police captain on West Thirty-fifth Street about a horse that had been abandoned in the gutter to die, he gave the name of the owner, the name and address of the man who committed the act, and the name and address of a witness. When he complained to William H. Vanderbilt about a "dead lame" horse owned by the New York and Harlem Railroad, he gave the date and identified the horse as being attached to Fourth Avenue car number 30. "I have adopted a habit through life," he warned a judge who was delaying unreasonably on a horse-abandonment case, "of always pursuing a subject until it is brought to its legitimate conclusion."

TURTLES, THE LOST CAUSE

Early on, Bergh undertook to stir up the city through working on a spectacular case: the elimination of torments visited upon green turtles. The turtles, source of delectable soup and succulent steaks, were transported by sailing vessels from the tropics to the Fulton Fish Market in New York. The turtles lay on their backs for several weeks, without food or water, held in place by ropes strung through holes punched in their flippers. Bergh boarded a schooner engaged in the turtle trade, arrested the skipper and crew, and marched them off to The Tombs prison. He reinforced his case with a letter from Professor Louis Agassiz. The famous zoologist assured the ASPCA that turtles could feel hunger, thirst, and pain and had, besides, certain minimal rights. However, a skeptical judge acquitted the defendants on the grounds that a turtle was not an animal within the meaning of the law. The trial was a nine-day wonder, with the newspapers making extensive facetious comments on the nature of turtles and aggressive humanitarians.

"The day following," Bergh told a lecture audience later, "a morning paper [it was the *New York Herald*] devoted six columns to an account of the trial; and to the funny fellow who wrote the account I have always felt grateful, for it at once placed the Society before the public and let them know that there was a Society for the defense of the inferior animals.". . .

BERGH AND BARNUM

The ASPCA was a constant threat to Barnum in connection with his zoological activities. A typical incident occurred when the head of the anticruelty society heard that the boa constrictor in the Broadway menagerie was being fed live toads and lizards in the presence of paying customers. The resulting pressure from Bergh was so heavy that at one time Barnum had to send his snake to Hoboken in a suitcase to be fed beyond the reach of the ASPCA. But Barnum found a way to punish Bergh. He obtained the support of Professor Agassiz, who told him that snakes require live food, and expressed the doubt that the members of the ASPCA "would object to eating lobster because the lobster was boiled alive, or refuse oysters because they were cooked alive, or raw oysters because they must be swallowed alive." The president of Barnum's & Van Amburgh's Museum and Menagerie thereupon demanded an apology from the president of the ASPCA, and released the complete correspondence concerning the proper feeding of reptiles to the press. . . .

Respect and even liking developed between the two men after Bergh defended Barnum on an occasion when the latter was attacked for using elephant goads. The circus impresario began contributing to both the New York and Bridgeport, Connecticut, SPCAs, and announced that he was "the Bergh of Bridgeport!" When Barnum died in 1891 he left a bequest to the city of Bridgeport for the erection of a monument to Henry Bergh. The memorial was duly constructed, with water troughs on two levels for animals of various heights, and was topped with a statue of a horse. The horse was damaged beyond restoring when an automobile crashed into the memorial in 1964, but the rest of the monument still stands.

LATER CAMPAIGNS

As the years passed, the ASPCA kept a vigilant eye on the operation of the city dog pound, on the treatment of horses and mules along the Erie Canal, and on the handling of dairy cows in Brooklyn and on Long Island. Bergh intervened successfully when it was proposed to make a circus horse walk a tightrope stretched over the rapids below Niagara Falls. He is also credited with devising derricks and slings for raising large animals that had fallen into excavations and with the invention of the clay pigeon to replace live birds in trap shooting. . . .

Henry Bergh's newsworthiness, his frequent entanglements with powerful commercial interests, and his striking personality and appearance all served to keep the ASPCA and its president in the news. Because of his sad-eyed countenance and what the comic press saw as his wildly romantic objectives, the cartoonists of the day inevitably delineated him as a nineteenth-century Don Quixote, mounted upon a bony Rosinante. The *New York Sunday Mercury,* which represented the point of view of sportsmen, assaulted Bergh editorially as "An Ass That Should Have His Ears Cropped." Using the technique of the *reductio ad absurdum,* the humorous newspaper *Wild Oats* suggested that the ASPCA had created a new social atmosphere in which "Cockroaches . . . insist on sharing the best. . . . Rats insist on having a chair at the table. . . . goats put on airs . . . hogs grunt delightedly . . . [as] unlimited sway is given to the very humane Bergh." But the significance of the satire aimed at the animal cause was this: while ridicule papered over the disturbing ethical challenges, the laughter masked a queasy conscience.

According to sprightly anecdotes circulated after Bergh had become a celebrity, he had as a child manifested a special sensitivity to the welfare of animals which included an earnest effort to persuade his parents to give up mousetraps, insect powder, and flypaper, and it was reported with relish in the New York weekly review of metropolitan life and the arts, *The Arcadian,* that young Bergh had once cured an aged mouse of neuralgia with Mrs. Winslow's Soothing Syrup. The journal also announced that Bergh would shortly introduce a bill in Congress to make it illegal to eat oysters.

A rumor often appeared in print that Bergh was a vegetarian, which granted him a theoretical consistency while neatly categorizing him as a crank. But it was not true. Bergh allowed in his philosophy for what he termed "necessary killing." At one time, indeed, he tried to introduce horsemeat as an article of diet. Characteristically, the move was attempted in the interest of the horse, a quick death being preferable to Bergh's eyes to the fate that awaited the victims of the horse dealers.

The physical courage of the president of the ASPCA was often tested. He received numerous threatening letters advising him to leave town. One postcard named the day and hour when he would be assassinated. A drayman, arrested for overloading, took a cut at Bergh with a piece of strap iron, but fortunately missed. And the society was always accused of choosing the wrong targets. The "dairymaids" thought Bergh ought to confine his attentions to the butchers. The butchers favored vigorous action against cockfighting. Kit Burns, the impresario of the dogfights, warned: "Your society is doing a noble work, sir, yes, a magnificent work, but let me tell you, when it interferes in dog fighting, it digs its own grave."

The ASPCA was also charged with bearing down on the poor while excusing the rich. But Bergh found his path full of tacks when he tried to call to account members of the business and social elite. The courts held, for example, that unless an officer of a corporation that owned horses personally hit a horse on the head with a shovel or personally abandoned it in the street, he could not be held accountable. But on the whole, the press came to support the ASPCA, accepted Bergh as a sage, and printed his views on things in general.

MEDIATOR FOR THE UPPER AND LOWER ANIMALS

As president of the society, Bergh received no pay for his work, and in fact turned over a substantial endowment to the society. New York City always remained his special domain, and its citizens came to regard indulgently, even proudly, the old gentleman with the kindly yet dyspeptic face, low voice, and old-school manners who, when he stopped a teamster and saw a crowd gathering, would seize the opportunity to deliver a little talk on Americanism. It always included the thought that free men who make their own laws ought to obey their statutes. In all that he did for animals, he always had a further objective in view, which he wrote out in French just three years before he died: *Les hommes seront justes envers les hommes, quand ils seront charitables envers les animaux* ("Men will be just to men when they are kind to animals").

The criticism was often leveled against the ASPCA that it was more concerned with improving the condition of animals than of men. This still remains a stock argument advanced by the opponents of animal protection activities. Bergh pointed out in reply that if the animals had to wait their turn until all human affairs were perfectly adjusted, they would still be waiting at the Second Coming. Neither the movement to alleviate the suffering of the lower animals nor justice for men, he insisted, excluded the other.

Henry Bergh kept bachelor hall during his later years in his brownstone house at 429 Fifth Avenue, with two nephews, a clutter of objets d'art, and his long memories. His wife had been an invalid for years, living at a home in Utica, New York, where she died in 1887. During the blizzard of '88 Bergh died in his Fifth Avenue home, and was immediately recognized as a man who had created a profound alteration in the moral climate of nineteenth-century America. James Gordon Bennett's *New York Herald,* which had gotten so much mileage out of Bergh's foibles, eulogized him. The *New York Citizen,* an old antagonist, announced "the man who loved his fellow animal is mourned by his fellow man. . . ."

Recognition took many forms. Milwaukee, like Bridgeport, erected a monument. Columbia University became the seat of a Henry Bergh Foundation for the promotion of humane education, and Henry Ward Beecher, the popular pulpit orator of the period, thought it both proper and probable that the founder of the ASPCA and his furred and feathered wards would be joyfully reunited in a human-animal heaven. It is a success story quite outside the rags-to-riches tradition that Henry Bergh, born to affluence, achieved his fulfillment in the role of "mediator," as he himself once said, "for the upper and lower animals." There is no evidence that Henry Bergh was especially well grounded in the speculative origins of humanitarianism. He was not a zoologist, theologian, or thinker absorbed in theoretical questions. He resembled, rather, the "righteous man" of Proverbs who regarded the life of his beast because that was the way of life of a just and good man.

Henry Spira and Grassroots Activism

PETER SINGER

Peter Singer, whose 1975 book *Animal Liberation* would popularize and remold the animal rights movement, taught a course of the same name at New York University a year before the book's publication. One of his students was Henry Spira, a former merchant seaman who had already spent most of his adult life fighting for the rights of oppressed humans. Galvanized by Singer's words but unimpressed by the movement's track record and methods, Spira went on to spearhead a major series of public campaigns whose string of successes against one well-funded institution after another would give animal activism an unprecedented legitimacy. Here Singer recounts how Spira employed what would become his trademark methodical tenacity to end a series of experiments on cats at New York's Museum of Natural History. Peter Singer's other works include *Democracy and Disobedience* and *Practical Ethics*.

I n 1974, New York University advertised that Peter Singer would teach a continuing education course titled "Animal Liberation," consisting of one two-hour evening seminar a week over the span of six weeks. The topics covered included the ethics of animal liberation, a short history of speciesism, factory farming, animal experimentation, arguments for ethical vegetarianism, and objections to animal liberation. . . .

The course attracted about twenty students, most of them already involved in working for animals in some way. The format allowed plenty of time for discussion, so we all got to know one another rather well. One man stood out from the others. He certainly wasn't a typical "animal person." His whole appearance was different: His voice had too much of the accent of the New York working class. The way he put things was so blunt and earthy that at times I thought I was listening to a character from a gangster movie. His clothes were crumpled, his hair tousled. In general, he struck me as an unlikely type of person to enroll in an adult education course about animal liberation. But he was there, and I couldn't help liking the direct way he had of saying what was on his mind. His name was Henry Spira. . . .

For Henry, the course helped to confirm his view that animals are at the bottom of the heap, as far as oppression and exploitation are concerned, and that they therefore most need our help. "During that semester, between classroom and conversations, it all began to gell." Gradually during the course he became a vegetarian, first giving up red meat, then chicken, and then fish. He had resolved his personal discomfort at cuddling one animal and eating another. But he wasn't going to leave it at that. . . .

About eight people took up Henry's invitation to meet in his apartment, on the corner of Central Park West and Eighty-fifth Street, to see what they could do to put the ideas of animal liberation into practice.

Spira's Strategy

A few of us met and planned what we could do. We did not want to build a tax-exempt charity to raise money in order to be able to raise more money. We wanted to adapt to the animal movement the traditions of struggle which had proven effective in the civil rights movement, the union movement and the women's movement. We knew that we were surrounded by systems of oppression, all related and reinforcing each other, but in order to influence the course of events we knew that we must focus sharply on a single significant injustice, on one clearly limited goal. Moreover that goal must be achievable. The animal movement had been starved of victories. It desperately needed a success which could then be used as a stepping stone toward still larger struggles and more significant victories.

It seems safe to assume that most of the small group of people who turned up at Henry's apartment for that first meeting would have wondered if they really had any hope of achieving anything. Without much debate, they decided to start with the issue of experiments on animals; but they knew that they could look back on a century of antivivisection activity in Britain, the United States, and many European countries that had had absolutely no impact on animal experiments.

Henry was aware of this background, but he was not daunted by it. He had read the newsletters put out by the traditional antivivisection organizations and didn't wonder at their abysmal record of achievement:

> It didn't make any sense to me, to put out a publication, to tell people about atrocities, and ask them to send money so we can tell you next month about more atrocities. Meanwhile, the atrocities keep increasing, the treasuries of the antivivisection groups keep increasing, and it doesn't help one solitary animal.

> It just defies common sense to me why people would be doing that. What's the point in giving people an ulcer, getting people upset, getting them frustrated, and telling them, what we're going to do is frustrate you next month, isn't that nice?

Henry's experience of campaigning for human rights led him to a different approach:

> Certainly, self-righteous anti-vivisection societies had been hollering, "Abolition! All or Nothing!" But that didn't help the laboratory animals, since while the anti-vivisection groups had been hollering, the number of animals used in United States laboratories had zoomed from a few thousand to over 70 million. That was a pitiful track record, and it seemed a good idea to rethink strategies which have a century-long record of failure.

There was a difference between the way I had presented the issues in the classes and the way Henry was thinking about them: "In selecting material for his course and his book, Singer based his priorities on the number of the victims and the intensity of their suffering. In one way this was obviously right, but my personal concern was rather: what can we do about it.". . .

THE TARGET

Henry started gathering information about animal experiments at institutions in New York City. In the summer of 1975, he saw a report about sex research on animals published by United Action for Animals, an antivivisection organization. Included in the experiments described in the report were some conducted on cats at the American Museum of Natural History. The museum, one of New York's major public attractions, was on Central Park West just five blocks south of where Henry lived. He had walked past it hundreds of times, but—like the crowds of visitors who passed through its doors to look at its dinosaur skeletons and geological specimens—he had had no idea that up on the fifth floor, experiments were being conducted on animals.

The fact that the experimental subjects were cats was significant. Ethically, in Henry's view, it does not make any difference whether an experiment is done on a cat, a hamster, or a rat: They are all sensitive creatures, capable of feeling pain. But he knew that it would be easier to arouse members of the public to protest against experiments on animals to which they could easily relate. Since dogs and cats are by far the most commonly kept companion animals, experiments on them made an ideal target.

Better still, from the point of view of Henry's plans, was the fact that these experiments were about the sexual behavior of the cats. No claim could be made that the experiments would lead to a cure for some fatal disease. The experimenters would have a hard time explaining why their research on the sexual behavior of cats would be of any great value to the community.

Next, the experiments were funded by the National Institute of Child Health and Human Development—a member of the National Institutes of Health (NIH), the principal government funding agency for medical research. In other words, the experiments were being paid for from revenue raised by taxation. The link between the experiments and the purposes for which the institute was established was tenuous at best. Since no one wants public tax money wasted or misused, that made the experiments particularly vulnerable. Even more vital was the fact that as a government agency, the NIH would have to comply with the Freedom of Information Act and provide documents relating to its funding of the experiments.

Finally, the experiments were clearly distressing for the cats. They were being mutilated in various ways so experimenters could observe the effects that removal of their senses had on their sexual behavior. A description of the mutilations would be easy for the public to understand and could be counted on to arouse their sympathy for the cats. Henry started describing the experiments to people he knew who had no connection with the animal movement, to see what reactions they elicited. They were shocked. . . .

At the museum, cats had their sense of smell destroyed, their sense of touch deadened by cutting nerves in their sex organs, and parts of their brains removed. The mutilated animals were then scored on their sexual performance in various situations. For example, in a paper titled "Olfactory Deprivation and Mating Behavior," [Dr. Lester] Aronson had published tables, complete with standard deviations, for "mean frequency of mounts" for cats who had had their sense of smell destroyed by surgery. In grant applications, the experimenters proposed blinding and deafening cats as well, although these experiments had not yet been carried out. After the experiments the cats were killed and their brains studied.

In 1974 alone, the experimenters had used seventy-four cats. Each set of taxpayer-funded experiments had led to the conclusion that further experiments were needed, and the researchers had been funded to mutilate more cats. . . .

THE CAMPAIGN

Henry sent a letter to officials at the museum, telling them what he had learned as a result of his freedom of information

The Demographics of American Animal Rights Activists

The results of independent 1990 direct-mail and personal surveys by Oregon State University (OSU) and Utah State University (USU) tended to suggest that most animal rights members are well educated, Caucasian, urban, female, under fifty years of age, and/or employed in professional positions.

Characteristic	OSU %	USU %
Sex		
Male	31.6	21.7
Female	68.4	78.3
Age		
29 and under	41.9	23.2
30 to 49	48.0	56.6
50 and over	6.4	20.0
Race		
White	92.9	96.9
Nonwhite	7.1	3.1
Education		
High school diploma, GED, or less	12.3	17.9
Bachelor's degree or some college	40.2	48.4
Some graduate school	7.1	NA
Graduate/professional degree	18.7	33.3
Income		
$19,999 or less	19.0	18.4
$20,000 to $49,999	46.1	42.5
$50,000 or more	18.7	38.9
Residence		
Urban (over 10,000 population)	85.0	73.4
Rural	10.0	26.6
Don't know/Did not answer	5.0	NA
Occupation		
Professional, business, or executive status	44.0	46.0

Harold D. Guither, *Animal Rights: History and Scope of a Radical Social Movement.* Carbondale: Southern Illinois University Press, 1998, p. 71.

request and suggesting a meeting to discuss the future of the experiments. From the group's point of view, this was a strategy with no downside. The goal was not to have a big public campaign for its own sake, but to stop the experiments. Perhaps the easiest way to get the museum to do that was to allow it to cease the research without losing face. Confronted with the prospect of a damaging campaign exposing the kind of experiments it was doing, the museum could have said that it had found out everything it needed to know, and hence there was no need for the experiments to continue. If that happened, then the group would have achieved its goal and could move on to another target. If, on the other hand, the museum refused to end the experiments, then the group would be able to say that they had tried to start a dialogue with the museum but that the door had been shut in their faces.

There was no response to the letter. Phone calls were equally unavailing. Henry even signed up for a course at the museum, hoping to get an opportunity to discuss the problem with one of its scientists, but to no avail. When he learned that Lester Aronson was to give a lecture at the museum, he went to that too, but Aronson refused to talk about his cat research with a mere layperson.

Henry's next step was to go to the *New York Times,* hoping that it would pick up the story. It did nothing with it. He turned to less authoritative, but more sympathetic, media. Pegeen and Ed Fitzgerald hosted a popular daily talk show on a New York radio station. They were long-standing antivivisectionists and needed little prompting to describe the experiments and stir their listeners to protest them. This led to the museum receiving, in June, 400 letters of protest about the experiments.

The campaign gained further invaluable publicity when *Our Town*, a free Manhattan weekly, published a long article by Henry giving full details of the experiments and of the museum's failure to respond to the objections to them. Henry also circulated his materials to other animal organizations, inviting them to make use of them and to join him in protesting the experiments.

The first demonstration outside the museum, supported by such organizations as the Society for Animal Rights and Friends of Animals, took place in July. The demonstrators carried placards and gave out leaflets describing the experiments. They did not ask people to refuse to go into the museum. That would have put most visitors in a difficult situation, since the visitors had come there, often with their children, looking forward to seeing the museum's displays. Instead, the demonstrators made use of the fact that the museum had no fixed admission charge. Admission was by donation, but the museum suggested a donation of $3.00. The picketers gave visitors a penny and suggested that they use it as their donation. In that way, the visitors could show in a tangible way their opposition to the experiments, save themselves some money, and still see the museum.

Gradually, the mainstream media began to take an interest. Their attitude showed the wisdom of selecting a target that could be seen to be objectionable even by those who were not against all animal experiments. In Chicago, for example, the *Sun-Times* published an article called "Cutting Up Cats to Study Sex—What Fun!" in which the writer, Roger Simon, took aim at the museum director's defense—which Henry had ensured was widely publicized—of the freedom to conduct research without regard to its "demonstrable practical value":

> I am not against the cutting up of animals if it might do some good to somebody some day. But before I blinded cats for 14 years, I would like somebody to tell me that there might be some "demonstrable practical value" somewhere down the road.

The demonstrations continued every weekend for more than a year. The demonstrators included such stalwarts as Sonia Cortis, a retired cabaret singer, then in her sixties, who protested outside the museum with a bullhorn every weekend for the entire duration of the campaign. At the height of the demonstrations, a thousand people took part and briefly blocked the entrance in a symbolic protest. On another occasion, a petition against the experiments, with thousands of signatures, was used to make a scroll that was unrolled across the front of the museum. At other times there may have been only a handful of demonstrators, but there was no letting up. The idea was to send a message to the museum that they weren't going away until the experiments were stopped and the labs dismantled.

When people carried their placards into the museum, officials said that they would have anyone who came into the museum with a sign arrested. The campaigners then had T-shirts printed with pictures of cats and slogans calling on the museum to stop its experiments. Protesters wore the shirts into the museum, which could hardly ask them to remove them.

At the end of each demonstration, the demonstrators went across the road to Central Park, and Henry told them what had been happening in the campaign, so that they would feel that they weren't going to be demonstrating at the museum forever. A bullhorn was passed around, and the demonstrators were invited to say what they had heard, thought, or done about the campaign during the past week.

The campaign took care not to present itself as opposed to scientific research as such. It said that it supported science, but that experiments of this sort gave science a bad name. To inspire young people to take up science as a career, the campaigners argued, it was necessary to stop experiments that were brutalizing and basically meaningless.

Meanwhile, Henry and his supporters were working on other fronts as well. In its publications, the museum regularly thanked its many benefactors, including the state of New York, the city of New York, public foundations, major corporations, wealthy individuals, and artists who donated their films and their skills to the museum. All of these were contacted and asked not to support the museum while it continued the cat experiments. The editors of *Discover America,* a travel magazine that had in the past publicized exhibitions at the museum, wrote to the museum's director saying that they would not mention the museum again while the experiments continued.

Campaign supporters who owned stock in corporations that gave money to the museum were asked to move a shareholders' resolution to stop further donations until the experiments were ended. Everyone was asked to contact their elected federal, state, and city representatives and ask them to stop the waste of tax monies on meaningless research that was creating more victims and helping no one. . . .

The museum responded to the campaign by setting in motion a review by its own animal welfare committee. The review found that the project was in compliance with federal guidelines for the use of laboratory animals. The favorable finding was not surprising, because the review was carried out by a committee of three: Lester Aronson; his assistant, Madeline Cooper; and the consulting veterinarian to the project. . . .

One congressman, however, was open-minded enough—and received enough letters from his constituents—to go and take a look. At the time, Ed Koch, later to be mayor of New York, was a relatively junior congressman from Manhattan. He later told Congress about his visit to the museum:

> I said to the doctor who was explaining what was happening: "What do you do here? What is the purpose of this experiment?" And she said, "Well, the purpose is to look at the effect of hyper- and hypo-sexuality in cats. We find," said she, "that if you take a normal male cat and you place that cat in a room with a female cat that is in heat, the male cat would mount the female cat."
>
> I said, "That sounds very reasonable to me."
>
> Then she said, "Now if you take a cat, a male cat, and you put lesions in its brain—"
>
> I interrupted and asked, "What are lesions?"
>
> She said, "Well you destroy part of the brain cells."
>
> I asked, "What happens then?"
>
> She said, "Well, if you take that male cat that has lesions in

its brain and you place it in a room with a female cat and a female rabbit, the cat will mount the rabbit."

I said to her, "How does that rabbit feel about all this?"

There was no response.

Then I said to this professor, "Now, tell me, after you have taken a deranged male cat with brain lesions and you place it in a room and you find that it is going to mount a rabbit instead of a female cat, what have you got?"

There was no response.

. . . I said, "How much has this cost the government?"

She said, "$435,000."

Members of Congress found this hilarious, but they also thought it ridiculous that so much government money had been spent for this kind of nonsense. Koch wrote to the National Institutes of Health asking why it was continuing to fund the experiments, and 120 other members of Congress wrote letters to the NIH about the experiments as well. Since the entire NIH budget was ultimately dependent on Congress, it was not something that the NIH could ignore.

Letters from the public had also been arriving at the National Institutes of Health in large numbers. The *New York Times* reported Dr. William Sadler, head of the branch of the NIH that had funded the experiments, saying that a deluge of complaints from the public and inquiries from Congress had brought the operation of his office to a standstill. After initially approving the findings of the museum's animal welfare committee, the NIH subsequently decided that a review by the experimenters themselves was not good enough. . . .

The mainstream media gradually took notice of the new phenomenon of animal rights. The *New York Times, Chicago Tribune, Christian Science Monitor, Newsweek,* and NBC TV's news service were among those to cover its most dramatic manifestation, the museum protests. The NIH had responded to the

121 members of Congress by establishing a review of the funding of the cat experiments and of its general funding guidelines regarding animal experimentation; but it showed no urgency in bringing the review to a conclusion.

THE VICTORY

The weekly demonstrations continued through the winter of 1976–1977 and all of the following spring. So, too, did the experiments. But, meanwhile, developments were taking place that would bring them to an end. In February, Aronson wrote to Donald Clark, chief of the Office of Grants and Contracts at the National Institute of Child Health and Human Development, which had been funding his research, saying that he would not seek renewal of his grant when it terminated on August 31. He gave two reasons for this. The first was that he would retire in July. (He was going to be sixty-six in April.) The second was that "in view of the recent attacks by the antivivisectionist groups, I believe that the museum is not the most suitable place for this research since we are much more vulnerable and have weaker defenses against such attacks than a number of other types of institutions."

Aronson did, however, request that the existing grant be extended for one year in order "to terminate the project in an orderly manner." Clark replied seeking further information, which Aronson provided in a letter outlining four experiments that he wanted to complete during the period of the extension. In most cases, the completion involved analyzing data already obtained, rather than further experimentation on living cats; but one of the proposed experiments included additional "behavioral observations." Despite this request, the museum began to tell protesters that the experiments would end in August, when the grant terminated and Aronson retired.

Since Henry had continued to use freedom of information legislation to obtain NIH documents, he knew that while the museum was telling the public that the experiments would end in August, Aronson's request for an extension envisaged some experimentation beyond August. So the demonstrations continued. In May 1977, a full-page advertisement appeared in the *New York Times,* asking, "In the name of sanity, is this where you want your tax dollars to go? Stop the cat-torture at the Museum of Natural History." The advertisement, paid for by radio host Pegeen Fitzgerald, featured a large photograph of the head of a cat held in a stereotaxic machine, of the kind used in the cat experiments. The text below referred to the museum's announcement that the experiments would end in August and then said: *"But they weren't telling the truth. And now they are asking the NIH for more funds to continue the cat-sex projects."* The advertisement asked readers to write to their congressional representatives and to officials of the city of New York, asking them to withhold "the $5 million subsidy the museum wants" until the experiments were stopped.

Aronson's request for an extension had said that the experiments would be nearly complete by the end of August 1977. The NIH decided that they would have to stop altogether at that point. On May 6, Clark notified Aronson that his grant had been extended for only three months, until November 30, 1977; furthermore, "Research efforts during this extension shall be limited to the analysis of data already collected as of August 31, 1977, on the projects described in the 16th year continuation application and the preparation of the terminal progress report."

In theory, Aronson could have obtained financial support from the museum to complete his "behavioral observations." But the museum itself was under too much pressure for this to be a real option. During the annual budget discussions of the New York City Council, Paul O'Dwyer, president of the council, asked the budget director to contact the museum to elicit a promise to discontinue the experiments—and said that he wanted the promise before the budget was passed. On June 1, 1977, O'Dwyer wrote to a supporter of the campaign against the museum telling him that the museum had agreed to stop the experiments after August 1977. On August 22 an NIH official confirmed, in a letter to Henry, that Aronson's grant would end on August 31, except for the three-month extension to analyze data collected prior to that date, and that there were no grant applications "in the pipeline" from the Department of Animal Behavior of the American Museum of Natural History.

Meanwhile, and quite independently of the group with which he had been working on the campaign against the museum, Henry had encouraged an activist to go ahead with a different form of attack. In August, people in Hillsdale, New Jersey, where Aronson lived, received an anonymous mailing:

DO YOU KNOW THIS MAN?

Lester R. Aronson is your neighbor! He lives at 47 Cedar Street in your town of Hillsdale. His telephone number is (201) 666-0175.

For more than forty years Lester R. Aronson has been earn-ing his living performing animal sex experiments. Attached is a more detailed description of his work and a partial bib-liography of his publications. While this partial bibliogra-phy is concerned only with experiments on cats, Lester R. Aronson has done the same type of experiments on nu-merous species of fish, on the leopard frog, and on hamsters.

After you have read the enclosed information why don't you telephone Lester Aronson and tell him what you really think of him and of Madeline Cooper.

Attached to the letter was one of the campaign's flyers, de-scribing the experiments, and a list of twenty-one publications by Aronson and Cooper, with such titles as "Genital Depriva-tion and Sexual Behavior in Male Cats" and "Persistence of High Levels of Sexual Behavior in Male Cats Following Ab-lation of the Olfactory Bulbs." A similar mailing was sent to people living near Madeline Cooper, except that this included an extract from the museum's own grant proposal justifying Cooper's salary. The extract refers to establishing the follow-ing groups of animals for experimentation:

1. Blinded—Enucleation of both orbits
   A. Experienced adults
   B. Kittens blinded at three months
2. Anosmic—olfactory bulbs of the brain destroyed
   A. Experienced adults
   B. Kittens made anosmic at three months

The extract also included a section headed "Significance of the Research," which stated that "this research offers a new approach to the study of factors influencing the decline of sexual behavior after castration."

Henry calls such a strategy "Dada tactics." Just as the Dada artist Marcel Duchamp had made us look at a urinal in a different way by exhibiting it in an art gallery, so Henry wanted us to look differently at a scientist's publications and grant proposals by taking them outside the context of the laboratory and the university. In doing it at this time, when he knew that the campaign against the cat sex experiments had been won, he was looking ahead to a broader goal: to change the culture of science, in which such work was taken as normal. The real target of the mailings was not Aronson and Cooper—although if they found their neighbors less friendly than they had been, Henry was not going to shed tears over that. The objective was to have an impact on other scientists, especially those at an early stage of their career, who might be thinking about areas of research to pursue. To reach that target, Henry sent—again anonymously—copies of the mailings to the National Society for Medical Research, a Washington-based lobby group that sees the defense of animal experimentation against its critics as one of its major activities. The National Society for Medical Research put a story about the mailings on the front page of its monthly *Bulletin,* which was exactly what Henry had hoped it would do with it. Thousands of scientists were led to think about the possibility that their neighbors, too, might one day receive extracts from their grant proposals

When the end of the cat sex experiments became official, Aronson and the museum tried to deny the protesters victory by saying that the experiments had been completed anyway.

While Aronson certainly was at the age at which many people retire, he had himself requested a full year's extension for work that included some behavioral observations. This made it difficult for him to maintain that the experiments were stopping because all the work had been done.

In December, the protesters were allowed to visit the area where the labs had been. By then, they had been dismantled. In the museum's *Annual Report,* the director said that, in the future, the museum's research would put "greater emphasis on natural populations of animals and on field research, as opposed to physiologically-oriented laboratory research with domesticated or laboratory-bred animals." The victory was complete.

Confessions of a Former Vivisectionist

DONALD J. BARNES

Donald J. Barnes studied psychology at Ohio State University before working as a clinical psychologist and then as a research psychologist at the United States Air Force School of Aerospace Medicine at Brooks Air Force Base, Texas. Here he recounts how his
experience in Texas as an administrator of experiments irradiating
rhesus monkeys formed the basis of his gradual defection from animal research and the awakening of a much broader ethical sensibility. Barnes later became director of the Washington, D.C., office of
the National Antivivisection Society (NAVS).

'Don,' an acquaintance of mine said recently, 'I don't
mean to question your commitment to the principles
of antivivisection, but you were a vivisector for sixteen years.'
What caused such a quick and radical change in your beliefs?'
I have been asked the same question many times, and by one
person more than any other . . . myself. The answer has
changed as my values have changed, but consistently and in the
same direction. Let's take a chronological look at the evolution
of my values in order to try to understand.

In early 1941, just a few months before my fifth birthday,
my parents somehow managed to buy a 20-acre farm in
Southern California. . . .

Animals were integral to our existence. We raised pigs, cattle and chickens for our meat, eggs and dairy products,
churned our own butter and drank our milk as it came from
the cow, without pasteurization or homogenization. We treated
our animals with love and respect, but always in the knowl-

edge that they were on earth not for themselves but to serve us. Butchering was accomplished as expediently as possible with a hatchet and a chopping block for the fowl and a well-placed bullet for the larger animals. Their deaths raised enigmatic questions in my mind but were soon accepted as necessary, for that was the ethos of the farm.

When I was about seven years old (and my brother nine), our father bought us a burro. We had wanted a horse for some time but had been convinced that a horse was economically unjustifiable, as it would contribute nothing but pleasure to the family farm. We had a tractor with huge metal wheels, almost an antique, so we couldn't even use a horse for ploughing. We soon learned that our burro was not to be simply a plaything for us. As my father pruned the branches of the fruit trees or cut down the corn stalks from the field, my brother and I loaded them on the cart and hauled them away from the field or orchard. There is much hauling to be done on a farm, and before we knew it we were performing this essential function daily. Even so, the burro and I became close friends and we spent many blissful hours exploring the surrounding countryside together. . . .

After several years our family moved to Colorado and the life on the farm was over for ever. But now I was taken hunting and fishing, and I became proficient in both. . . .

PROJECT X

In 1960, while studying for a Ph.D. in clinical psychology and ever mindful of the ethics involved in working with psychiatric patients, I was given a position as graduate teaching assistant at the Ohio State University. My job was to teach principles of learning to second-year college students through the use of operant-conditioning techniques applied to laboratory rats. This was no problem for me, given that my entire background consisted of using other animals for my sake, and I glibly demonstrated the effectiveness of various techniques of training, including the use of electric shock as 'negative reinforcement'.

Six years later, having completed my internship and graduated from the US Air Force Officers Training School, I was assigned to head up the laboratory when the Air Force decided to develop a capability to determine the effects of pulsed ionizing radiation upon the behaviour of non-human primates. (To the Department of Defense, a psychologist is a psychologist: it didn't matter that I was a clinical psychologist.) I was given a relatively large budget ($200,000 to $300,000 per year) and freedom to set up the programme I wanted. I had a crew of enlisted and civilian workers, most of them with college degrees. I was given the opportunity to travel to other laboratories, to speak to funding agencies, to consult with other scientists. . . .

The gastro-intestinal system is affected early in the course of radiation injury. Hence we were not at liberty to use food, or 'positive reinforcement' to train the monkeys, for if they stopped 'working' we could not attribute the work stoppage to their inability to work. The animals might simply not feel like eating. We were therefore constrained to use shock avoidance, or 'negative reinforcement', in our experiments. We felt that we must provide the animals with the strongest incentive in order to avoid interpretational difficulties based upon 'motivation'. We therefore bought specially designed shock units from Behavioral Research Systems Electronics. These shock units delivered between 0 and 50 millamperes at 12,000 volts. The output from the shock units was connected to 'shock plates', metal plates under the monkeys' feet and mounted on strong springs to ensure contact with the feet. It was impossible to measure the amount of shock each animal received as skin toughness, perspiration, spring tension, the specific shock unit, etc., were all relatively uncontrolled. The training situation therefore became totally empirical in that the shock unit was turned up until the primate began to respond. In many cases this was a very high shock level, as most of the monkeys were very young and passive and tended to withdraw rather than to strike out when hurt. The more aggressive animals received fewer shocks because they responded more often and were therefore more likely to emit the response desired by the experimenter, at which point the shock would be terminated. But woe to the monkey who withdrew, who began to self-mutilate, who tried to escape: I've seen more than one monkey die from cardiac fibrillation occasioned by repeated shocking. . . .

A MATTER OF NATIONAL SECURITY

I was, of course, given a reason for this research. I was told that the Air Force needed to know the survivability/vulnerability of its weapons systems. In other words, it needed to know where the systems were weakest so that it could bolster up that part of the system. Much research had been accomplished to 'harden' the electronics against the effects of radiation, but the human was also a basic component of most Air Force weapons systems (i.e., airplanes). Hence, it was argued, the vulnerability of the human 'subsystem' demanded definition.

It became my job to determine probability estimates of aircrew functioning following nuclear radiation. If the pilot (co-pilot, bombardier, etc.) became comatose following the receipt of 5,000 rads, why spend an exorbitant amount of time and money 'hardening' the electronic components to withstand 10,000, 15,000 or 20,000 rads? Also, if the human simply underwent a period of 'early transient incapacitation' and could operate the weapons system fifteen or twenty minutes after irradiation, how could we develop an automatic pilot which would get the crew member through this period of incapacitation and still enable him (sexist but accurate) to complete his mission?

These are real questions to the military planner; as an employee of the Department of Defense, they became real problems for me. I'm sure that I don't have to point to the lack of humane consideration inherent in this situation. In contrast to most biomedical research, even the human is seen as expendable to the mission; the goal is to assure that the mission is completed, that the bombs are dropped. No one expects the human operators of these weapons systems to return from their missions. What possible chance of personal consideration does a non-human have in such an environment?

The obvious solution: take the human out of the weapons system. Even though the technology to do exactly that has existed for a decade, it will not be done. Why? Because the future of the US Air Force depends upon having a person in the cockpit. The US Air Force is an entrenched bureaucratic institution. It is self-perpetuating and has erected defence mechanisms to prevent its own annihilation while developing other defensive strategies to defend the United States against invasion; both systems are sophisticated and 'hardened' against attack. In order to protect the status quo, projects which maintain it are approved; those which threaten its continuation are disapproved. If we can't take the human out of the system, we must find a way to ensure that the system works with the human in it. Hence, billions of dollars are spent on justifying the existing bureaucratic apparatus.

1,000 MONKEYS LATER

In this role, I accepted the problems as my superiors outlined them for me. How, indeed, does one determine the vulnerability of the human operator to radiation?

First, one must accept an anthropocentric point of view—that is, human welfare is the first priority. Second, one must, at least implicitly (as in my case), assume that the ends justify the means. There is no substitute for humans in biomedical research designed to learn about humans, but one cannot accept this fact if convinced that the problem must be solved. So a surrogate must be found for those experiments which would prove harmful to humans. The non-human primate would appear to be our closest relative; he is the obvious choice.

If there were an extrapolative index, a formula for predicting human behaviour from the behaviour of non-human primates, biomedical science would have a wealth of information. Many of the 'problems' presented to me would have been solved years and years ago, for millions of non-human primates have been sacrificed to this end. There is no such formula. But I didn't realize this simple fact and, being convinced that non-human animals exist for human purposes, blindly accepted the premise that 'close is better than nothing' and set about developing an ambitious programme to irradiate trained monkeys in order to extrapolate the results to hypothetical human situations. Over 1,000 monkeys later, several events occurred which caused me to step back and re-evaluate my position. Although I cannot point to a single causative factor in my conversion from experimenter to animal rights activist, I can recall some of the events.

I must confess that, for some years, I had entertained suspicions about the utility of the data we were gathering. I made a few token attempts to ascertain both the destination and the purpose of the technical reports we published but now acknowledge my eagerness to accept assurances from those in command that we were, in fact, providing a real service to the US Air Force and, hence, to the defence of the free world. I used those assurances as blinkers to avoid the reality of what I saw in the field, and even though I did not always wear them comfortably, they did serve to protect me from the insecurities associated with the potential loss of status and income.

As each day passes it becomes increasingly difficult to comprehend how I was able to close my eyes to the artificiality of the research I was doing. The data we gathered on the behavioural effects of ionizing radiation were used as inputs to 'models' of the operational systems. By this stage the numbers themselves had become 'truths'. The fact that they had been obtained from non-human primates in highly artificial situations was forgotten or ignored. The very fact that they existed to be utilized as inputs to computer-modelled 'war games' justified their validity.

THE PETER PRINCIPLE

And then, one day, the blinkers slipped off, and I found myself in a very serious confrontation with Dr Roy DeHart, Commander, US Air Force School of Aerospace Medicine. I tried to point out that, given a nuclear confrontation, it is highly unlikely that operational commanders will go to charts and figures based upon data from the rhesus monkey to gain estimates of probable force strength or second-strike capability. Dr De-Hart insisted that the data will be invaluable, asserting, 'They don't know the data are based on animal studies.' Needless to say, this confrontation proved devastating to my status as a Principal Investigator at the School of Aerospace Medicine!

In retrospect, I realize that the slow changes in my perception of the research I was doing were accompanied by changes on the empathic, as well as on the intellectual, level. For example, on several occasions during the sixteen years I did research on non-human primates, I took it upon myself to destroy irradiated animals. Although not trained as a physiologist, I found I had the facility to locate a vein while many technicians could not. Rather than cause the monkey further suffering, I began to fill in when the veterinarian was absent. On each occasion a thought occurred to me: 'Do I have the "right" to do this?' I know now that a subliminal voice answered 'No!' but I felt I had no choice. At that particular moment I did not; later it was easy to concentrate on other issues.

In 1979, just over a year before I would leave the laboratory to work for the dignity of non-human animals, my boss approached me with a request: would I talk to a young statistician who had just come into our laboratories to work with us? He had apparently become quite upset upon seeing the monkeys receive electric shock for failing to perform their 'duties' correctly and had commented on the inhumanity of the project. Could I defuse this potentially dangerous situation? Of course! I gave this fellow all the trite arguments. I told him of the 'necessity' for the research; I told him of the reason for using electric shock; I told him why we had to use monkeys. He bought the argument; in the process I began to unconvince myself.

Shortly thereafter I was ordered to radiate four trained rhesus monkeys with 360 rads of gamma radiation and to determine the effect of such radiation upon the monkeys' behaviour over the next ten hours. I objected to doing this experiment for the following reasons. First, I had become an expert on the behavioural effects of ionizing radiation in the rhesus monkey; I knew that 360 rads would not affect the performance of the monkeys during the ten hour post-irradiation observation period. Second, with even the most elegant of experimental designs, a subject population of four is statistically inadequate; even if all four monkeys behaved in exactly the same way following radiation, the results would be scientifically invalid. Third, I had fallen out of favour with my superiors by this time as a result of my questioning of the entire project and had been relegated to the laboratory. I knew these monkeys. I was becoming more and more particular about how they were 'utilized'. I didn't want to 'use' these animals in a meaningless project. This is not to say that I would have balked at using them in a project I considered to be important; I had not yet reached that point in my conversion. I took my objections to a staff meeting and presented my position.

The other professionals, including my immediate supervisor, agreed that the experiment would be a negative one; the monkeys would demonstrate no behavioural changes during the 10-hour post-irradiation observation period. They further agreed that the experiment could be done by analysis of existing data, by a thorough literature review. Even so, my immediate superior was frightened to authorize this procedure and would not do so. He did, however, promise to discuss the matter with his supervisor.

The farther one goes up the chain of command, the less competent technical advice is available, states the Peter Principle. This was no exception; I was ordered to accomplish the experiment for political reasons. My reaction was anything but acquiescence; steps were subsequently taken to get rid of me, as I had become a thorn in the side of the bureaucracy. I was fired.

LIVING WITH CHANGED AWARENESS

As I reflect upon this situation, I see that values based upon an unpopular ethic are a luxury that many people cannot afford to conceptualize, let alone to embrace. I was being stirred by some disquieting thoughts and feelings, to be sure, but I didn't understand them. As far as I was concerned, I was caught up in a bureaucratic morass, being punished for questioning authority, feeling self-righteous because I knew that it was scientifically improper to waste valuable resources (animals) in the pursuit of poor science. Whatever empathy existed with the laboratory animals was still in its own cage, locked away from my thoughts.

I was hurt, embarrassed and angry. I looked for ammunition, for tools of retribution. I called in the Inspector General, alleging mismanagement and waste of government resources. I filed for reinstatement with the proper authorities. I talked to the press. I wrote to humane organizations and, in the process of composing these letters, began to realize, perhaps for the first time, that my work and the research efforts of my peers had been both inhumane and without redeeming value.

As a biomedical research scientist, I had been shielded almost completely from contact with organizations within the animal advocacy movement. It wasn't so much that I had been ordered not to communicate with individuals or organizations concerned with the rights of laboratory animals, but a bias against any antivivisection philosophy was a 'natural' part of the laboratory environment. During my sixteen years in the laboratory the morality and ethics of using laboratory animals were never broached in either formal or informal meetings prior to my raising the issues during the waning days of my tenure as a vivisector. On at least two occasions support personnel were chastised for unnecessary abuse of their non-human charges, but the question of the cruelty of the research itself remained buried in the all-encompassing and 'beneficent' embrace of medical science.

In my anger and frustration, I had a flash of insight. The research I had been doing, and which was continuing in my absence, was not merely scientifically improper: it was inhumane. I was appalled at my own past insensitivity and determined to put a stop to those projects which I knew to be both invalid and cruel, but I had no idea who to contact. Like so many other people, I had not taken the time or made the effort to become informed about the plight of non-human animals. Two groups came to mind from distant memories: the Society for the Prevention of Cruelty to Animals (SPCA) and the Humane Society of the United States (HSUS). I wrote to the latter organization, and my letter was referred to Dr Andrew Rowan, who replied with interest and recommended that I contact Dr Shirley McGreal of the International Primate Protection League (IPPL). I did so, and a lively correspondence grew up between myself and Dr McGreal—a correspondence which would eventually lead me into the humane movement.

I won my case for reinstatement and returned to the School of Aerospace Medicine, not to work with animals, for I could no longer do that, but to do research on alternatives to the use of animals. After three months I recommended that the research be terminated. This was not accepted, and I was ordered back to the laboratory. I resigned my position and found employment in the humane movement.

My values are very different today from what they were in 1980. In retrospect, I realize that I held tightly to my conditioned beliefs, releasing them only as they were pried from me by logic and evidence of their inappropriateness. In 1980 I could be pressed to separate research with non-human animals into 'better' or 'poorer' categories. The residual logic of 'necessary medical research' remained to some extent; the anthropocentric view faded slowly away, to be replaced by a broader view of increased respect for other life forms. As a consequence, meat was omitted from my diet, leather from my wardrobe and rodeos and circuses from my options for entertainment. My feelings at the sight of a fur coat changed from grudging admiration to nonchalance, to pity, to disgust and frustration.

Change requires the reconceptualization of many, if not all, of our habits. I didn't change my views quickly, nor did I change them without struggle or resentment. I only hope that in changing my own views I have become able to bring about similar changes in the views of those who unthinkingly continue to experiment today.

Cleveland Amory and the Black Beauty Ranch

MICHAEL BLUMENTHAL

Cleveland Amory, a prominent humorist and humanitarian whose works included *The Cat and the Curmudgeon* (the middle installment of a trilogy) and *Man Kind? Our Incredible War on Wildlife*, was well-known for his founding of the animal rights organization Fund for Animals, serving without pay as its president from its inception in 1967 until his death in 1998. But in addition to this, inspired by his lifelong love of Anna Sewell's novel *Black Beauty*, Amory also established the Black Beauty ranch, a 1,460-acre refuge that provided shelter for abused animals from chimpanzees to burros to elephants. His intention was to create a sanctuary where its inhabitants would roam unfettered and unbothered by human taskmasters. Michael Blumenthal, an Austin-based poet, novelist, and essayist, recounts a visit to the ranch shortly following the scattering of Amory's ashes there.

It is early October, a fairly typical day in the life of Chris Byrne, the resident manager of the Fund for Animals Black Beauty Ranch in the East Texas town of Murchison. But it's not going to be a typical month: In less than two weeks the ranch's founder and presiding spirit, 81-year-old Cleveland Amory, will die the kind of death he would have wished for any of its six-hundred-plus resident animals—in his sleep, and at home.

On this particular morning, however, Byrne has just returned from Denver, where he has picked up a pair of white-handed gibbons from the Denver Zoo. Before that he had been to Indianapolis, where he had consulted with a group of veterinarians and elephant managers on what to do about the lame hind leg of a thirteen-year-old African elephant named Babe. Now Byrne has to be briefed by the ranch's handful of employees about what has taken place during his absence, and he has to begin constructing a more permanent, more humane shelter for the gibbons, which, at this moment, are ensconced in a small cage next to the elephant barn.

Not exactly your typical Texas ranch, this is a place where, as you drive through the front gate just a mile or so off FM 1803, you're greeted by a sign reading "Drive Carefully: Animals at Play." This 1,460-acre spread is a haven for animals that have been injured or abused or, in some cases, are merely unwanted—and the incarnation of the dream of one man: writer, social historian, television critic, and animal rights advocate extraordinaire Cleveland Amory. This is a Ranch of Dreams.

A LIFELONG OBSESSION

As a child, Amory—who had a lifelong obsession with Anna Sewell's classic novel, *Black Beauty*—had a very specific dream. "It was not long after reading *Black Beauty* for the first of many times," he wrote in his 1997 book about the ranch, *Ranch of Dreams*, "that I had a dream that one day I would have a place which would embody everything Black Beauty loved about his final home. I dreamed that I would go even a step further—at my place none of the horses would ever wear a bit or blinkers or check reins, or in fact have any reins at all, because they would never pull a cart, a carriage, a cab, or anything else. Indeed, they would never even be ridden—they would just run free."

From the moment my eight-year-old son, Noah, and I arrive at the ranch, its inhabitants—who range from ringed doves to greater elands—do their best to let us know that we're here, if not exactly by the grace of God, by their consent. Just minutes after we get out of the car and head toward Byrne's state-of-the-art elephant barn, for instance, a 10,000-pound African elephant named Conga—who came to the ranch from a roadside zoo in Florida, where she had suffered second- and third-degree sunburn when she was forced to sit on a park bench and twirl an umbrella—welcomes me by sending a slightly viscous spray my way.

As I follow Byrne and volunteer veterinarian Leigh Wilson on their daily tour of inspections, greetings, and feedings, it occurs to me that if Amory had been an animal, Black Beauty Ranch is the kind of place where he would have wanted to end up. The words on the ranch's gate ("I have nothing to fear, / And here my story ends./ My troubles are all over, / And I am at home") are taken from the final lines of *Black Beauty*, but the lines inscribed on a plaque at the Statue of Liberty ("Give me your tired, your poor, / Your huddled masses yearning to breathe free") would be just as apt—although the ranch can't take in every homeless or abused waif. Decisions are made by Byrne on a case-by-case basis and depend on the availability of space and the suitability of the ranch's environment for each prospective tenant.

Amory established the Fund for Animals, the ranch's parent organization, in 1967. He was a self-proclaimed curmudgeon (his book *The Cat and the Curmudgeon*, the second of three about his cat Polar Bear, was published in 1990) whose 1974 classic, *Man Kind? Our Incredible War on Wildlife*, is widely credited with launching the anti-hunting movement in this country—and a man you wouldn't want to be in charge of making a Sophie's choice between you and your pet burro. "It would be a horrible world if everything were on two legs," he once told an interviewer, staring his fellow two-legged creature in the eye.

In *Ranch of Dreams* Amory admitted that East Texas was "about as curious a place for a Bostonian to choose as could be imagined. I did not know anything about Texas when I picked it," he wrote. "Indeed, before I knew much about Texas, I firmly believed that all Texans thought that animals were good for just three things—to make money off of, to eat, and to shoot." Amory soon discovered that, in addition to being home to large areas of Bermuda grass, the ideal grazing pasture for most hoofed animals, East Texas was "something very different" from what he had first imagined. "The first time I saw Murchison, Texas," he confessed, "I had to rub my eyes to believe I was not in New England."

Like Amory, Chris Byrne—who was born in Wimbledon, England, 48 years ago—is a person obsessed with the animal victims of the world. The web of scars on his right hand—the combined artwork of a puma, a bobcat, and a rhesus monkey—testifies to the fact that his line of work isn't for the faint of heart or the purely sentimental. Byrne and Ringo, a rhesus monkey who won't let another human being come within three feet of him without baring his teeth and lashing out with his claws, stand grooming each other. "I suppose you might say I get along better with animals than with humans," says Byrne. When asked why Ringo seems to exempt him from his rage, Byrne says, "I guess we have something in common."

At age six Byrne became so enamored of a Welsh pony a local Gypsy woman used to deliver firewood that he persuaded her to let him look after it in exchange for delivering the wood. He came to Black Beauty eight years ago after working as a stuntman and an animal trainer in the U.S. and Australia, including a period when he took care of the DuPont family's horses. "My early childhood was almost entirely animal deprived," he tells me, "and I suppose that's partly why I became so obsessed with animals."

Among the lifestyle changes of the various ranch staffers and volunteers, however, it's probably Leigh Wilson's that is the most clearly symbolic. Trained as a psychologist at Colorado State University in Fort Collins, Wilson spent nearly twenty years living and working in Alaska before "burning out" on her two-legged subjects and, at the age of forty, deciding to attend veterinary school.

RANCH RESIDENTS

As Byrne and Wilson introduce me to some of the ranch's residents, the animals' stories begin to sound like the life histories of war veterans. Babe, who now shares the elephant enclosure with Conga and a Sri Lankan refugee from the Ringling Brothers and Barnum and Bailey Circus named Tara, was standing beside her mother in Africa when she was killed by hunters during a culling. Babe was then shipped to an American circus in an undersized crate, where she badly banged up two of her legs and her head, which is still misshapen. While performing with the circus, she further damaged her right hind leg—which is curled backward in what can only be described as a kind of clubfoot—when she was hit by a larger elephant while chained. After Babe arrived at the ranch, Byrne decided to have her leg evaluated at Texas A&M, a decision that entailed borrowing a trailer big enough to transport the 3,400-pound elephant, installing lights and an observation camera in it, and persuading the Texas Department of Public Safety to provide scales normally used for weighing semi-trailers. At A&M, veterinarians decided that a fiberglass boot should be fabricated for Babe's leg, but so far the university's engineers have been unable to design one that Babe can tolerate. So Byrne has begun consulting with Larry Gallupo of the University of California at Davis School of Veterinary Medicine about alternative treatments.

Black Beauty's most famous resident, however, is a 25-year-old chimp named Nim Chimpsky, whose early life is chronicled in two books bearing his name and who seems, during our visit, to take inordinate pleasure in untying Noah's sneakers. Nim was born at the University of Oklahoma's Institute for Primate Studies on November 21, 1973. When he was just three days old, he was sent to the New York lab of Herbert Terrace, a Columbia University psychologist who was doing research in behavioral psychology and who named him after—who else?—MIT linguist and political activist Noam Chomsky. During the course of the next four years—until Terrace's funding tapered off—Nim lived with private families and researchers in New York and learned to communicate in American Sign Language, using more than two hundred signs. After he was returned to the Institute for Primate Studies, Cleveland Amory prevailed upon the University of Oklahoma to let Nim live out his days at Black Beauty Ranch, where he has been for the past fifteen years, at present in the company of three other chimps: Midge, Kitty, and Lulu Belle.

But it's not the chimps or the elephants or the bobcats that are the ranch's real raison d'etre. In 1979 the National Park Service decided to shoot the burros in the Grand Canyon because their numbers were getting out of hand and, the Park Service said, they weren't indigenous to the canyon. That decision, which Amory called "a declaration of war on the burros," so energized and mobilized the Fund for Animals that it hired the New York advertising firm Young and Rubicam to place a fundraising ad in *Parade* magazine showing a picture of a young burro under the headline "If You Turn This Page, This Burro Will Be Shot." Months of negotiation, fundraising, and litigation led to the fund's purchase of an 85-acre plot near Murchison and to an agreement with the Park Service to let it rescue the burros. Over a two-year period, using a helicopter and a sling—and with the help of world champion roper Dave Ericsson of Arizona—the new Black Beauty Ranch managed to airlift 577 burros out of the canyon and relocate them in East Texas.

More recently, the relationship between the ranch and the Park Service has taken a happier turn. When a part of the Mojave Desert was designated a national preserve in 1994, the Park Service decided that the burros there were damaging the area's native plant life. This time, it contacted the Fund for Animals to see if they could work together to relocate the animals. An agreement was reached under which the ranch will accept some three hundred feral burros a year for adoption. On September 12 a shipment of fifty jacks arrived, followed by a shipment of forty more jacks and ten jennies on the twenty-third. . . .

WHY CAN'T WE JUST BE KIND

"My ranch," Amory wrote of his boyhood dream, "would most definitely not be a place for circus acts. No animal would stand on two legs or sit on a stool or jump through hoops or do tricks or acts or any other kind of stunt." And, as we pull away from the ranch—past Shiloh, Atlantic City's last diving horse, and One-eyed Jack, the buffalo found wandering around a Pennsylvania feedlot, and Peg, a three-legged cat who crawled up the driveway eighteen years ago with her leg caught in an animal trap, and Conga, who no longer has to sit on a bench twirling an umbrella—it is clear that here was a man who made good on his dream. "They're able to give such love and respect to us," Amory once said of the occupants of his East Texas ark. "Why can't we do it for them? Why can't we just be kind?"

Unlike Mark Antony in Shakespeare's *Julius Caesar*, I had wanted to write this piece to praise Cleveland Amory, not to bury him. But fate intervened, and during the last week of October, Amory's ashes were placed in a large saltshaker tied around the neck of Friendly, one of the first burros rescued from the Grand Canyon back in 1979, and scattered about the ranch he so loved. "We're going to keep going just as we have been," Byrne says on the phone. "Just the way Cleveland would have wanted it." He is working on a stone monument to Amory that will stand beside the monument to his beloved cat, Polar Bear, whom he rescued from starvation and cold on a long-ago Christmas Eve. The cat's marker is inscribed with the words "Beneath these stones lie the mortal remains of The Cat Who Came for Christmas, Beloved 'Polar Bear' 1977–1992. 'Til we meet again."

Now, true to Amory's wish, he and his beloved Polar Bear, the Curmudgeon and the Cat, have met again. "I have nothing to fear, / And here my story ends. / My troubles are all over, / And I am at home."

CHAPTER 3

PHILOSOPHIES AND CRITICISMS

AMERICAN
SOCIAL
MOVEMENTS

Why Animals Have Rights

TOM REGAN

Animals deserve respect, argues author and animal rights philosopher Tom Regan, not because "it is good to be kind" but because as sentient creatures they satisfy the same criteria humans possess for being valuable "subjects of a life." According to Regan, the "utilitarianism" view held by fellow animal rights scholar and frequent collaborator Peter Singer with its goal of achieving "the greatest good for all parties involved," though ideal in principle, is ultimately less tenable than Regan's rights theory because concepts such as "greatest good" are wildly subjective to interpretation. Tom Regan is a former professor of philosophy at North Carolina State University and a leading scholar on the topic of animal rights. His other works include (with Andrew Linzey) *Animals and Christianity: A Book of Readings* and *All That Dwell Therein: Essays on Animal Rights and Environmental Ethics.*

How to proceed? We begin by asking how the moral status of animals has been understood by thinkers who deny that animals have rights. Then we test the mettle of their ideas by seeing how well they stand up under the heat of fair criticism. If we start our thinking in this way we soon find that some people believe that we have no duties directly to animals, that we owe nothing to them, that we can do nothing that wrongs them. Rather we can do wrong acts that involve animals and so we have duties *regarding* them, though none *to* them. Such views may be called *indirect duty views.* By way of illustration—suppose your neighbor kicks your dog. Then your neighbor has done something wrong, but not to your dog. The wrong that has been done is a wrong to you. After all it is wrong to upset people and your neighbor's kicking your dog upsets you so you are the one who is wronged not your dog. Or again—by kicking your dog your neighbor damages your property. And since it is wrong to damage another person's property, your neighbor has done something wrong—to you, of course, not to your dog. Your neighbor no more wrongs your dog than your car would be wronged if the windshield were smashed. Your neighbor's duties involving your dog are indirect duties to you. More generally, all of our duties regarding animals are indirect duties to one another—to humanity.

How could someone try to justify such a view? Someone might say that your dog doesn't feel anything and so isn't hurt by your neighbor's kick, doesn't care about the pain since none is felt, is as unaware of anything as is your windshield. Someone might say this, but no rational person will, since, among other considerations, such a view will commit anyone who holds it to the position that no human beings feel pain either—that human beings also don't care about what happens to them. A second possibility is that though both humans and your dog are hurt when kicked, it is only human pain that matters. But, again, no rational person can believe this. Pain is pain wherever it occurs. If your neighbor's causing you pain is wrong because of the pain that is caused, we cannot rationally ignore or dismiss the moral relevance of the pain that your dog feels.

Philosophers who hold indirect duty views—and many still do—have come to understand that they must avoid the two defects just noted: that is, both the view that animals don't feel anything as well as the idea that only human pain can be morally relevant. Among such thinkers the sort of view now favored is one or another form of what is called *contractarianism*.

CONTRACTARIANISM EXPLAINED

Here, very crudely, is the root idea: morality consists of a set of rules that individuals voluntarily agree to abide by, as we do when we sign a contract (hence the name contractarianism).

Those who understand and accept the terms of the contract are covered directly; they have rights created and recognized by, and protected in, the contract. And these contractors can also have protection spelled out for others who, though they lack the ability to understand morality and so cannot sign the contract themselves, are loved or cherished by those who can. Thus young children, for example, are unable to sign contracts and lack rights. But they are protected by the contract nonetheless because of the sentimental interests of others, most notably their parents. So we have, then, duties involving these children, duties regarding them, but no duties to them. Our duties in their case are indirect duties to other human beings, usually their parents.

As for animals, since they cannot understand contracts, they obviously cannot sign; and since they cannot sign, they have no rights. Like children, however, some animals are the object of the sentimental interest of others. You, for example, love your dog or cat. So those animals that enough people care about (companion animals, whales, baby seals, the American bald eagle), though they lack rights themselves, will be protected because of the sentimental interests of people. I have, then, according to contractarianism, no duty directly to your dog or any other animal, not even the duty not to cause them pain or suffering; my duty not to hurt them is a duty I have to those people who care about what happens to them. As for other animals, where no or little sentimental interest is present—in the case of farm animals, for example, or laboratory rats—what duties we have grow weaker and weaker, perhaps to the vanishing point. The pain and death they endure, though real, are not wrong if no one cares about them.

When it comes to the moral status of animals, contractarianism could be a hard view to refute if it were an adequate theoretical approach to the moral status of human beings. It is not adequate in this latter respect, however, which makes the question of its adequacy in the former case, regarding animals, utterly moot. For consideration: morality, according to the (crude) contractarian position before us, consists of rules that people agree to abide by. What people? Well, enough to make a difference—enough, that is, *collectively* to have the power to enforce the rules that are drawn up in the contract. That is very well and good for the signatories but not so good for anyone who is not asked to sign. And there is nothing in contractarianism of the sort we are discussing that guarantees or requires that everyone will have a chance to participate equally in framing rules of morality. The result is that this approach to ethics could sanction the most blatant forms of social, economic, moral, and political injustice, ranging from a repressive caste system to systematic racial or sexual discrimination. Might, according to this theory, does make right. Let those who are the victims of injustice suffer as they will. It matters not so long as no one else—no contractor, or too few of them—cares about it. Such a theory takes one's moral breath away . . . as if, for example, there would be nothing wrong with apartheid in South Africa if few white South Africans were upset by it. A theory with so little to recommend it at the level of the ethics of our treatment of our fellow humans cannot have anything more to recommend it when it comes to the ethics of how we treat our fellow animals. . . .

THE CRUELTY-KINDNESS VIEW

Indirect duty views, then, including the best among them, fail to command our rational assent. Whatever ethical theory we should accept rationally, therefore, it must at least recognize that we have some duties directly to animals, just as we have some duties directly to each other. The next two theories I'll sketch attempt to meet this requirement.

The first I call the cruelty-kindness view. Simply stated, this says that we have a direct duty to be kind to animals and a direct duty not to be cruel to them. Despite the familiar, reassuring ring of these ideas, I do not believe that this view offers an adequate theory. To make this clearer, consider kindness. A kind person acts from a certain type of motive—compassion or concern, for example. And that is a virtue. But there is no guarantee that a kind act is a right act. If I am a generous racist, for example, I will be inclined to act kindly towards members of my own race, favoring their interests above those of others. My kindness would be real and, so far as it goes, good. But I trust it is too obvious to require argument that my kind acts may not be above moral reproach—may, in fact, be positively wrong because rooted in injustice. So kindness, notwithstanding its status as a virtue to be encouraged, simply will not carry the weight of a theory of right action.

Some Problems with Tom Regan's Philosophy

Though author Ted Benton goes on in this essay to commend Tom Regan's attempt to develop a view of moral justice that crosses the species barrier, here he notes two of the potentially smoky details in Regan's thesis: that of Regan's cut-off point for rights-holders and the difficulty in assessing human accountability when the rights of eligible animals are infringed.

A . . . difficulty in Regan's position concerns the range of beings which could be given moral protection from abuse—the scope of the rights view. There are several aspects here. First, the immense majority of animal species are offered no protection whatsoever from Regan's argument. The right to respectful treatment derives from possession of 'inherent value', and the criterion of this, for Regan, is that an individual counts as 'subject-of-a-life'. . . . The teeming millions of insects and other invertebrates, amphibians, reptiles, fish, birds and mammals at the earliest stages of infancy all would appear to be objects of complete moral indifference. The difficulty is, indeed, sharpened by Regan's insistence that inherent value cannot be a matter of degree: either one has it or one does not, and anyone who has it has it equally with everyone else who

Cruelty fares no better. People or their acts are cruel if they display either a lack of sympathy for or, worse, the presence of enjoyment in another's suffering. Cruelty in all its guises is a bad thing, a tragic human failing. But just as a person's being motivated by kindness does not guarantee that he or she does what is right, so the absence of cruelty does not ensure that he or she avoids doing what is wrong. Many people who perform abortions, for example, are not cruel, sadistic people. But that

has. For Regan, this requirement follows from the need to avoid any parley with the detested perfectionist views of justice. Either, therefore, a being does satisfy the subject-of-a-life criterion and so possesses equal rights with human individuals, or it does not, in which case it has no moral status at all. . . .

The question of individualism, indeed, does arise immediately in connection with [another] difficulty in Regan's position: the specific analysis of rights which he advocates. . . . Should we assign responsibility to the operatives who administer and maintain the animals and the physical plant, to their managers, or to the business executives who run the enterprise, or to the investors in the pension schemes who supply its capital, or to the food processors and retailers who demand standardized and predictable supplies of meat at set prices, or to consumers who demand cheap food and ask no questions, or to legislators who fail to outlaw these practices, to a civil service which fails to enforce what legislation there is, or to a citizenry that fails to act against abuse? If individual responsibility is shared, it is shared so thinly that no one may feel the issue is one of overriding priority.

Ted Benton, *Natural Relations: Ecology, Animal Rights, and Social Justice*. New York: Verso, 1993, pp. 87–90.

fact alone does not settle the terribly difficult question of the morality of abortion. The case is no different when we examine the ethics of our treatment of animals. So, yes, let us be for kindness and against cruelty. But let us not suppose that being for the one and against the other answers questions about moral right and wrong.

PROS AND CONS OF UTILITARIANISM

Some people think that the theory we are looking for is *utilitarianism*. A utilitarian accepts two moral principles. The first is that of equality: everyone's interests count, and similar interests must be counted as having similar weight or importance. White or black, American or Iranian, human or animal—everyone's pain or frustration matters, and matters just as much as the equivalent pain or frustration of anyone else. The second principle a utilitarian accepts is that of utility: do the act that will bring about the best balance between satisfaction and frustration for everyone affected by the outcome.

As a utilitarian, then, here is how I am to approach the task of deciding what I morally ought to do: I must ask who will be affected if I choose to do one thing rather than another, how much each individual will be affected, and where the best results are most likely to lie—which option, in other words, is most likely to bring about the best results, the best balance between satisfaction and frustration. That option, whatever it may be, is the one I ought to choose. That is where my moral duty lies.

The great appeal of utilitarianism rests with its uncompromising *egalitarianism:* everyone's interests count and count as much as the like interests of everyone else. The kind of odious discrimination that some forms of contractarianism can justify—discrimination based on race or sex, for example—seems disallowed in principle by utilitarianism, as is speciesism, systematic discrimination based on species membership.

The equality we find in utilitarianism, however, is not the sort an advocate of animal or human rights should have in mind. Utilitarianism has no room for the equal rights of different individuals because it has no room for their equal inherent value or worth. What has value for the utilitarian is the satisfaction of an individual's interests, not the individual whose interests they are. A universe in which you satisfy your desire for water, food, and warmth is, other things being equal, better than a universe in which these desires are frustrated. And the same is true in the case of an animal with similar desires. But neither you nor the animal have any value in your own right. Only your feelings do.

Here is an analogy to help make the philosophical point clearer: a cup contains different liquids, sometimes sweet, sometimes bitter, sometimes a mixture of the two. What has value are the liquids: the sweeter the better, the bitterer the worse. The cup, the container, has no value. It is what goes into it, not what they go into, that has value. For the utilitarian, you and I are like the cup; we have no value as individuals and thus no equal value. What has value is what goes into us, what we serve as receptacles for; our feelings of satisfaction have positive value, our feelings of frustration negative value.

Serious problems arise for utilitarianism when we remind ourselves that it enjoins us to bring about the best consequences. What does this mean? It doesn't mean the best consequences for me alone, or for my family or friends, or any other person taken individually. No, what we must do is, roughly, as follows: we must add up (somehow!) the separate satisfactions and frustrations of everyone likely to be affected by our choice, the satisfactions in one column, the frustrations in the other. We must total each column for each of the options before us. That is what it means to say the theory is aggregative. And then we must choose that option which is most likely to bring about the best balance of totalled satisfactions over totalled frustrations. Whatever act would lead to this outcome is the one we ought morally to perform—it is where our moral duty lies. And that act quite clearly might not be the same one that would bring about the best results for me personally, or for my family or friends, or for a lab animal. The best aggregated consequences for everyone concerned are not necessarily the best for each individual.

That utilitarianism is an aggregative theory—different individuals' satisfactions or frustrations are added, or summed, or totalled—is the key objection to this theory. My Aunt Bea is old, inactive, a cranky, sour person, though not physically ill. She prefers to go on living. She is also rather rich, I could make a fortune if I could get my hands on her money, money she intends to give me in any event, after she dies, but which she refuses to give me now. In order to avoid a huge tax bite, I plan to donate a handsome sum of my profits to a local children's hospital. Many, many children will benefit from my generosity, and much joy will be brought to their parents, relatives, and friends. If I don't get the money rather soon, all these ambitions will come to naught. The once-in-a-lifetime opportunity to make a real killing will be gone. Why, then, not kill my Aunt Bea? Oh, of course I *might* get caught. But I'm no fool and, besides, her doctor can be counted on to cooperate (he has an eye for the same investment and I happen to know a good deal about his shady past). The deed can be done . . . professionally, shall we say. There is very little chance of getting caught. And as for my conscience being guilt ridden, I am a resourceful sort of fellow and will take more than sufficient comfort—as I lie on the beach at Acapulco—in contemplating the joy and health I have brought to so many others.

Suppose Aunt Bea is killed and the rest of the story comes out as told. Would I have done anything wrong? Anything immoral? One would have thought that I had. Not according to utilitarianism. Since what I have done has brought about the best balance between totalled satisfaction and frustration for all those affected by the outcome, my action is not wrong. Indeed, in killing Aunt Bea the physician and I did what duty required.

This same kind of argument can be repeated in all sorts of cases, illustrating, time after time, how the utilitarian's position leads to results that impartial people find morally callous. It is wrong to kill my Aunt Bea in the name of bringing about the best results for others. A good end does not justify an evil means. Any adequate moral theory will have to explain why this is so. Utilitarianism fails in this respect and so cannot be the theory we seek.

INHERENT VALUE AND THE RIGHTS VIEW

What to do? Where to begin anew? The place to begin, I think, is with the utilitarian's view of the value of the individual—or, rather, the lack of value. In its place, suppose we consider that you and I, for example, do have value as individuals—what we'll call *inherent value*. To say we have such value is to say that we are something more than, something different from, mere receptacles. Moreover, to ensure that we do not pave the way for such injustices as slavery or sexual discrimination, we must believe that all who have inherent value have it equally, regardless of their sex, race, religion, birthplace, and so on. Similarly to be discarded as irrelevant are one's talents or skills, intelligence and wealth, personality or pathology, whether one is loved and admired or despised and loathed. The genius and the retarded child, the prince and the pauper, the brain surgeon and the fruit vendor, Mother Teresa and the most unscrupulous used-car salesman—all have inherent value, all possess it equally, and all have an equal right to be treated with respect, to be treated in ways that do not reduce them to the status of things, as if they existed as resources for others. My value as an individual is independent of my usefulness to you. Yours is not dependent on your usefulness to me. For either of us to treat the other in ways that fail to show respect for the other's independent value is to act immorally, to violate the individual's rights.

Some of the rational virtues of this view—what I call the *rights view*—should be evident. Unlike (crude) contractarianism, for example, the rights view in *principle* denies the moral tolerability of any and all forms of racial, sexual, or social discrimination; and unlike utilitarianism, the view in *principle* denies that we can justify good results by using evil means that violate an individual's rights—denies, for example, that it could be moral to kill my Aunt Bea to harvest beneficial consequences for others. That would be to sanction the disrespectful treatment of the individual in the name of the social good, something the rights view will not—categorically will not— ever allow.

The rights view, I believe, is rationally the most satisfactory moral theory. It surpasses all other theories in the degree to which it illuminates and explains the foundation of our duties to one another—the domain of human morality. On this score it has the best reasons, the best arguments on its side. Of course, if it were possible to show that only human beings are included within its scope, then a person like myself, who believes in animal rights, would be obliged to look elsewhere.

But attempts to limit its scope to humans only can be shown to be rationally defective. Animals, it is true, lack many of the abilities humans possess. They can't read, do higher mathematics, build a bookcase, or make *baba ghanoush*. Neither can many human beings, however, and yet we don't (and shouldn't) say that they (these humans) therefore have less inherent value, less of a right to be treated with respect, than do others. It is the *similarities* between those human beings who most clearly, most noncontroversially have such value (the people reading this, for example), not our differences, that matter most. And the really crucial, the basic similarity is simply this: we are each of us the experiencing subject of a life, a conscious creature having an individual welfare that has importance to us whatever our usefulness to others. We want and prefer things, believe and feel things, recall and expect things. And all these dimensions of our life including our pleasure and pain, our enjoyment and suffering, our satisfaction and frustration, our continued existence or our untimely death—all make a difference to the quality of our life as lived, as experienced, by us as individuals. As the same is true of those animals that concern us (the ones that are eaten and trapped, for example), they too must be viewed as the experiencing subjects of a life, with inherent value of their own.

Some there are who resist the idea that animals have inherent value. "Only humans have such value," they profess. How might this narrow view be defended? Shall we say that only humans have the requisite intelligence, or autonomy, or reason? But there are many, many humans who fail to meet these standards and yet are reasonably viewed as having value above and beyond their usefulness to others. Shall we claim that only humans belong to the right species, the species *Homo sapiens*? But this is blatant speciesism. Will it be said, then, that all—and only—humans have immortal souls? Then our opponents have their work cut out for them. I am myself not ill-disposed to the proposition that there are immortal souls. Personally, I profoundly hope I have one. But I would not want to rest my position on a controversial ethical issue on the even more controversial question about who or what has an immortal soul. That is to dig one's hole deeper, not to climb out. Rationally, it is better to resolve moral issues without making more controversial assumptions than are needed. The question of who has inherent value is such a question, one that is resolved more rationally without the introduction of the idea of immortal souls than by its use.

Well, perhaps some will say that animals have some inherent value, only less than we have. Once again, however, attempts to defend this view can be shown to lack rational justification. What could be the basis of our having more inherent value than animals? Their lack of reason, or autonomy, or intellect? Only if we are willing to make the same judgment in the case of humans who are similarly deficient. But it is not true that such humans—the retarded child, for example, or the mentally deranged—have less inherent value than you or I. Neither, then, can we rationally sustain the view that animals like them in being the experiencing subjects of a life have less inherent value. *All* who have inherent value have it *equally*, whether they be human animals or not.

Inherent value, then, belongs equally to those who are the experiencing subjects of a life. Whether it belongs to others—to rocks and rivers, trees and glaciers, for example—we do not know and may never know. But neither do we need to know, if we are to make the case for animal rights. We do not need to know, for example, how many people are eligible to vote in the next presidential election before we can know whether I am. Similarly, we do not need to know how many individuals have inherent value before we can know that some do. When it comes to the case for animal rights, then, what we need to know is whether the animals that, in our culture, are routinely eaten, hunted, and used in our laboratories, for example, are like us in being subjects of a life. And we do know this. We do know that many—literally, billions and billions—of these animals are the subjects of a life in the sense explained and so have inherent value if we do. And since, in order to arrive at the best theory of our duties to one another, we must recognize our equal inherent value as individuals, reason—not sentiment, not emotion—reason compels us to recognize the equal inherent value of these animals and, with this, their equal right to be treated with respect.

Animals Are Moral Creatures Deserving of Fair Treatment

BERNARD E. ROLLIN

The German philosopher Immanuel Kant once wrote in his *Lectures on Ethics* that "Animals are . . . merely a means to an end. That end is man." His conclusion was based on the grounds that humans can reason but animals cannot. Here Bernard E. Rollin argues that animals can and do perform cognitive reasoning but that we purposely blind ourselves to the evidence, partly out of guilt but more because Kant's view has held sway among the majority for so long. If people grant moral concern to children, the comatose, and the insane, then, according to Rollin, they have no basis for denying consideration to other life forms with highly developed brains and nervous systems. Bernard E. Rollin is professor of philosophy, physiology, and biophysics at Colorado State University, Fort Collins. His books include *The Unheeded Cry* and *Farm Animal Welfare: Social, Bioethical, and Research Issues*.

I t is often argued that man has been granted dominion over the rest of nature by God. This claim is also put non-theologically when it is asserted that man stands at the apex of the evolutionary pyramid. Once again, holding theological skepticism in abeyance, we may unearth a profound philosophical point in discussing this claim. Even if man has been placed by God at the peak of the Great Chain of Being, or even in command of it, it does not follow that the creatures beneath him may be treated by him in any way he sees fit. (The Bible, in fact, as we shall see, clearly and explicitly counters this claim in the many passages devoted to kindness towards animals.) Correlatively, even if we can sensibly talk about an objective "top" of the evolutionary scale (which I doubt, since in evolutionary terms there is only survival, non-survival, reproductive success, and adaptation), the same point holds. Being at the top does not entail that one can treat the creatures beneath in any way one chooses. (Ironically, Darwinism has historically been used both to justify exclusion of animals from moral concern, because of human supremacy, and to justify inclusion of animals within the scope of moral concern, because of the evolutionary continuity between men and animals!)

To better understand our rejection of the moral relevance of human "supremacy," one must consider what sense can be made of the claim that man is at the "top." Of course, since man creates the ratings, he can do as he chooses, but what is the criterion of superiority? Surely it is not longevity, adaptability, and reproductive success, else turtles, cockroaches, and rats would be at the top. Is it intelligence? But why does intelligence score highest? Ultimately, perhaps, because intelligence allows us to control, vanquish, dominate, and destroy all other creatures. If this is the case, it is power that puts us on top of the pyramid. But if power provides grounds for including or excluding creatures from the scope of moral concern, we have essentially accepted the legitimacy of the thesis that "might makes right" and have, in a real sense, done away with all morality altogether. If we do accept this thesis, we cannot avoid extending it to people as well, and it thus becomes perfectly moral for Nazis to exterminate the Jews, muggers to prey on old people, the majority to oppress the minority, and the government to do as it sees fit to any of us. Furthermore, as has often been pointed out, it follows from this claim that if an extraterrestrial alien civilization were intellectually, technologically, and militarily superior to us, it would be perfectly justified in enslaving or eating or exterminating human beings.

Some may be tempted to assert that might does, in a fundamental sense, make right. After all, those in power do call all the shots. But this is to ignore a very basic distinction. While those in power are indeed in a position to impose their will on others, and even to *call* what they decree "right," that does not of course mean that it is *in fact* right. I may, at the point of a gun, force you to call black "white" and white "black," but that would not make black into white and white into black. To accept the principle that might makes right is to vitiate all talk of justice and injustice, to render meaningless any claims about what ought to be the case. Even to assert that it is right that might makes right or it ought to be the case that might makes right is self-defeating, for the very possibility of making the assertion presupposes some notion of right above and beyond that created by superior force, since, presumably, the person who holds that position holds it even if *in fact* what is considered right happens to be determined at that time by something other than superior force, for example, religious tradition. . . .

REASON, LANGUAGE, AND MORAL CONCERN

We turn now to the most serious and important criterion of demarcation that has historically served to delineate the scope of moral concern. At least since Plato and Aristotle, and even in the Catholic tradition, the notion of the soul providing the basis for excluding animals from moral concern has been given philosophical content by equating the soul with the rational faculty or the ability to reason. Men are rational, or at least have the capacity for rational thought, while animals do not, and for this reason, the scope of morality does not extend beyond men. This claim that only men are rational has traditionally been linked to another criterion used to distinguish men from animals, the claim that only men possess language or the ability to use what are called "conventional signs." (This is often put in various other ways—men use symbols, animals have only signs or signals; men use artificial signs, animals are restricted to natural or instinctual signs, etc.) The great philosopher René Descartes saw the possession of language as the only real evidence we have that other beings have minds like ours and could think, feel, and reason. For Descartes, animals were just machines and were thus incapable of thinking or feeling. This

Cartesian view was terribly important as a justification for the burgeoning science of physiology, since it provided a convenient rationale for ignoring the "apparent" suffering that experimentation engendered. Many Cartesians, such as the residents of the famous Port-Royal Abbey, were actively involved in research on animals, research that was shocking to contemporaries who had not accepted Cartesianism. The influence of Descartes, coupled with the development of ingenious machinery in the eighteenth century that could behave in lifelike ways, has left its mark on the Western mind, and to some extent current thought about animals is still very Cartesian. . . .

The position linking rationality, language, and moral status may very briefly be schematized as follows:

1. Only men are rational.
2. Only men possess language.
3. Only men are objects of moral concern.

Although a great number of thinkers have historically entertained this view and it is still quite prevalent today, remarkably little has been done to spell out or defend the connections between (1), (2), and (3). There are, after all, many questions to be asked here. We may ask, for example, what is rationality, and what grounds do we have for asserting that only men possess it? We may further ask, what is the connection between rationality and language? Is language evidence for rationality, as Descartes suggests, or is language somehow the essence of rationality? And most important for our purposes, we are faced with the question of why the possession of rationality and language is morally relevant, i.e., makes a difference to morality.

It is easy to see, of course, why rationality would be important for a being to be considered a *moral agent,* that is, a being whose actions and intentions can be assessed as right and wrong, good and bad. We are certainly not inclined to hold anyone responsible for his actions if he is incapable of reason—even our laws reflect this notion. We do not hold children, the insane, or idiots morally or legally responsible for their actions. But it is, of course, not obvious that one must be capable of being a moral agent before one can be considered an object of moral concern. In fact, we certainly consider children and the insane to fall within the scope of moral concern even though we do not hold them responsible or consider them to be moral agents. So our other questions still remain. . . .

KANT'S THEORY OF REASON

One major philosopher whose work explores the questions we have been raising is Immanuel Kant, the great German philosopher of the Enlightenment. In fact, Kant's moral theory can be seen as an attempt to extract all of morality, both being a moral agent and being a moral object, from a particular concept of rationality. In this attempt, Kant represents an articulation of a tradition begun in Greek moral thought (by which he was influenced), and an amplification of the position taken by Descartes. In his discussion, Kant argues that only rational beings can count as moral agents and, even more important for our purposes, that the scope of moral concern extends only to rational beings. . . .

The notion of reason is central to the philosophy of Kant, who was a major figure in the Age of Reason. For him, the bases of science and ethics needed to be logically proved, much as theorems in geometry are proved, not merely assumed or derived from experience. In his major work, *The Critique of Pure Reason,* Kant devotes a good deal of attention to explaining and justifying reason, and defining what it means to be a rational being. Kant was very much opposed to the British empiricist tradition, the tradition that based all knowledge on sense experience or perception, and that had culminated in the skeptical writings of David Hume. Hume, like an early Pavlov, had concluded that reason was merely habit, custom, and conditioning, and that if men could be said to reason, so too could animals. . . .

Kant proceeds by stressing man's ability to arrive at what philosophers call *a priori* knowledge, that is, knowledge that cannot be shown to be false by experience and can be known to be true simply by thought. A good example of *a priori* knowledge is "The sum of the angles of a Euclidean triangle is 180 degrees." As we all know from studying geometry, we can prove that by reason, and once we have proved it, we can know that it must always be true. Kant ingeniously shows that science rests upon certain items of knowledge that we can know *a priori,* and for this reason, a number of things in science *are* certain, contrary to Hume's claim. The important point for our purposes is Kant's claim that only human beings can possess *a priori* knowledge, and only the possession of *a priori* knowledge can allow a being to go beyond the particular instances one finds in sense experience of the world and assert judgments that claim universality, not tied to specific times and places. This for Kant is the essential meaning of rationality. Since only men can entertain, understand, apprehend, and formulate statements that are universal in scope, only men are rational. This is because, according to Kant, animals are tied to stimulus and response reactions. An animal may respond to *this* particular fire in a way that indicates its awareness that *this* fire is dangerous here and now, but only man has the mental capacity to understand and formulate an assertion like "all fires, wherever and whenever they may occur, are potentially dangerous.". . .

In any event, it follows clearly for Kant that since only human beings are rational beings, only human beings fall within the scope of moral concern. As far as animals are concerned, they have only instrumental value; that is, any worth they may have stems from their usefulness for humans. In his *Lectures on Ethics,* Kant actually says this:

Animals are . . . merely as means to an end. That end is man.

Kant does assert that we should avoid cruelty, but only for the reasons . . . that cruelty to animals can lead to cruelty towards men, or that an animal is human property, and to damage that animal is to harm a person.

This then is a sketch of the argument that thinkers in the tradition of Kant might advance to justify excluding animals from the scope of moral concern. . . .

The Ordinary Notion of Rationality

While it is certainly the case that the ability to universalize and generalize is a major aspect of what we call "rational," there are many cases of rationality in which we do not make even implicit reference to universalization. For example, we speak of the rationality of a man's swerving into a snow bank to avoid colliding with a truck, or we speak of the rationality of one's giving up in a fight when the opponent has clearly outmatched him. Interestingly enough, animals such as dogs can and do engage in this sort of behavior, and, in this sense, seem to behave perfectly "rationally." In point of fact, we regularly speak of animal behavior as being rational, not only in ordinary discourse, but in our scientific works on animal behavior. In fact, a good deal of our psychological research that studies the learning behavior of animals is based on an implicit assumption that human cognitive behavior bears significant analogies to animal intellectual processes. . . .

For example, I had a highly intelligent German shepherd that I acquired when he was an adult. One extremely hot day, while my wife was filling the horses' tank from a high-pressure hose, the dog approached her, clearly wanting a drink. Not having a bowl handy, she turned the hose towards the ground, and the dog attempted to drink but was thwarted by the extreme pressure. Undaunted, he proceeded to dig a hole beneath the stream, allowed the water to pool, and drank his fill.

One of the best stories I have ever run across in this area was told by a German trainer of police dogs. He relates that he had trained a police dog in Berlin to apprehend suspects and hold them by the arm unharmed until the officer arrived. Only if the suspect resisted was the dog to bite, and then only to disable the offensive arm. On the dog's first day at work, he was patrolling a large public park along with his handler. They came upon a robbery in progress, being perpetrated by two men. When the men caught sight of the dog, they broke and ran towards a fork in the path, where both took off in different directions on the theory that the dog could not pursue both. The dog chased one suspect up the left fork, apprehended him, *disabled his leg,* left him, proceeded up the right fork, and held the second man by the arm, unharmed. The dog had never been trained to attack the leg.

As I said, anyone who has lived with animals can tell such stories, and many such incidents have been filmed and documented. It seems to me only common sense to call such behavior rational and to say that such animals reason. We all know, of course, that common sense is often wrong, as when it tells us that the earth does not move. But still, in order to abandon common sense, one needs strong counter-evidence or powerful philosophical or scientific arguments that demonstrate its inadequacy. And to my knowledge, such evidence and argument have not hitherto been forthcoming. . . .

MORAL THEORY AND OUR WORLD VIEW

Thus we have tried to argue that any living thing, insofar as it evidences interests, with or without the ability to suffer, is worthy of being an object of moral concern. Insofar as we can inform ourselves of the interests of a creature, we must at least look at that creature with moral categories. Certainly, from a psychological point of view, those creatures whose interests are most readily understood by us, and that are most like ours, will be most readily granted moral status. On the other hand, we must recall that this is also the case in ordinary human morality—we are powerfully inclined to favor people to whom we are related, or whom we know, or who live in our neighborhood or state or country, or who dress and look as we do. And, though rational reflection can provide no defense for these inclinations, we persist in them.

Certainly, visible signs of the ability to suffer, which betoken in the creature conscious negative correlates of thwarted needs, will always most readily seize our imagination and empathy. This leads to an important point: The limits of what we are *psychologically* capable of being concerned about must serve as a curb on the pretensions of any moral theory, else our arguments degenerate into merely scholastic exercises or intellectual oddities. . . . Few philosophers have made this point, since our psychological abilities are changeable and variable, and philosophers seek eternal verities. The one exception is perhaps [philosopher David J.] Hume, who stressed the importance of sympathy and fellow-feeling for moral theory. And it is certainly difficult for a person of our era to have much fellow-feeling with a spider. Yet it is precisely *because* human empathy can change that we must stress the vast range of creatures that must enter within the scope of moral concern, for only in this way can we hope to effect changes in what human psychology can accept as morally palatable.

The much used notion of *gestalt shift,* drawn from gestalt perceptual psychology, is of great relevance here. A gestalt shift is a change in perspective on the same data, as when we suddenly see a person in a new light or realize we have a crush on the girl next door. . . .

I suddenly realize that the girl next door is incredibly desirable, though I have seen her a thousand times. I can recall one of my own gestalt shifts in this regard. After moving to Colorado, I immensely enjoyed hiking into the mountains and trout fishing. I found the fight that the trout gave me exhilarating and therapeutic, a test of my skill and an outlet for tension, much like negotiating a motocross course on a motorcycle. One day, for no obvious reason, I suddenly realized that the good fight that fifteen-inch rainbow trout was giving me was its struggle to survive, born of pain and fear. My perception shifted; I could no longer fish for fun.

I also recall a conversation I had with a well-known parasitologist, who does much research with protozoa. We were discussing some of my ideas on the moral status of animals when he turned to me and somewhat hesitatingly, as if he were somehow ashamed, confessed that the more he worked with protozoa, the more he understood their *telos* and their life, the more he could *empathize* with them, and the more loath he was to destroy them. This embarrassed him, because . . . such empathetic understanding is foreign to current scientific practice. But the fact is, he had undergone a gestalt shift and was seeing the protozoa as objects of moral concern, not merely as things in test tubes.

Another interesting example concerns the scientist . . . who works with planaria or flatworms. As he became more and more aware of their behavior, and studied them in greater detail, he began to see them, in his words, as "little men in worm suits." This example illustrates an important point. Perhaps this sort of anthropomorphism is in some cases psychologically necessary as a stage in developing moral consciousness, for it provides us with a fulcrum for our gestalt shifts. Eventually, one can put the human connection aside and value the creature in its own right, but before this can take place, it is possible that we must move them from the realm of things to the realm of people. It is for this reason that anthropomorphic depictions of animals, as in Disney movies and cartoons, are not necessarily bad as a first step in education. They are pernicious only if a child does not transcend them and appreciate the creature in terms of its *telos*. For eventually, he or she will see through the anthropomorphism and realize that dogs do not understand English and write messages with their paws, and that woodpeckers do not converse with hunters. If he has not learned to value the creature for what it is, he may move in the opposite direction, dismissing any concern for the animal as "childish" since it has, after all, turned out to be totally unlike a person.

This, then, is one task of a moral philosophy, whether it argues for extension of rights to people who are enslaved, or whether it argues for extending the scope of moral concern to other creatures. It serves not to effect changes in behavior overnight; such hopes would be utopian. But it does serve to prepare thinking people for the moral gestalt shift that is a necessary prerequisite to any genuine and enduring change in conduct. No one can be argued into morality, any more than one can be argued into religion. But argument can prepare the ground and plant the seeds that may grow into new moral viewpoints and show anomalies in one's ordinary perspective that ready us for the possibility of a new, revolutionary shift in attitude. Any thoughtful individual must either refute our arguments or else, however haltingly, begin at least to think about applying his moral discourse to non-human beings.

The Animal Rights Movement Is Dangerous to Scientific Progress

FREDERICK K. GOODWIN AND ADRIAN R. MORRISON

The animal rights movement knows not of what it speaks when leveling charges against the scientific research community, argue authors Frederick K. Goodwin, a former director of the National Institute of Mental Health, and Adrian R. Morrison, a professor of veterinary medicine at the University of Pennsylvania. Using animals as research subjects provides necessary knowledge of how the mind and body function which will prove beneficial not only to humans but also to untold future generations of animals. Goodwin and Morrison claim that resistance to experimentation using animals is grounded in a superstitious distrust and ignorance of the scientific method and that legislation curtailing such research disregards the many medical advances made possible by the use of animal subjects. This essay is excerpted from an article that originally appeared in *Cerebrum: The Dana Forum on Brain Science.*

T wenty years ago, animal research became the target of a new generation of anti-vivisectionists: the radical "animal rights movement." That movement, which views animals as moral agents on a par with people, has promoted a profoundly confused philosophy that equates animal research with the enslavement of human beings.

Scientists responded to this movement by proposing to strengthen the standards and regulation of animal research and care. But even as the handling of research animals became ever more restricted, the animal rights campaign became ever more demanding and violent. Scientists working with animals, especially those involved in brain and behavioral research, were assaulted in their laboratories, harassed in their homes, and threatened with death.

In Europe, scientists have long been the target of actual terrorism, now identified as such by the United Kingdom. Indeed, the neuroscientist Colin Blakemore at Oxford University, who studies brain activity in cats, literally lives under siege. Police must protect his home, which has been assaulted with his frightened wife and daughters in residence. Why? He spoke out in support of the obvious necessity of using animals to advance medical science—to alleviate the suffering of human beings—and has been in danger ever since that principled act. In 1998, Blakemore and other European scientists were marked for death by animal rights terrorists, and Blakemore lived for months under round-the-clock police protection.

Although for a few years American researchers enjoyed relative peace, animal rights activists struck last spring [1999] at the University of Minnesota, causing thousands of dollars in damage. A scientist studying hearing at the University of California at San Francisco is now suffering what Blakemore has endured for years. But biomedical research is coming under another kind of siege.

THE EROSION OF HUMAN RIGHTS

There has been a campaign in New Zealand to give the great apes constitutional rights, an outgrowth of the ideas of the animal rights movement and the Great Ape Project, which seeks to award apes the same rights as those possessed by humans. Last year in Germany, the ruling Social Democratic and Green parties introduced legislation stating that animals have the right to be "respected as fellow creatures," and to be protected from "avoidable pain." Two recent developments in the United States suggest that we may be entering a dangerous era in thinking about animals.

In the first, a U.S. court recognized the legal standing of an individual to sue the federal government in order to force changes in animal-welfare regulations. In that case, the individual claimed "harm" as a result of seeing animals mistreated, in his opinion, at a roadside zoo; the plaintiff held the Department of Agriculture responsible. However, in deciding the merits of the case, an appeals court later found that USDA was not responsible for the individual's alleged harm, and declined to order any change in the current regulations.

In the second, animal rights groups are pushing USDA to include rats and mice under the Animal Welfare Act.

The campaign to end the use of animals in biomedical research is based upon a complete misunderstanding of how scientists work, what research requires, and what has made possible our era's outpouring of lifesaving advances in medicine. Unfortunately, neither their misunderstanding of science nor their misguided philosophy has prevented activists from becoming an increasingly powerful, militant force—one now threatening the discovery of new medical treatments and preventive strategies for serious illnesses.

To understand the animal rights movement, we must distinguish its objectives from those of animal welfare organizations. Typically, such organizations as local societies for the prevention of cruelty to animals will care for strays, teach good animal care, run neutering programs, and build animal shelters. Acting as the stewards of animals, especially those not in a position to care for themselves, these organizations uphold our traditional values of humane, caring treatment of sentient creatures.

Animal rights organizations, on the other hand, invest their energies in campaigning against various uses of animals, including research. They start with a completely different philosophy, summed up by Peter Singer, the acknowledged founder of the animal rights movement, in his 1975 book, *Animal Liberation*. Singer, now De Camp Professor of Bioethics at Princeton University, argues that sentient creatures—all those capable of feeling pain—must essentially be considered moral equivalents to human beings, certainly as equivalent to the severely brain-damaged and to human infants before the age of reasoning. Anyone who dismisses any sentient creature as merely an animal to be used for human benefit is guilty of "speciesism," a prejudice morally equivalent to racism and sexism. (Singer, who is Australian, does not base his opposition to animal research on the concept of rights; his American counterpart, University of North Carolina philosophy professor Tom Regan, does.)

TARGETING SCIENTIFIC RESEARCH

On the political front, Ingrid Newkirk, the national director of People for the Ethical Treatment of Animals (PETA), asserted in 1983 that "animal liberationists do not separate out the human animal, so there is no rational basis for saying that a human being has special rights. A rat is a pig is a dog is a boy. They're all mammals." She has also said, "Six million Jews died in concentration camps, but six billion broiler chickens will die this year in slaughterhouses." Chris DeRose, who heads an organization called In Defense of Animals, said recently that even if the death of one rat would cure all disease, that death still would not be right, because we are all equal.

Despite PETA's view that broiler chickens are the moral equivalent of murdered Jews, animal rights activists decided early on to target scientific researchers, not farmers, although more than 99 percent of the animals used by people are for food (or clothing, or killed either in pounds or by hunters) and just a fraction of 1 percent for research. Singer has said that the strategic decision to level protests against science was made because farmers are organized and politically powerful (and live in rural areas, which makes them hard to get at). In contrast, scientists are not politically organized, live in urban areas, and can be hard put to explain their work in lay language.

Neuroscientists have been a frequent target. Two key fields of neuroscience, behavioral and addiction research, were highlighted in Singer's book. High-profile laboratory invasions have targeted scientists engaged in brain research. For example,

PETA, which adheres to Singer's philosophy, established itself by infiltrating the laboratory of neuroscientist Edward Taub in Silver Spring, Maryland, in 1981, and "exposing" deficient laboratory conditions with photographs that purported to show animal mistreatment. Taub, however, has noted that no one else in the lab observed the conditions in the PETA photographs, and he is supported by the sworn statements of seven people, including a USDA inspector, who testified at Taub's subsequent trial. At the time, Taub was investigating how monkeys perform complex tasks with certain nerve pathways in their arms severed, work that was the basis for the subsequent development of improved methods for stroke rehabilitation.

In 1984, PETA exploited the Animal Liberation Front's invasion of the University of Pennsylvania Head Injury Research Laboratory by cleverly editing videotapes taken in the raid and using the resulting composite as a fund raising tool. In subsequent literature, PETA made it clear that alleged mistreatment of animals was not the real issue. In PETA's view, animals cannot be used to alleviate health problems of people, period. Even after more stringent government controls over animal research were in place (by 1985) Texas Tech sleep researcher John Orem suffered a raid in 1989 that resulted in $40,000 worth of damage to his laboratory. In this and other cases, however, the critical damage is to the scientist's will to continue research.

FOES OF REASON

Many factors have contributed to the climate of moral confusion surrounding the use of animals in research and to the apparent willingness of many people to credit the bizarre ideas of the animal rights activists.

For one thing, we are victims of our own health care successes. We have enjoyed such a victory over infectious diseases that baby boomers and subsequent generations do not even remember polio and other dreaded infectious diseases, and have little sense of how amazing it was when antibiotics were first developed. With the eradication of so many deadly infectious diseases, antibiotics have become something that you take for incidental minor infection. The healthiest generation in history is a ripe target for the anti-science nonsense pushed by the animal rightists.

Second, America has sustained a steady, devastating decline in scientific literacy. Our high school students consistently rank below those of other developed countries. As a result, most people, especially young people, do not understand what the scientific method is really about.

Additionally, Americans today spend little time around animals other than house pets. It is worth remembering that just before World War II one in four of us lived on a farm; now it is one in 50. What do most urban and suburban kids know about animals, other than what they see in cartoons?

Such factors have helped propel the ever-tightening regulation of research, stifling the creativity that is its essence and posing a threat to the human well-being that is its goal. Many major discoveries in the history of medicine have come about by serendipity, when a scientist has had his sights trained on an entirely different topic of research. The story behind the initial discovery that lithium, an elemental substance on the periodic table, might have therapeutic benefits illustrates this serendipity and demonstrates how basic research with animals can lead to major medical advances.

In that case, Australian psychiatrist John Cade asked what might be wrong in the brains of patients with manic-depressive illness and wondered whether a substance called urea would have therapeutic value. Testing his hypothesis on guinea pigs, Cade gave them a salt form of urea, which happened to contain lithium. The guinea pigs became unexpectedly calm. Further experimentation revealed that the urea had nothing to do with this result; it was caused by the lithium—a complete surprise to Cade. Having laid his foundation with animal research, Cade extended his findings by giving lithium to manic patients, who experienced an alleviation of their manic excitement without being sedated. This single discovery has revolutionized treatment of manic-depressive illness, easing the lives of millions and saving billions of dollars along the way. At the same time, it has opened whole new productive areas for brain research.

No one could have predicted the outcome of Cade's initial experiment with urea. There was no way to list in advance what the health benefits of using guinea pigs would be. That would have required knowing the answer to a question that had not yet been asked. If one already knows the answer, research is unnecessary.

ANIMAL SUBJECTS ARE NECESSARY

In 1976, before the animal rights controversy arose, the National Institutes of Health sponsored a study by Julius H. Comroe Jr. and R.D. Dripps to ascertain if government funding of basic biomedical research had been a good investment. The authors asked practicing cardiologists what they regarded as the 10 leading medical advances of their lifetimes; the scientists named such advances as cardiac surgery, drug treatment of hypertension, and medical treatment of cardiac insufficiency. Comroe and Dripps then traced the scientific ancestry of each of these discoveries and found that 40 percent of the studies leading to the advances originated from work in a different, seemingly unrelated field of research. Animal research was fundamental to many of these studies. Regulations that require justification of animal research in terms of its specific outcomes, rather than the clarity of the hypotheses and strength of the research design, may end much of the creative research now under way.

Less than a quarter of the studies in biomedicine involve animals (and more than 90 percent of those are rats and mice), but anyone working in the field will tell you that such animal studies are indispensable. One cannot develop an understanding of a chemical or a gene, then try to ascertain its role in a complex human organism with billions of cells and dozens of organs, without first knowing how it works in the biological systems of animals. The animal model enables a scientist to understand what is happening at a level of detail that could not be reached in humans.

The great kidney transplant pioneer Dr. Thomas E. Starzl

was once asked why he used dogs in his work. He explained that, in his first series of operations, he had transplanted kidneys into a number of subjects, and that the majority of them died. After figuring out what had enabled a few to survive, he revised his techniques and operated on a similar group of subjects; a majority of them survived. In his third group of subjects, only one or two died, and in his fourth group all survived. The important point, said Starzl, was that the first three groups of subjects were dogs; the fourth group consisted of human babies. Had Starzl begun his series of experimental operations on people, he would have killed at least 15 people. Yet there are activists who believe, in the name of animal rights, that that is what Starzl should have done. . . .

WHAT THE ACTIVISTS SAY

Activists assert that animal research is cruel. But their argument misses the point that experimenters usually want to disturb the animal as little as possible, since their goal is to study its natural response to whatever is being tested. An estimated 7 percent of research does employ procedures causing pain in order to understand pain mechanisms in the central nervous system. This kind of experimentation has enabled us to develop effective painkillers.

Activists claim that animal experiments are duplicative. The reality is that today only one out of four grant requests is funded, a highly competitive situation that makes duplicative research scarce. But research does have to be replicated before the results are accepted; and progress usually arises from a series of small discoveries, all elaborating on or overlapping one another. When activists talk about duplication, they betray a fundamental misunderstanding of how science progresses. Nor do they understand scientists. What highly trained, creative individual wants to do exactly what someone has already done?

Activists urge prevention rather than treatment. They say we should urge people to adopt measures such as an altered diet or increased exercise to prevent major illness, so that we would not need so many new treatments. But much of what we have discovered about preventive measures has itself resulted from animal research. You cannot get most cancers to grow in a test tube; you need whole animal studies.

Activists argue that we should use alternatives to animal research. A favorite example is computer simulations. But where do they think the data that are entered into computers come from? To get real answers, one has to feed computers real physiological data. There is an argument that researchers should use PET scans, which can provide an image of how a living human organ is functioning, as a way of avoiding the use of animals. It took Lou Sokoloff at the National Institute of Mental Health eight years of animal research to develop the PET scan methodology.

There are many other arguments. Activists say animal research diverts funds from medical treatment. But the United States spends only 37 cents on animal studies for every $100 it spends on treatment. We could divert all our research funds into treatment, and it would have no impact on sick people.

Activists say that pets are at risk, but more than 90 percent of the animals used in research are rodents. At the same time, about five million unwanted cats and dogs are killed in shelters every year, which comes to about 50 animals killed in shelters for every one that must be sacrificed in research. One reason so many animals are killed in shelters is that animal rights organizations have diverted much of the funding from animal welfare organizations, so they cannot run adoption or neutering programs as well as they could with more funds.

THE DANGER ACTIVISTS POSE TO RESEARCH

Despite the weakness of their arguments, the animal rights activists have taken their toll on research. Nothing impairs creativity like fear. Today, scientists who work with animals are often segregated in high-security, bunker-like buildings, separated from their colleagues. In effect, biomedical research budgets are reduced by the costs of increased security and compliance with new regulations.

But the situation could get even worse. If the individual who sued the USDA had succeeded in gaining standing to sue on behalf of animals, a precedent would have been established that could have led to mischief by those who would impede research. Should a future case succeed, an activist "plant" in a laboratory need only claim distress at the way animals are being treated to bring a nuisance lawsuit against the laboratory. Even now, an accusation of wrongdoing, no matter how trumped-up, will lead to weeks or months of work stoppage while the laboratory is being investigated by government agencies.

Including rats and mice (as well as birds) under the Animal Welfare Act, as the USDA has been urged to do, is more complicated. Viewed superficially, the proposal is not unreasonable. Rats and mice are animals, after all, and deserving of appropriate care. Their exclusion from oversight by the Department of Agriculture reflects the department's decision to focus available funds on monitoring the well-being of such animals as primates, dogs, and cats. But one need not be overly cynical to suspect that the real motive behind the push for inclusion is not a desire to protect the rodents' welfare so much as a wish to impede research by all means possible. Bureaucracy is expensive and enervating. The fact that the person leading this effort, John McArdle, once suggested in an interview that brain-dead humans are reasonable substitutes for animals as research subjects speaks volumes about the real agenda here.

Is there a proven problem concerning the welfare of these animals? The Association for the Assessment and Accreditation of Laboratory Animal Care International (AAALAC), the extra-governmental organization that intensively examines animal care programs at institutions striving to receive AAALAC's highly desirable seal of approval, has estimated that 90 percent of the rats and mice used in research are already overseen by either AAALAC inspections or those required by the U.S. Public Health Service. Many nonacademic institutions, such as pharmaceutical companies and commercial breeders, are covered by AAALAC inspections. Thus, the USDA would needlessly duplicate oversight programs already in place.

We live in an age of moral self-doubt. Some scientists and other individuals associated with biomedical research in supportive roles have begun to feel guilt over their use of animals. That has spawned a group calling itself the "troubled middle" (a rather presumptuous phrase, suggesting that only they care about the issues raised by animal research). Indeed, a whole industry has grown up around this sense of guilt, with constant, somewhat repetitive conferences focusing on how to oversee research, how to be the perfect member of an Institutional Animal Care and Use Committee, and how to find alternatives to using animals. These topics are not unworthy, but the conferences give short shrift to the perspectives of working scientists, who rarely appear as major speakers.

Progress toward increased human well-being cannot flourish amid such self-doubt. Scientists and members of the public who support their work must recognize that they are engaged in a struggle for minds. Their own minds therefore must be clear about what justifies animal research when necessary: that human beings are special. Researchers and others must appreciate the value of such work, and must be ready to state unequivocally and publicly that human life comes first. We who work with animals, and those who support the benefits of that work, have made a moral choice, and we must be willing to stand by it.

The Animal Rights Movement Has Sold Out to "New Welfarists"

GARY L. FRANCIONE

Though many in the animal rights movement endorse diversity and compassion, Gary L. Francione argues that such broad generalizations render the issues cloudy and such confusion shows in the movement's repeated and increasing approval of useless "animal welfare" reforms such as the American Wildlife Act and provisions for "humane slaughter." According to Francione, these "new welfarists," though well-intentioned and whose number includes even such rights "extremists" as People for the Ethical Treatment of Animals (PETA), mistakenly believe that incremental improvements in animal welfare regulation will someday lead to the abolition of animal exploitation. Gary L. Francione is a professor at Rutgers School of Law. His other books include, with Alan Watson, *Introduction to Animal Rights: Your Child or the Dog?* and, with William M. Kunstler, *Animals, Property, and the Law*.

Although virtually all modern animal advocates describe their various positions as embodying "rights" views in their fund-raising literature and in the media, many leaders of the movement now explicitly dismiss the importance of rights notions. For example, Don Barnes, education director at the National Anti-Vivisection Society (NAVS), argues that the distinction between animal rights and animal welfare is "artificial" and that it is "elitist" to maintain that the rights position and the welfarist positions are inconsistent.

According to Kim W. Stallwood, editor of the *Animals' Agenda*, there are many different philosophical theories concerning animals, but none of these can be defended as better than any others. Stallwood labels the animal rights position "utopian" and cautions that "some animal rights proponents use particular philosophical theories as yardsticks to measure" fidelity to animal rights ideology. He argues that such efforts are "artificially constructed devices" that are "divisive" of movement unity and are "elitist."

Zoe Weil of the American Anti-Vivisection Society (AAVS) maintains that the philosophical differences between rights and welfare are irrelevant and that only "compassion, concern and respect for animals" matter. According to Weil, "Animal welfare *does* mean something good and positive." The AAVS magazine promotes publications that endorse more "humane" methods of experimentation. Carol Adams, of Feminists for Animal Rights (FAR), claims that rights are patriarchal and that we should go "beyond animal rights" and accept that "sympathy, compassion, and caring are the ground upon which theory about human treatment of animals should be constructed."

Even the more so-called "radical" animal "rights" groups have distanced themselves from animal rights. For example, Ingrid E. Newkirk, director of People for the Ethical Treatment of Animals (PETA), maintains that the "all-or-nothing" position of animal rights is "unrealistic," and argues in favor of animal welfare. According to Alex Pacheco of PETA, as long as people just "care" about animals, it does not matter whether they adopt the animal rights philosophy. PETA's mission statement contains no mention of animal rights.

This rejection of rights theory by supposed rights advocates is becoming increasingly apparent. For example, in 1990, animal advocates held a "march for animal rights" in Washington, D.C. The theme of the march was explicitly to vindicate animal rights, and a highlight of the march was the presentation of the Declaration of the Rights of Animals, which provided that animals "have the right to live free from human exploitation, whether in the name of science or sport, exhibition or service, food or fashion," and the "right to live in harmony with their nature rather than according to human desires." Absent from the 1990 march was the Humane Society of the United States (HSUS), whose chief executive, John Hoyt, criticized the animal rights view as threatening the "kind of respectability that [HSUS] and a number of other organizations have worked hard to achieve in order to distinguish the legitimate animal *protection* movement from the more radical elements."

Animal advocates have planned another march for June 23, 1996. A major sponsor of the 1996 march will be HSUS, along with other groups, such as PETA, which were once considered "more radical." But the original promotional materials for the 1996 march did not mention "rights" at all and, instead, used the expression "animal protection." The march organizers invite animal advocates to join the "largest gathering" in the "history of the *humane* movement." They seek to bring "our message to mainstream audiences around the world" through the "resources of ethical corporations" and "compassionate celebrities and legislators." The tone of the 1996 march is clearly more moderate than that of the 1990 march, and it reflects the deliberate and explicit rejection of animal rights by many animal advocacy groups.

In sum, the dominant view among the organized animal movement is that the distinction between animal welfare and animal rights is, as one leading animal advocate put it, a "distinction without a difference."

What Is "New Welfarism?"

This rejection of rights by animal advocates does not necessarily mean that all of these advocates have simply embraced some version of classical welfarism. Many modern animal advocates see the abolition of animal exploitation as a long-term goal, but they see welfarist reform, which seeks to reduce animal suffering, as setting the course for the interim strategy. For example, Henry Spira, of Animal Rights International (ARI), "sees no contradiction between working for abolition and accepting reform. '[Reform] is basically about strategies, [abolition] is the ultimate goal. . . . The two aren't contradictory.'" Finsen and Finsen have observed, "The ultimate goals of the animal rights movement are clearly different from those of the humane movement," but "many within the movement see the possibility—or even the necessity—of achieving those goals by gradual and reformist means" employed by welfarists. This view posits some sort of causal relationship between welfare and rights such that pursuing welfarist reform will lead eventually to the abolition of all institutionalized animal exploitation.

Many animal advocates see rights theory as seeking the complete and immediate abolition of institutionalized exploitation, and they regard this as unrealistic or "utopian" and as incapable of providing a specific program of change leading to the abolition of animal exploitation. This is what Newkirk means when she characterizes animal rights as involving an "all-or-nothing" approach, and what Stallwood means when he characterizes animal rights as a "utopian" approach. In Spira's words, "If you push for all or nothing, what you get is nothing."

In addition, many animal advocates believe that the only pragmatic way to achieve animal rights is to pursue welfarist reforms as a short-term tactic. For example, Newkirk endorses a rights position and ultimately seeks the abolition of animal exploitation, but she argues that "total victory, like checkmate, cannot be achieved in one move" and that we must endorse the moral orthodoxy of animal welfare as involving necessary "steps in the direction" of animal rights. Newkirk argues that animal welfare facilitates a "springboard into animal rights." Her comments help to elucidate why PETA, a supposedly "radical" organization, joined with the most conservative animal welfare groups, such as HSUS and the Animal Welfare Institute (AWI), in support of the 1985 amendments to the federal Animal Welfare Act. Those amendments explicitly reinforce the moral orthodoxy that exploiting animals is acceptable, and it may be argued quite plausibly that not one animal has been helped as a result of those amendments. So, although PETA espouses an abolitionist *end,* it maintains that at least some welfarist *means* are both a causally efficacious and morally acceptable way of getting to that end. . . .

An important and predictable consequence of this coupling of rights ends with welfarist means is that even though "rights" advocates see abolition as a long-term goal, many animal advocates, seeing that both welfarists and "rightists" pursue the same welfarist strategy, have adopted the position that there is *no difference* between animal welfare and animal rights. As long as a person is "compassionate" and "cares" about animals and wants to reduce their suffering, then that is all that is necessary to be an animal advocate. For example, Barnes claims that "the different ideologies arrive at the same conclusion: humans have definite responsibilities to minimize the pain and suffering around them." He states that the distinctions between animal rights and animal welfare are "artificial" and that animal advocacy requires only that "a person [feel] compassion toward other animals and [seek] to aid their plight." Barnes claims that "this whole business that we have to have a philosophical framework and ideology for which we can raise our banners, well, I just don't think that's true, and it's elitist to say so." Similarly, Stallwood states that no action intended to reduce animal suffering should be rejected because it is "considered unworthy of some politically correct theory."

I consider this position—that the means to the long-term goal of animal rights is short-term welfarist reform—the "new welfarism" and its advocates the "new welfarists.". . .

INTRAMOVEMENT CONFUSION: WHO IS AN EXPLOITER?

Once we abandon animal rights idealism in favor of a standard that requires only that we "care" or feel "compassion" toward other animals, it becomes impossible any longer to differentiate animal rights theory from welfarist notions that are accepted by virtually everyone—*including animal exploiters.* In a 1995 article in *Vegetarian Times,* investigative journalist Jack

Rosenberger provided a list of organizations that purport to be animal *welfare* organizations but really promote the "interests of meat companies, trappers, hunters, furriers, and vivisectors." For example, the American Animal Welfare Federation is, according to its stated position, constituted "to promote the humane use and general welfare of animals, and to educate the public about the vital distinction between animal welfare and animal rights." According to a spokesperson for the organization, funding is provided by the fur, meat, and pet industries, hunting interests, and "other pro-animal-use individuals and organizations." Ted Nugent, rock star and zealous defender of bow hunting, is a member of the group's board of directors. Rosenberger's list includes five other groups that ostensibly promote animal welfare but are really nothing more than trade groups for animal exploiters. Moreover, everyone— from governmental agencies such as the National Institutes of Health and the U.S. Department of Agriculture to the quasi-governmental research organizations such as the Institute for Laboratory Animal Resources and associations such as the American Meat Institute—embraces the principle of animal welfare: that animals ought to be treated "humanely" and that no "unnecessary" suffering ought to be inflicted on them.

The response of many animal advocates to this posture is not, as one might expect, to distance themselves from animal welfare. Ironically, many animal advocates interpret exploiters' embrace of animal welfare as an attempt to drive a wedge between animal rights advocates and animal welfare advocates rather than to identify their differences. Any attempt to distinguish rights from welfare is perceived to be "divisive," to threaten destruction of the movement by violating the imperative that animal advocates must all "stick together." In an attempt to avoid this disintegration, the animal protection movement no longer endorses a philosophical concept of animal rights; instead, it endorses the principle that as long as we "care" or have "compassion" for animals, then we are all walking the same road. We should, so the common wisdom goes, focus on the common "enemy": the animal "exploiter." The problem is that in some cases there may be very little difference between the position of the animal advocate and the animal exploiter. And if any difference is one of degree (more or less), how does this effect our notion that the animal rights movement is, as commentators have argued and as most animal advocates believe, *qualitatively* different from the animal welfare views that have dominated thinking about these issues since the mid-nineteenth century? . . .

NEW WELFARISM AND THE FEDERAL ANIMAL WELFARE ACT

Although Great Britain in 1876 passed the first statute regulating the activities of those who used animals in experiments, numerous American legislative efforts to regulate the use of animals in experiments were unsuccessful until 1966, when Congress passed the Laboratory Animal Welfare Act, which, when amended in 1970, became known as the federal Animal Welfare Act (AWA). The AWA was also amended in 1975, 1985, and 1990. . . .

Those who supported the legislation made it clear that they did not oppose animal experimentation per se, and that they did not want to affect the content or conduct of research.

What is most important for the present discussion is that the AWA, although originally passed in 1966, was not amended in any significant way until 1985—at what was arguably the height of the emerging animal rights movement. . . .

Despite the momentum that the movement had achieved by 1985, the legislative result was disappointing, to say the least. Congress refused to move from the position—adopted in 1966—that Congress would not do anything to interfere with the actual content or conduct of research, and would only regulate issues of animal husbandry. . . . I argue [that] . . . once regulation affects only or primarily issues of husbandry, and once it is accepted that those who use the animals get to determine questions of scientific necessity, then the law will, as a practical matter, regulate (and prohibit) only those uses of animals that involve the *gratuitous* infliction of suffering and death.

Nevertheless, the animal rights movement rallied around the 1985 AWA amendments and refused to support the more progressive measures urged by Friends of Animals (FoA) or the International Society for Animal Rights (ISAR).

Many animal advocates recognized that the 1985 amendments were problematic: the amendments were "written with a great deal of input from the scientific community and, for the most part, [were] viewed as just another paper curtain." Nevertheless, the animal advocacy community was urged to support the amendments: "The word of the wise in the animal rights movement is: don't drop the ball now; work to get currently-pending legislation passed. But next time, get it together and get it right.". . .

Animal advocates supported the legislation because it purported to limit "survival" surgery, or the use of a single animal for multiple surgeries from which the animal is permitted to recover. The 1985 amendments provided that experimenters may not use an animal for "more than one major operative experiment from which it is allowed to recover." But the legislation added that multiple survival surgeries would be permitted when "scientifically necessary" or condoned by the secretary. In essence, Congress enacted a rule with a loophole large enough to negate it entirely. . . .

Moreover, the 1985 amendments not only failed to provide any real protection for animals; they arguably made it more difficult for the public to obtain information about animal use in federally funded experiments. A provision of the law imposes substantial criminal penalties on any animal care committee member who releases "any confidential information of the research facility," including information pertaining to the "trade secrets, processes, operations, style of work, or apparatus" or "the identity, confidential statistical data, amount or source of any income, profits, losses, or expenditures of the research facility." It is clear from other provisions that Congress was referring to proprietary information, such as trade secrets and patentable inventions, but research facilities have relied on this provision in both refusing to provide information to the public about experiments and in chilling the free speech rights of committee members who may wish to discuss publicly issues concerning experimentation at the particular facility.

Despite the fact that the 1985 amendments represented nothing but complete capitulation to the desire of the research community to continue doing business as usual, "groups that supported the amendments included NAVS [the National Anti-Vivisection Society], PETA, the Humane Society and most other animal-rights and animal-welfare organizations." HSUS vice-president Wayne Pacelle defended movement support of the amendments: "If animal suffering was relieved even to a small extent then a good purpose was served. If 60 animals are going to suffer, and we can stop 30 of them from suffering, by God we're going to do it. We're not just going to stand by and do nothing if we can't get all 60." There is, of course, no empirical evidence that the 1985 amendments did *anything* to decrease animal suffering. Indeed, USDA annual enforcement reports indicate that the supposedly fundamental shift to a largely local supervision scheme represented by the animal care committee has not had much effect on the total number of animals used or on the numbers of animals used in painful experiments without the benefit of pain relief. . . .

PETA AND THE ASPEN HILL SANCTUARY

In 1991, it was disclosed that PETA had killed healthy rabbits and roosters at its sanctuary, Aspen Hill, located in Silver Spring, Maryland. Although fund-raising literature for Aspen Hill claimed that animals at Aspen Hill would receive a "permanent home" there, the rabbits and roosters, which had been "rescued" from abusive situations, were killed by lethal injection, as animals are now killed in animal shelters that are supposed to be distinguished from animal sanctuaries.

When questioned about this matter, PETA's Ingrid Newkirk stated that PETA has "never been opposed to the humane killing of animals." Newkirk defended the killings as "euthanasia": "'Euthanasia means mercy killing,' she said.

'What we are opposed to is unnecessary slaughter of animals for frivolous reasons.'" The Aspen Hill killings were supposedly necessary because, according to PETA spokespersons, PETA "just [didn't] have the money" to build facilities for the animals. Newkirk stated that PETA would "not overcrowd our animals. . . . We really didn't have anything else to do." This contention is difficult to understand not only in light of PETA's supposedly radical animal rights philosophy but in consideration of PETA's budget, which, at the time of the Aspen Hill killings, was in excess of $6 million per year. Moreover, popular media regularly feature PETA employees traveling around the globe to accompany rock stars who promote animal rights or to stage antifur demonstrations in Rome, Japan, and countless other places. Presumably, these activities involve considerable financial expenditures.

It should be noted that Newkirk also argued that these animals were not really at the sanctuary permanently, but were only in an "interim situation" that did not make their killing inconsistent with PETA's statements about Aspen Hill in its fund-raising literature. Again, it is difficult to know what to make of such a contention. Assuming that the animals are rightholders and that they have a right to live their out their natural lives—a right that PETA seemed to recognize explicitly in its literature promoting Aspen Hill—then it is irrelevant that the rabbits were in an "interim" situation, whatever that means. Animals are either rightholders or they are not. If they are, then it is incoherent to say that humans can still deprive them of their most fundamental interests because of human convenience. No one doubts that PETA could have afforded to accommodate the animals; the point is that PETA made a decision to spend funds for other purposes, most of which have no direct impact on animals anyway. But then, how does Aspen Hill differ from the shelter whose purpose is to provide a humane death? And how is it any different from the dog owner who has her dog "put to sleep" because the dog is no longer convenient to the owner's lifestyle? PETA may have believed that funds spent on its educational campaigns would help more animals, but so does the person who says, "I will kill some animals today in the hope that I will obtain greater benefits for even more animals at some point in the future." It is precisely this sort of trade-off that characterizes the reasoning behind most institutionalized animal exploitation.

Reports suggested that some of the rabbits needed veterinary attention. But even if so, that would not have meant either that they needed to be killed or that the need for minor veterinary care morally justified their killing. And there was also never a suggestion that the decision to kill the roosters involved any concern about their ill health. I am in no way claiming to question PETA's motivation in this matter, but it is difficult, if not impossible, to square any coherent notion of animal rights with the killing of healthy animals, especially at a sanctuary that, as Jasper and Nelkin observe, is supposed to represent a "rights" improvement over the welfarist's notion that we are obligated only to provide a "humane" death.

Again, the Aspen Hill matter resonates with the view that all that matters to animal advocacy is "compassion" for animals and that the "different ideologies arrive at the same conclusion." That view is simply not true. PETA surely has "compassion" for animals and seeks to improve their plight. But that does not end the matter. It is now necessary to decide what to do with *these* particular rabbits and roosters. To the extent that the decision made is to kill animals that do not absolutely require to be killed for reasons that would similarly justify the euthanasia of *any* moral agent, the different ideologies do not lead to the same conclusion. Indeed, that is why Jasper and Nelkin argue that the sanctuary approach is the "rights" alternative to the welfarist view that the purpose of shelters is to provide a "humane death."

I do not doubt that the roosters and rabbits at Aspen Hill were killed "humanely," in the sense that their death was inflicted with an absolute minimum of pain and suffering. I am absolutely certain that the killings were performed with "compassion." But that does not make the killings right. The animals had interests other than the simple right to be free of pain and suffering. If that were the only interest that animals had, then it would be acceptable to eat animals who were raised and killed "humanely." And, as I pointed out earlier, that is precisely the position that Peter Singer takes in *Animal Liberation*. But the rights advocate believes that although animals certainly have an interest in avoiding pain and suffering, they have other interests as well, such as not being treated as means to ends within a system of institutionalized exploitation that causes the pain and suffering in the first instance. For the animal rights advocate, "happy" slavery *is still slavery*. This is not to say that the rights position is correct on this ground alone; it is only to establish that the two views, despite the claims of the new welfarists, lead to very different results.

Again, there was virtually no intramovement coverage of the Aspen Hill issue. In its "news shorts" section the *Animals' Agenda* had a single paragraph on the incident in which *Agenda* reported that the "PETA chairman pointed out that the group has never opposed euthanasia as a last-resort alternative to letting animals suffer." The *Agenda* "news short" did not discuss the fact that there was no indication of any need to kill any of these animals apart from the need created by PETA's decision not to spend the funds necessary to obviate the killings. And PETA continues to be identified by some with the very concept of animal rights. In my view, this is less an indication of attempts to cover up inappropriate or even outrageous behavior than it is more seriously a failure by some advocates to see the problem. This failure is understandable; in a movement that valorizes "compassion" above all other virtues, it should come as no surprise that the actions of "compassionate" people are excused even when those actions fly in the face of any coherent understanding of animal rights theory. But the confusion is compounded in light of wholly incorrect assertions that the "different ideologies arrive at the same conclusion." Animal rights theory would *not* lead to the same conclusion, and in this case, the difference certainly did make a difference—at least as far as the rabbits and roosters who were killed were concerned.

A DISTINCTION WITHOUT A DIFFERENCE

Many in the movement endorse "diversity" and urge that anyone who "cares" for animals, or who has "compassion" for animals, is really "walking along the same road" with those whose long-term goal is the abolition of animal exploitation. This desire to embrace "diversity" in the movement leads to positions that are difficult to understand and that make it difficult to formulate criteria for distinguishing who is the "exploiter" and who is not. For many new welfarists, the only criterion for belonging to the animal movement is having "compassion toward other animals" and a desire to "aid their plight." Any other criteria are considered to be exclusionary or "elitist."

If, however, the only difference between those whom Singer refers to as "exploiters" and at least some leaders of the animal rights movement is that the latter "feel compassion," then truly *this* is a "distinction without a difference" and is useless in helping to understand how the modern movement differs from its historical predecessors or from those whom it purports to oppose.

CHAPTER 4

LANDMARK CASES

AMERICAN
SOCIAL
MOVEMENTS

The Legal Defense for Releasing Captive Dolphins

GAVAN DAWS

When two lab students unaffiliated with any animal rights group systematically planned and executed the release of a pair of captive female bottlenose dolphins from a Honolulu marine biological facility in 1977, they anticipated enjoying public support based on their having taken the "moral high ground," but neither the judge nor an admittedly sympathetic jury considered their actions as anything other than property theft. As author Gavan Daws explains, though most media outlets covering the event sided with the laboratory, the publicity attracted by the case inspired similar marine "liberations" in both the United States and Japan and set the stage for more organized acts of dissent in the 1980s. Gavan Daws is also the author of *Shoal of Time* and *Dream of Islands* and coauthor of *Archipelago: Islands of Indonesia.*

B etween midnight on 29 May and dawn on 30 May 1977, two captive female Atlantic bottlenose dolphins held under the control of the University of Hawaii's Institute of Marine Biology at the Marine Vertebrate Laboratory of Comparative Psychology, Kewalo Basin, Honolulu, were lifted from their circular concrete isolation tanks, carried on stretchers to a panel van fitted with foam padding, driven to a fishing and surfing beach an hour from the city, and turned loose before sunrise in the Pacific.

The two men who organized the release of the dolphins, Kenneth W. Le Vasseur and Steven C. Sipman, lived on the lab-

From "'Animal Liberation' as Crime: The Hawaii Dolphin Case," by Gavan Daws, *Ethics and Animals,* edited by Harlan B. Miller and William H. Williams (Clifton, NJ: The Humana Press, 1983). Copyright © 1983 by Gavan Daws. Reprinted with permission.

oratory premises at Kewalo. They had been students of the laboratory's director, Dr. Louis M. Herman, in his animal psychology classes at the University of Hawaii. Herman, whose research at Kewalo was funded by the National Science Foundation, originally made use of Le Vasseur and Sipman, among many other students, to assist in carrying out behavioral experiments on the two dolphins. One of the dolphins, called Puka, had been in her tank at Kewalo since 1969; before that, she had been for many years an experimental subject in Navy and Navy-sponsored research and operations–related programs. The other dolphin, Kea, also came to Kewalo by way of the Navy, in 1972. (She replaced a dolphin named Nana who had been found dead in her tank one morning, of causes not altogether satisfactorily explained by the autopsy results.) In 1975 Le Vasseur moved into a room on the laboratory premises. Sipman became his immediate neighbor there in 1976. By the start of 1977 both Le Vasseur and Sipman, on the basis of what they saw happening at the laboratory, had become disenchanted with the idea of using dolphins in close captivity for rigorous scientific experimentation, and at the time they released the dolphins it had been many months since they had taken any part in the experimental program; they were doing maintenance work, principally cleaning the dolphins' tanks, in return for free rent.

Once the dolphins were in the ocean, Le Vasseur and Sipman went back to Honolulu and called a press conference to announce what they had done. They realized that the release of the dolphins might appear on the face of things to be criminal. But they did not consider themselves to be criminals. In fact, they took the view that if there was a crime, it was the crime of keeping dolphins—intelligent, highly aware creatures, with no criminal record of their own—in solitary confinement, in small concrete tanks, made to do repetitive experiments, for life.

THE "UNDERSEA RAILROAD"

Le Vasseur and Sipman were not systematic animal rights philosophers. They were students of dolphins whose personal experience at Kewalo led them to become animal rights activists. Neither were Le Vasseur and Sipman systematic thinkers about the law. Indeed they had not so much as consulted an attorney before they released the dolphins. Their view was that the release was morally right, and they believed the force of their act would compel the law to recognize as much. What they had done was intended to be exemplary. They wanted to convince other people—the world—that dolphins should be free. In their view, no matter what rights humans might claim over animals, no matter what assertions scientists might make about the importance of extending human knowledge, nothing was of more importance than the right of the dolphins Puka and Kea—and, by extension, all dolphins—to be free.

Le Vasseur and Sipman, in short, saw themselves as liberators. When the dolphins were taken from the tanks, a message was left behind identifying the releasers as the 'Undersea Railroad,' a reference to the Underground Railroad, the abolitionists' slave-freeing network of pre–Civil War days. Along the Underground Railroad in the 1850s, it sometimes happened that juries refused to convict people charged with smuggling slaves to freedom. That was the kind of vindication Le Vasseur and Sipman were looking for. If they were to be charged with a crime, then—so they believed—the evidence that could be brought forward about the nature of the dolphin would be persuasive that there was no crime, could be no crime, in freeing a captive dolphin.

What happened was that Le Vasseur and Sipman were charged with first-degree theft, a felony. In substance, the indictment ran that on or about 29 May 1977 they obtained or exerted unauthorized control over property valued at more than $200 belonging to the University of Hawaii Institute of Marine Biology, to wit, two dolphins, with the intent of depriving the owner of the property. . . .

Prosecuting attorney Stephen B. Tom did not have to address the question of dolphin rights, much less argue a negative case on the issue; he had merely to prove beyond a reasonable doubt that the elements of theft set out in the indictment were satisfied. Le Vasseur had never denied taking the dolphins from the laboratory and putting them in the ocean. He had even agreed to be photographed for a magazine article, between the date of the release and the date of his trial, standing in the water where the release took place, with Sipman and the attorney who took his case. So there was the most public of admissions from the defendant. No one could argue that the dolphins were worth less than $200. There were perhaps some minor uncertainties about where ownership of the dolphins finally rested; with the Institute of Marine Biology, the National Science Foundation, or the Navy. No matter—if Le Vasseur had taken the dolphins with intent to deprive, this was theft. With the possible exception of intent to deprive, the major elements seemed to be incontrovertibly present; Tom could approach the case in a straightforward way.

The defense, perforce, would have to be innovative. . . . Might it be argued that Le Vasseur acted out of *necessity?* Le Vasseur would testify to his belief that the continued incarceration of the dolphins at Kewalo in bad physical conditions, and their subjection to a demanding experimental regimen, was damaging to their health and well-being and might even result in their death. Though taking them out of this situation was in a strict sense a criminal act, leaving them would have been the greater evil. This 'choice of evils' defense is not widely reported in case law, but it is contained in the Model Penal Code that has been enacted in a number of states, and was made part of the Hawaii penal code when it was revised during the early 1970s.

"CHOICE OF EVILS" DEFENSE

Before the choice of evils defense could stand, a number of tests would have to be met. It would have to be shown that the threatened harm to the dolphins was imminent, and that no lawful alternative was open to Le Vasseur. Then it would be for the court to agree that the evil Le Vasseur committed in breaking the law to release the dolphins was less than the evil that would have been perpetuated had he *not* released them.

The defense of necessity or 'choice of evils' emerges from conduct that the actor believes to be necessary to avoid an imminent harm or evil to himself or to 'another.' Who, in this case, might be 'another'? The definition in the Hawaii Penal Code includes under the category of 'another,' where relevant, the United States, the State of Hawaii, other states and their political subdivisions. So if it could be shown that what was happening to the dolphins in captivity at Kewalo constituted a violation of federal or state statutes or regulations, then that was a harm or evil to 'another,' so defined, and Le Vasseur's release of the dolphins might be seen as a legitimate choice of evils.

The more central definition of 'another' is 'any other person'; and this, of course, was the consideration that bore most closely on questions of animal rights. Could it be sustainably argued that a dolphin by its nature and characteristics deserved to be treated under the law as a *person*? Le Vasseur clearly thought so. Here he was on ground mapped out by those who hold that any useful definition of 'person' framed so as to include *every* human being without exception must at the same time include *some* animals. One way commonly used to illustrate this proposition is to compare—in point of intelligence, communicative ability, and so on—a massively retarded and disabled human infant, incapable of speech, social activity, or even self-preservation, with a physically self-reliant, intelligent and sociable chimpanzee able to use one of the languages developed for two-way human–primate communication. Clearly in this instance, the chimpanzee would qualify as more 'human' than the human infant in every important respect but the purely biological. Le Vasseur would be able, through expert witnesses, to bring evidence of the exceptional size and structure of the dolphin brain; the remarkable communicative abilities of the dolphin; and the sophisticated, apparently mindful individual and social behavior of the dolphin, especially in its relation with humans. On the basis of this sort of evidence, the dolphin would seem to rank with the primates as possessing characteristics that might qualify it as a person for purposes of a choice of evils defense.

If a dolphin could be defined as a person, it could not be defined as property. Le Vasseur could not be convicted of theft. And the legal situation with respect to animal rights, at least the rights of dolphins, would be radically altered.

JUDGE DOI'S POSITION

What, then, happened to these lines of argument in court? Before trial proper began, Judge Doi made rulings that determined the course of everything that followed. He defined dolphins as property, not as persons—as a matter of law. A dolphin could not be 'another person' under the penal code. Accordingly, Doi refused to allow the choice of evils defense: 'This is going to be tried as a theft case, pure and simple,' not 'this choice of evil . . . is a dolphin going to be considered a person? This is not going to be the area of trial at all as far as the court is concerned, and I will rule right now that it is irrelevant . . .'

[Le Vasseur's attorney John F.] Schweigert moved to have Doi disqualified for prejudice because he would not even allow an offer of proof on the choice of evils defense. The move failed. Schweigert then asked leave to go to federal court for injunctive relief on the basis that Thirteenth Amendment rights in respect of involuntary servitude might be extended to dolphins. This failed. Judge Doi said: 'We get to dolphins, we get to orangutans, chimpanzees, dogs, cats. I don't know at what level you say intelligence is insufficient to have that animal or thing, or whatever you want to call it, a human being under the penal code. I'm saying that they're not under the penal code, and that's my answer. I may be in error, but that's my legal proposition here at this level.'

During Schweigert's conduct of voir dire [questioning of potential jury candidates to determine their impartiality] of the jury panel, Doi ruled that questions on potential jurors' attitudes to dolphin rights were irrelevant. This provoked Schweigert to move—unsuccessfully—for a mistrial because Doi had foreclosed questioning on the moral issue.

Throughout the subsequent days of testimony, Schweigert kept trying to open the trial up, to get to the issue of rights of dolphins, looking for a way around Doi's rulings on dolphins as property and on the choice of evils defense. This resulted in innumerable bench conferences. (The court reporter, a man of many years' experience, could not recall a trial in which the attorneys and the judge spent so much time in colloquy out of hearing of jury, spectators, and the press.) . . .

LE VASSEUR TAKES THE STAND

Trial, from the empaneling of the jury to the handing down of the verdict, extended over eight days of court time. Prosecutor Tom's presentation of the state's case was clear, economical, and precise, hewing closely to establishing the elements of theft. Schweigert, in his opening statement for the defense, spoke about the exceptional nature of dolphins as animals; bad and rapidly deteriorating physical conditions at the laboratory; a punishing regimen for the dolphins, involving overwork, reductions in their food rations, the total isolation they endured, deprived of the company of other dolphins, even of contact with humans in the tank, deprived of all toys that they had formerly enjoyed playing with—to the point where Puka, having refused to take part consistently in experimental sessions, developed self-destructive behaviors symptomatic of deep disturbance and unhealth, and finally became extremely lethargic, 'comatose.' Le Vasseur, seeing this, fearing that death would be the outcome, and knowing there was no law he could turn to, believed himself authorized, in the interest of the dolphins' well-being, to release them. The release was not a theft in that Le Vasseur did not intend to gain anything for himself. It was intended to highlight conditions at the laboratory. It would not permanently deprive Louis Herman and the Institute of Marine Biology of the use of the dolphins—Schweigert proposed to show that Puka and Kea could be recovered from the ocean, and that they were in fact alive to be recovered. . . .

Le Vasseur took the stand in his own defense. Doi had ruled that he could testify to 'all the things he observed and made him believe that he had to do what he did.' Within the constraints of a theft trial, this gave Le Vasseur and Schweigert considerable latitude, and Le Vasseur stayed on the stand most of one day, going into minute detail about his observations of deteriorating conditions at the laboratory; increased stress on the dolphins, particularly Puka; Puka's increasingly worrying behavior—erratic participation in experiments, interspersed with periods of total noncooperation, neurotic jaw-snapping, tail-slapping, coughing for hours at a time at night, beating her head against experimental apparatus and drawing blood. Schweigert took Le Vasseur at length through the decision to release the dolphins, the planning for the release (which took weeks to organize), and the way the release was carried out.

Testimony completed, the attorneys for state and defense submitted their proposed instructions to the jury. None of the substantive instructions proposed by Schweigert were used. In other words, he had made no impression on Judge Doi with his arguments about the theory of the case. The instructions to the jury were basically those of the prosecution, of a sort that might have been given in any theft case where the elements of theft had been well established.

After eight days of hearing testimony and argument, the jury took less than an hour to convict Le Vasseur of the felony of first-degree theft. . . .

THE SENTENCING OF LE VASSEUR

Le Vasseur could be sentenced to anything between a period of probation and five years' jail. In arriving at sentence, Doi spoke of the necessity of deterrence, the defendant as an individual being submerged in the 'overall picture' because of 'larger considerations that came into play: the seriousness of the offence involved,' and the 'deterrent or nondeterrent effect of any sentence that may be imposed on him.' Le Vasseur had no criminal record of any kind. On the other hand, 'release of the dolphins was an act which caused irreparable injury to many who were directly involved in dolphin-research and learning which caused great monetary loss and which may have . . . sentenced the dolphins, themselves, to death in . . . unfamiliar waters.' In sum, said Doi, 'there is nothing in the Defendant's personal background which indicates that he should receive harsh treatment. On the other hand, even assuming that he had good motives in doing what he did, the seriousness of his conduct in taking vigilante action cannot be condoned nor encouraged by this Court.' Doi sentenced Le Vasseur to five years' probation, as a special condition of which he was to spend six months in jail. . . .

The Intermediate Court of Appeals considered this not excessive, but pointed out that the sentence could be reduced if the criminal court saw fit to do so. In August, 1980, Judge Harold Y. Shintaku, having heard from both prosecution and defense, reduced the sentence so that Le Vasseur, as part of his probation, would serve no time in jail, but would instead be required to do four hundred hours of community service.

LEGACY OF THE KEWALO DOLPHIN CASE

This outcome could be seen as less than satisfactory for defense and prosecution alike. The defense failed to make its point—that, for legal purposes, dolphins should not be regarded as property but should be assigned 'person-like' rights. The prosecution got a conviction that was upheld on appeal, but failed, at final sentencing, to make its point—that 'vigilante' action to release captive dolphins was a serious matter, deserving of jail.

Both sides had a second chance to make their case. The trial of Le Vasseur's codefendant, Steven C. Sipman, was eventually brought on at the end of November, 1981, four years almost to the day after Le Vasseur's trial. The principal argument of the defense went to the question of *intent:* Sipman's state of mind was such that he did not consider dolphins to be property; thus in removing the dolphins from the tanks at Kewalo he could not have intended to commit the crime of theft, one element of which is depriving an owner of property. Sipman was able to testify at length, as Le Vasseur had been able to; but neither judge nor jury was persuaded by the defense argument, and Sipman was found guilty of first degree theft, as Le

Vasseur had been. Interestingly, some members of the jury remarked afterwards that they sympathized with Sipman, and said that in his place they might very well have acted as he did; but the law was the law, and under the law they had to find him guilty. In their discussions, they even mentioned the analogy between dolphins in captivity as property and slaves in Southern states as property, and concluded that however reprehensible slavery might have been, they would have had to convict a slave-liberator just as they had convicted Sipman—obeying the provisions of existing law.

In pre–Civil War days, juries sometimes refused to convict those who took it on themselves to liberate slaves by removing them from the control of their owners. This came to be known as "jury nullification" of what was seen to be bad law. This doctrine was discussed again at the time of trials of anti-Vietnam protestors in the 1960s, but has not been brought to bear in any significant way in the courtroom.

Since Le Vasseur and Sipman released Puka and Kea from Kewalo, there have been other instances of "vigilante" action to release captive marine mammals in the United States and in Japan. And the animal rights or animal liberation movement continues to search for the best legal forum for presenting its case.

Henry Spira and the Draize Campaign

In 1978, after the successful culmination of his campaign against the New York Museum of Natural History that resulted in the dismantling of its study on castrated cats, activist Henry Spira turned his attentions to Revlon, the world's largest cosmetics corporation, which tested the toxicity of its products by applying substances to the eyes of albino rabbits. This procedure is known as the Draize test, which was widely in use not just by cosmetics companies but the vast majority of corporations producing household products of all varieties. Spira's efforts involved the organization and maintenance of a delicate coalition of scientists, activists, and public relations personnel, as well as numerous letters, demonstrations, and meetings with Revlon spokespeople. As animal rights activist and author Peter Singer describes, Spira's trademark tenacity ultimately paid off again. This account is excerpted from Peter Singer's biography of Henry Spira, *Ethics into Action*. Peter Singer is a professor of bioethics at Princeton University and the author of *Animal Liberation* and *Practical Ethics*.

C osmetics and other substances are tested for eye damage. Here the standard method is the Draize test, named after J.H. Draize. Rabbits are the animals most often used. Concentrated solutions of the product to be tested are dripped into the rabbits' eyes, sometimes repeatedly over a period of several days. The damage is then measured according to the size of the area injured, the degree of swelling and redness, and other types of injury. One researcher employed by a large chemical company has described the highest level of reaction as follows: "Total loss of vision due to serious internal injury to cornea

Excerpted from *Ethics into Action: Henry Spira and the Animal Rights Movement,* by Peter Singer (Lanham, MD: Rowman & Littlefield Publishers, 1998). Copyright © 1998 by Rowman & Littlefield Publishers, Inc. Reprinted with permission.

174 • THE ANIMAL RIGHTS MOVEMENT

or internal structure. Animal holds eye shut urgently. May squeal, claw at eye, jump and try to escape."

By shutting or clawing at the eye, however, the rabbit may succeed in dislodging the substance. To prevent this the animals are now usually immobilized in holding devices from which only their heads protrude. In addition their eyes may be held permanently open by the use of metal clips which keep the eyelids apart. Thus the animals can obtain no relief at all from the burning irritation of substances placed in their eyes.

For thirty years, the Draize test had been widely used to test virtually anything that might get into a human eye. Could anything be done about it? . . .

The Draize test was a good target. . . . As Henry said, "people know what it feels like to get a little bit of soap in their eyes," and so they could identify with the rabbits undergoing the Draize test. And if anyone did have trouble identifying with the rabbits, it was easy to show, very vividly, just what it was like. The U.S. government's Consumer Products Safety Commission (CPSC) had produced a full-color film showing how to carry out the test. The film was intended to be used to train technicians, but anyone could buy a copy, and Henry did. From the same commission he also got a set of color slides illustrating various grades of damage to the eyes of rabbits who had undergone the Draize test. The slides were issued so that technicians could compare the eyeballs of the living rabbits in front of them with those of the rabbits in the slides. The film and slides were perfect campaigning tools: Their source meant that no one could claim that they gave a false or distorted impression of what the Draize test did to the eyes of rabbits.

Focusing on this test went beyond Henry's previous public campaigns, not only in the number of animals affected, but also in their species. Campaigning for cats and dogs made it easier to get a favorable response from the public, but at the same time, it reinforced the idea that if animals aren't lovable, they don't matter. Henry wanted to break out of that restriction and convey the idea that it is the capacity of an animal to suffer that really matters. But to try to go too far—by campaigning against tests done on rats, for example—would be to risk losing public support altogether. The Draize test was standardly performed on albino rabbits, because their lack of pigmentation meant that any damage caused to the eye was easier to see. White rabbits are a symbol of innocence, though, and probably lie somewhere between rats and dogs in terms of the sympathy they could be expected to arouse.

The Draize test was being performed across the United States by thousands of different corporations, but the success of the museum campaign had reinforced Henry's conviction that a winnable campaign needed a specific target. Cosmetics companies looked particularly vulnerable:

> We could pose the issue this way: is another shampoo worth blinding a rabbit? It was so incongruous for the cosmetics industry to be carrying out these tests. The cosmetics industry is trying to sell dreams, but the reality is that they are creating a nightmare for the rabbits. Exposing the reality of what they are doing threatens the whole image of the industry. Blinding rabbits isn't beautiful.

The frivolous nature of the products the industry was selling was also important: "I think that there are very few people on the street who'll say, 'Yeah, go around and blind rabbits to produce another mascara.'"

Once again, the Freedom of Information Act was essential to the campaign. Organizations carrying out experiments on animals in the United States are required to make annual returns to the Department of Agriculture showing the numbers of animals they are using and—when the experiment causes pain or distress without anesthesia—giving an explanation as to why no anesthetic was used. Henry requested the returns of the two leaders of the cosmetics industry, Revlon and Avon. They confirmed that both corporations were conducting the Draize test. Revlon's 1977 report showed that it had used 2,000 rabbits that year. The report also stated tersely that "no anesthesia is used in any of the above procedures. This is due to the nature of the studies involved.". . .

One-Hundredth of One Percent

To demand that Revlon cease testing its products on rabbits would lead to head-on conflict. Government regulations required corporations to provide evidence of the safety of their products, and there was no recognized alternative to the Draize test that would be accepted as evidence of safety for products that might get in someone's eye. To find an area of overlap between Revlon's interests and those of the animals, Henry decided not to ask for an immediate halt to Revlon's use of the Draize test but, instead, to seek Revlon's support for a research project to develop an alternative test that did not use animals. After scanning some financial information on the cosmetics industry, he calculated that if each corporation in the industry gave one-hundredth of 1 percent of their gross revenues, then $1.1 million would be available to fund a crash research program to develop an alternative to the Draize test. One-hundredth of 1 percent seemed a modest amount to put toward ending the suffering that cosmetics companies were inflicting on animals. For Revlon, it would amount to about $170,000 a year. The company spent $162 million on advertising alone.

Quite apart from the fact that asking Revlon for one-hundredth of 1 percent of its revenue would make the campaign winnable, whereas asking it to stop carrying out the Draize test would not, there was another strong reason for taking the first approach. If the whole cosmetics industry stopped doing the Draize test, that might save 10,000 rabbits a year; but the number of rabbits used in Draize tests for household goods, pharmaceuticals, pesticides, and raw chemicals would be at least ten times that. . . .

The campaign began in September 1978 with a letter from Leonard Rack and Henry to Frank Johnson, Revlon's vice president for public affairs, outlining some scientific ideas for methods that could replace animal testing in the cosmetics industry. These methods would, the letter asserted, "be faster, more economic, and more efficiently protective of the cosmetics user than current methods." The letter quoted Smyth's comments on the desirability of finding an alternative to the Draize test and gave detailed references to scientific papers that offered promising avenues for further exploration. The "humane aspect of substituting alternatives for animal testing" was referred to only in two sentences near the end of the five-page letter.

Months went by without any real response. To try to get the company to move things along, Henry bought one share of Revlon stock and went to the company's annual general meeting. At question time—after Revlon chairman and chief executive Michel Bergerac had announced the largest increase in dividends in the company's history—Henry rose to demand an end to the "cruel and grotesque" rabbit blinding tests Revlon was performing. Bergerac responded that "regrettably" the choice was between "having to harm animals or harming humans.". . .

Frank Johnson agreed to a meeting, and on the morning of June 28, Henry was ushered into Johnson's impressive office, overlooking Central Park. Johnson was friendly and seemed to listen to what Henry said, but he was vague about what Revlon was doing by way of research into methods of testing its products without the use of animals. Worse still, it became clear during the meeting that he had not passed on Rack's memo on alternatives to those involved in scientific research at Revlon. After the meeting, Henry held a postmortem with Rack, and they concluded that they were not being taken seriously. Henry wrote a letter in which he said that the failure to forward the memo to the company's own researchers "constitutes a breach of communicative faith as well as an inefficient use of our meeting time." He asked for "a timely response" to the specific proposals that he had made.

A month later, Henry wrote to Michel Bergerac:

Dear Mr. Bergerac,

Nine months ago we gave Mr. Frank Johnson a memo on alternatives to the use of live animals in cosmetic safety testing, a revised copy of which is attached. Our last letter, copy enclosed, was hand delivered on 6/28/79. It was followed by three phone calls to his secretary—and no response from

Mr. Johnson.

Though pleasant enough on a personal level, Mr. Johnson's actions signify unconcealed contempt and deliberate insult which may, to a considerable extent, represent a failure to recognize the potential value, to Revlon, of our attempted dialogue. It would also be a gross error for Mr. Johnson to mistake our patience and civility as meekness.

We do hope you'll take an intelligent interest in the possibilities suggested.

As Revlon continued to make polite but meaningless responses, Henry . . . outlined the goals of the coalition. From the start, it was clear that they went beyond abolishing the Draize test itself.

- To challenge the archaic ritual whereby regulatory agencies force the testing of every chemical on tens of millions of animals every year.
- To focus on a single, grotesque, massively used—and particularly vulnerable—animal test, the Draize eye mutilations, as a specific, concrete target.
- To set the precedent of replacing crude, painful, and outdated methods with elegant, modern, nonviolent science through a realistic, effective, and winnable campaign. . . .

The coalition grew to include more than 400 organizations, with a membership in the millions. The basic running costs were met by the larger societies, especially the Humane Society of the United States, the ASPCA, and the Chicago Anti-Cruelty Society. On one occasion the Humane Society sent out a mailing to 250,000 people on behalf of the coalition, and for a time it employed a part-time staff member to assist the coalition. Apart from that, the coalition had no paid employees. Henry himself was still working as a high school teacher and campaigning in his spare time. . . .

An essential plank of Revlon's defense of its use of the Draize test was that it was "used by agencies of the federal government concerned with the safety of consumer and chemical products." This careful phrasing was necessary, because the test was not strictly required by any federal government agency. Instead, the agencies demanded that companies supply adequate evidence of the safety of a product—or else they required that the product be sold with a label warning that its safety level was unknown. No major cosmetics or household products manufacturer was prepared to put such a label on its products. Since the agencies always accepted Draize test data as adequate evidence, and since no one knew of any other kind of evidence that they would accept as adequate, the manufacturers continued to use the Draize test.

In these circumstances, it was just as urgent to persuade the regulatory agencies to change their stance as it was to persuade the manufacturers to put money into developing alternatives. There would be no point in having alternative tests unless the agencies were prepared to accept results from them. So while the campaign against Revlon was going on, Henry was also lobbying government at various levels. This produced some success. In a move that revealed how utterly mindless the approach to the use of animals in safety testing had been before Henry started campaigning against it, the government's Interagency Regulatory Liaison Group issued a statement that "substances known to be corrosive may be assumed to be eye irritants" and should not be tested on the eyes of rabbits. Even *Chemical Week* applauded the move:

> It is true that the test has been overworked. No sensible person would require a Draize test to prove that caustic soda is an eye irritant—as has been done in the past. But governmental agencies are relaxing their requirements for Draize testing. This appears to be a result of the group's efforts, and for this, the coalition deserves unqualified praise.

In September, Senator David Durenberger, a Republican from Minnesota, addressed the U.S. Senate on the issue:

> The other evening I was watching the television show *20/20*. . . . One of the issues raised was the continued justification for the Draize test. I was embarrassed at the way Federal officials responded to questions posed by the re-

porter. For example, the reporter asked why the Federal Government utilizes such a painful test, and why the animal was not given pain medication. The official responded that "No one thought of it."

Durenberger submitted a resolution that referred to doubts about the reliability of the Draize test and then stated:

> Now therefore be it resolved, it is the sense of the Senate that the Consumer Product Safety Commission, the Environmental Protection Agency, and the Food and Drug Administration set aside research time and funding to develop and validate an alternative nonanimal testing procedure.

Such resolutions are not binding, but if they come to a vote—which is uncommon—they carry some weight with government agencies. The resolution was sent to a committee, where it languished for nearly two years. The Senate finally voted on it—and passed it—on August 11, 1982. By then, much else had already happened.

MAKING PROGRESS

To keep up the momentum against Revlon, on May 13, several hundred people gathered outside its head offices. Some were in rabbit costumes. The demonstration impressed Roger Shelley, then Revlon's vice president for investor relations:

> I remember one day at lunch an enormous demonstration on the Fifth Avenue side of the General Motors building, which was probably the most popular four corners in all of New York City, with the Plaza Hotel in the background, the General Motors building in the foreground, Central Park in one direction and Fifth Avenue heading downtown in the other, and there were hundreds and hundreds and hundreds of people . . . and in the middle there was every major science writer, science reporter, newspaper man, or TV science person in New York—all of whom were interviewing people. And that evening on the news and in the next morning's newspapers, we took a beating the likes of which no opponent of Muhammad Ali ever took.

Roger Shelley had good cause to remember that demonstration, because shortly after it, Frank Johnson, who had been handling the issue for Revlon, was removed from his position, and the task was given to Shelley. After working with investors, the change of job must have been a shock:

> I personally had to sign 20,000 letters. I got letters on Saturdays and Sundays prepared by my secretary, in shoe boxes waiting for me to sign, to people who wrote in. [We answered them] whether they were stockholders, whether they were customers, whether they were employees, whether they were animal rights people from all over the country. This produced writer's cramp . . . but more importantly, it gave a real focal point to the board of directors of Revlon . . . that we had to deal with this.

NEGOTIATING

Revlon's decision to replace Johnson with Shelley was a hopeful sign that the corporation might be moving beyond dealing with the issue at the level of public relations. Shelley decided to meet Henry as soon as he could. In contrast to the meetings in Johnson's office, they met privately at a cocktail lounge, where they both ordered soft drinks and began to talk. Shelley was expecting to have difficulty in finding common ground:

> I felt when I met Henry Spira [that] it was going to be a very contentious set of meetings, because Henry espoused—and quite well—the animal rights groups' feelings about animal testing in the cosmetics industry, and I, on the other hand, represented consumers, stockholders, employees, and a company, and on this issue there was plenty of opportunity for us to have opposite points of view.

> The first feeling I had of Henry, though, was that my preconception was wrong. One major and overriding factor about Henry which I and . . . Michel Bergerac felt in those days was that Henry understood the pressures on business. My first impression was: "Here's a man who has a very strong point of view, have no doubt about it, who is going

to make peace with us by making us do the right thing in his eye, but who would listen to us and who would be prepared to work something out that we could live with too."

While Shelley and Henry got to know each other and explore what the "right thing" that Revlon could live with might be, Henry took care that the pressure did not abate. Several smaller demonstrations were held, including one at Bloomingdale's. Supporters asked their local stores not to stock Revlon products; a twelve-year-old boy was reported to have persuaded three small department stores to stop selling Revlon cosmetics. The top-rating television network programs, *20/20* and *Speak Up America,* did stories on the Draize test campaign. The trade journal *Chemical Week* ran an article headed "Cosmetics Firms Feel Heat over the Draize Test." On October 7, a second full-page advertisement appeared in the *New York Times,* with a large picture of a hand putting something into the eye of a rabbit and the caption: "There must be a less ugly way for Revlon to test beauty products."

On November 29, the campaign went international, with simultaneous demonstrations in Britain, Germany, France, Australia, New Zealand, and South Africa. "Remember the Revlon Rabbits' Day" was especially big in Britain, where Jean Pink, founder of a rapidly growing organization called Animal Aid, involved at least 3,500 activists in every major British city, picketing High Street stores with Revlon counters and distributing 400,000 leaflets explaining the nature of the Draize test. Stickers saying REVLON TORTURES RABBITS began appearing in public places.

At Revlon, Shelley started talking to his superiors about the futility of hoping that the issue would just go away without any positive move on Revlon's part. Initially, he encountered some resistance from people who didn't want Revlon to be perceived as having backed down under pressure from the animal rights movement, but when he was able to reach past the level of management immediately above him, he found that those points of view were not held at the top of the company, nor the level just beneath it. . . . [The Board of Directors and the highest level of management] had a different agenda. Their agenda was that Revlon had been around for fifty years . . . , it was going to live a lot of years afterwards, and there comes a time when this hackneyed phrase of "corporate responsibility" does come into play.

By November, it was clear that Revlon was getting serious in thinking about putting money into alternatives. In a letter to Roger Shelley that addressed him as "Dear Roger" (in eighteen months of discussions and correspondence with Frank Johnson, it had always been "Dear Mr. Johnson"), Henry wrote that he was "deeply encouraged and grateful for your active interest in developing alternatives to the Draize eye test." The letter portrayed Revlon's situation in positive terms, as an opportunity for the industry leader to be "the pioneer in linking imaginative, elegant science with effective and efficient safety testing.". . .

Henry used his network of science advisers, particularly Andrew Rowan, to ensure that Revlon received letters from researchers indicating that they were interested in pursuing promising lines of research into alternatives to the Draize test if funds could be provided. After considering several proposals, Henry and Shelley agreed that Rockefeller University, on New York's Upper East Side, would be an ideal base for the search for an alternative. Previously known as the Rockefeller Institute for Medical Research, Rockefeller University was devoted exclusively to research and graduate education in the biomedical sciences. The sixteen Nobel Prizes awarded to its scientists were sufficient proof of its international leadership in research. For so eminent an institution to take the lead in research into alternatives to the use of animals would fulfill Henrys highest hopes. The status of the recipient of the funds was important, not only because the better the institution, the better the chance that it would come up with a viable alternative to the Draize test, but also because simply by conducting research in what had hitherto been an extremely low-status area of research, Rockefeller University would give an unprecedented boost to the whole field of in vitro toxicology. As Henry was later to put it: "It transformed the search for alternatives from some kind of flaky anti-vivisectionist issue to something that received large-scale support from a multibillion-dollar corporation and was linked with one of the most respected medical research institutions in the country."

Henry and Shelley met Dr. Dennis Stark, director of Rockefeller's Laboratory Animal Research Center, to tell him what they were interested in doing. When Stark was receptive to the idea of receiving a grant from Revlon for the purpose of developing an alternative to the Draize test, Shelley arranged a meeting between Bergerac and Dr. Joshua Lederberg, president of Rockefeller University and a Nobel laureate. The upshot was that Revlon agreed to give the university $750,000 over three years—more than the one-hundredth of 1 percent of their gross revenues that Henry had originally sought—to support research into nonanimal safety tests. Bergerac thought the proposal sufficiently important to take it to Revlon's Board of Directors. The board approved it unanimously. . . .

Henry had made a commitment to Revlon that the campaign against it would cease as soon as it made the commitment he was seeking. The campaign had worked so well, however, that there were some in the animal rights movement who wanted to keep it going as long as Revlon was still doing the Draize test. In Britain, Jean Pink vowed that "the demonstrations will continue." For Henry, this was a threat to his credibility, which he would need for the broader goals he had in mind. He therefore suggested to Pink, as well as to American groups that were keen to continue to harass Revlon, that—as Bergerac had indicated in his speech—the ball was now in the court of other cosmetics companies. Instead of continuing with the Revlon campaign, the coalition should get ready for a campaign against Avon.

Henry then wrote to David Mitchell, chairman of Avon Products, Inc.:

Undoubtedly, Revlon has set a standard with its $750,000 grant to Rockefeller University. . . . Revlon has shown that a corporate giant can have the vision to be responsive in a constructive, innovative and substantive fashion. We expect no less from Avon.

The letter mixed encouragement with a delicately veiled threat of demonstrations. Having watched what happened to Revlon, Avon needed little persuading. On March 18, 1981, the company issued a news release pledging a matching $750,000 donation to a fund created by the CTFA for research into alternatives to the Draize test.

The Silver Spring Monkeys Case

ALEX PACHECO WITH ANNA FRANCIONE

The autumn of 1981 marked the first time a federally funded research facility was ever legally tried for the mistreatment of its animal subjects. Here activist Alex Pacheco chronicles his conversion
to animal rights while employed at a Maryland research institute.
Pacheco recounts the abuses he saw perpetrated against the lab monkeys imprisoned there and the bittersweet outcome of the ensuing
high-profile legal case that brought the animal rights movement to
national prominence. Alex Pacheco is cofounder of the organization People for the Ethical Treatment of Animals (PETA). His
cowriter, Anna Francione, is an animal law professor at Rutgers University in New Jersey and coauthor of *Vivisection and Dissection in
the Classroom.*

I discovered animal rights in 1978, when I first entered a
slaughterhouse and witnessed the violent deaths of terrified dairy cows, pigs and chickens. What I saw changed my
life. Shaken by the slaughtering, I sought and joined the animal protection community. . . .

Upon moving to Washington, DC in 1980, I joined forces
with Ingrid Newkirk who had accomplished major victories
for animals in her eleven years as an animal law-enforcement
officer. By the spring of that year we had formed People for
the Ethical Treatment of Animals (PETA), both believing that
this young movement needed a grassroots group in the USA
that could spur people to use their time and talents to help animals gain liberation. Our emphasis was to be on animals used
in experimentation and food production, while at the same

time being out on the streets, bringing as many animal issues to the public's attention as we could.

In the summer of 1981, after my third year as a political science and environmental studies major at George Washington University, I discussed with Ingrid the need to gain some first-hand experience in a laboratory. It now shocks me to think how easily we fell upon the atrocities at the Institute for Behavioral Research (IBR), because it suggests that such conditions are common to many other facilities. I simply found IBR listed in the US Department of Agriculture directory of registered animal research facilities and chose it because it was a stone's throw from where I lived.

FIRST DAY ON THE JOB

I was greeted at IBR by a research assistant. I told him that I was seeking employment, and he referred me to Dr Taub. Taub took me into his office and explained that research was being conducted on surgically crippled primates to monitor the rehabilitation of impaired limbs. There were no paid positions available, he said, but he offered to check to see if they could use a volunteer. I called the next day, as he suggested, and was offered the opportunity to help Georgette Yakalis, his student protégé. On 11 May 1981 I began work and was given a tour by Taub himself.

The Institute was divided into two areas. The rooms near the front were used for work with humans. They appeared unremarkable. The animals were kept in the back. As we went through the doors to that section, I had my first indication that something was wrong. The smell was incredible, intensifying as we entered the colony room where the monkeys were kept. I was astonished as I began to comprehend the conditions before me. I saw filth caked on the wires of the cages, faeces piled in the bottom of the cages, urine and rust encrusting every surface. There, amid this rotting stench, sat sixteen crab-eating macaques and one rhesus monkey, their lives limited to metal boxes just 17¾ inches wide. In their desperation to assuage their hunger, they were picking forlornly at scraps and fragments of broken biscuits that had fallen through the wire into the sodden accumulations in the waste collection trays below. The cages had clearly not been cleaned properly for months. There were no dishes to keep the food away from the faeces, nothing for the animals to sit on but the jagged wires of the old cages, nothing for them to see but the filthy, faeces-splattered walls of that windowless room, only 15 ft. square.

In the following days the true nature of the monkeys' sad existence became apparent. Twelve of the seventeen monkeys had disabled limbs as a result of surgical interference (deafferentation) when they were juveniles. Sarah, then eight years old, had been alone in her cage since she was one day old, when she was purchased from Litton Laboratories and then forgotten. According to a later count, thirty-nine of the fingers on the monkeys' deafferented hands were severely deformed or missing, having been either torn or bitten off.

CONDITIONS UNFIT FOR MAN OR BEAST

Many of the monkeys were neurotic, particularly Chester, Sarah and Domitian. Like a maniac, Sarah would attack her foot and spin around incessantly, calling out like an infant. Domitian attacked his arm mercilessly and masturbated constantly. Chester saw himself as the troupe leader, powerless to defend his fellows, enraged at the world. It was astounding that Taub and the other researchers expected to gain any reproducible, let alone reliable, data from these animals, considering the condition of the animals themselves and of the colony and surgery rooms. The surgery room had to be seen to be believed. Records, human and monkey, were strewn everywhere, even under the operating table. Soiled, discarded clothes, old shoes and other personal items were scattered about the room. Because of a massive and long-standing rodent problem, rat droppings and urine covered everything, and live and dead cockroaches were in the drawers, on the floor and around the filthy scrub sink.

No one bothered to bandage the monkeys' injuries properly (on the few occasions when bandages were used at all), and antibiotics were administered only once; no lacerations or self-amputation injuries were ever cleaned. Whenever a bandage was applied, it was never changed, no matter how filthy or soiled it became. They were left on until they deteriorated to the point where they fell off the injured limb. Old, rotted fragments of bandage were stuck to the cage floors where they collected urine and faeces. The monkeys also suffered from a variety of wounds that were self-inflicted or inflicted by monkeys grabbing at them from adjoining cages. I saw discoloured, exposed muscle tissue on their arms. Two monkeys had bones protruding through their flesh. . . .

Even though I had made it plain to Taub that I had no laboratory experience, within a week of starting work I was put in charge of a pilot study. With the opportunity to work alone, I could better document the operation of the facility and the life the monkeys lived there. Taub called the study a 'displacement experiment'. I was given two monkeys and told to put them in separate cages in a room. The monkeys, Augustus and Hayden, were deprived of food for two to three days, and I was to go alone into their room, set up video equipment to record events and feed them about fifty raisins each. After some weeks I was to withhold their food for three days and then, instead of giving them the raisins, I was just to show them the raisins but no allow them to eat, and then record their frustrated reactions.

NOXIOUS STIMULI

Perhaps I was too recently initiated into this scientific environment, but I asked Taub and Yakalis three times what the purpose of the experiment was and what I should keep my eyes open for. On each occasion they responded that they hoped to find something 'interesting', in which case they 'could get [grant] funding'. It made me wonder if this typified scientific method. Working at IBR was becoming more and more of a strain. I was beginning to appreciate the monkeys as individuals and had especially close relationships with Billy, Sarah, and Domitian. Night after night, I agonized over what to do. . . .

After about a month I was put in charge of yet another experiment: the 'acute noxious stimuli test'. I was to take a monkey from the colony and strap him into a homemade immobilizing chair, where he would be held at the waist, ankles, wrists and neck. The acute noxious stimuli were to be applied with a pair of haemostats (surgical pliers) clamped and fastened on to the animal, and locked to the tightest notch. I was to observe which parts of the monkey's body felt pain. (The noxious stimuli used to be administered by using an 'open flame'—a cigarette lighter.) Taub's protocol . . . stated that the stimuli were to be applied to the monkeys every four months. The work was conducted in such a haphazard way that this schedule was never adhered to. As I was working alone, I was able to fabricate data to avoid hurting them.

Before beginning the test on my own I was instructed in how to apply the haemostats. Domitian was unfortunate enough to be chosen as the 'example' animal and was placed in the chair and the haemostat clamps were latched as tightly as possible on to his testicles. Terrified, he thrashed violently and screamed. This was repeated three times over a forty-five minute period so that I could witness a 'positive' reaction: an enraged creature, desperately thrashing against the restraints to escape the pain. That same day the surgical pliers were twice thrust into Domitian's mouth and raked against his teeth and gums. Such was my introduction to the acute noxious stimuli test.

HERBIE AND CALIGULA

By the time I was put in charge of administering the test on my own, I had requested (and received) a set of keys on the pretext of doing more work on the weekends and in the evenings. I was now freer to explore the entire laboratory and take photographs of the monkeys, the cages, the rodent droppings, the dried blood on the floors, the restraining chairs and so on.

Inside an ice-choked freezer I found two plastic bags labelled 'Herbie' and 'Caligula'. I asked Yakalis what had happened to these monkeys. She said that she did not know Herbie had died but that Caligula had developed gangrene from a filthy, unchanged bandage. She told me that Caligula had been in such bad shape that he had begun to mutilate his own chest cavity, and she then confided that putting him in a restraining device, and administering the noxious stimuli test, with his chest ripped open, and having to experience the stench of his rotting body, was the most disgusting thing she had ever done. After the acute pain test, she said, he was destroyed.

As time went on I discovered that I was not the only one who came in late at night. Several times, while taking pictures around midnight, my heart would jump as one of the two caretakers came in to pick up a paycheck or to 'clean' the colony room. The caretakers took turns coming into the laboratory at any time of the night, and as no schedules were assigned to them, they often did not come in at all. I also found that they were paid not by the number of hours they worked, nor by the number of cages they were supposed to clean, but simply by the number of rooms in their charge. They were paid $10 a day. The colony room, with seventeen monkeys, was only damp-mopped, because there was no drain in the floor to take any water away. Every few days the faecal trays, sometimes filled to the top, were emptied but never cleaned. To feed the monkeys, the caretakers would simply open the cage doors and throw in half a scoop of monkey chow— when and if they fed them at all. The markers I put in the chow cans indicated there were many days, often several at a time, when the monkeys went without food. When they were fed, the food would fall through the wire mesh into the faecal trays below, as no bowls or food receptacles were ever used. The employees usually worked carelessly and as fast as they could, getting out as soon as possible.

I soon began to take more photographs, hiding my camera and risking discovery by photographing the monkeys in the restraining chair during the day. At that point I was still under the impression that all animal experimentation was exempt from anti-cruelty code enforcement, so I still hadn't determined what action I would be able to initiate. There were many times when I felt very alone, unsure of whom I could approach with the evidence or of what recourse would be available to prevent Taub from continuing his practices.

PREPARING THE CASE AGAINST IBR

Then, after about two months, I found out that a revision of the Maryland statute had excluded language designed to exempt animal experimenters. Elated, I began to prepare my criminal case against Taub. One of the first things I had to do was to stop giving the monkeys the fresh fruit I was smuggling in for them. The food sacks which were clearly marked with an expiry date (after which the food is nutritionally deficient) had all expired four months before I started work at IBR. I realized that Taub would use any improvement in their health brought about by my independent feeding of them to defend his treatment of the animals. I also discovered that virtually all the medication in the laboratory had expired, some in 1979, others as far back as 1969. The broken and the intact containers were kept in a filthy refrigerator, strewn about next to a bag of putrefied apples that were actually covered with cobwebs. Near this refrigerator was the shell of another. This one had been converted into a chamber containing a plexiglass immobilizing chair. A monkey would be placed in the chamber, and electrodes attached to his body. The monkey would be forced to try to squeeze a bottle of fluid with his surgically crippled arm in order to stop the painful electric shock that coursed through his body. The ceiling and walls of the chamber were covered with blood. I remembered Taub's assistant, John Kunz, telling me that some monkeys would break their arms in desperate attempts to escape the chair and the intense electric shocks.

On several occasions things were so bad that I risked appearing suspiciously concerned about the primates and suggested that a veterinarian be called in to treat the most serious injuries. At one point Billy's arm was broken in two places and I repeatedly asked that a veterinarian be called. Then, it was finally openly admitted to me that they did not use a veterinarian. Billy's extremely swollen, broken arm was left untreated.

Conditions were so bad that it was clear that it would be crucial to bring in some expert witnesses who could vouch for the conditions I was witnessing. I cautiously approached five people with expertise in various related fields. They were Dr

Violence in the Movement or a Frame Job?

In 1990, Fran Trutt was convicted for the attempted murder two years earlier of U.S. Surgical Corporation chairman Leon Hirsch by pipe bomb. But testimony from key players in the drama suggested that Hirsch may have orchestrated the whole event to entrap Trutt and defame the animal rights movement. According to authors Lawrence Finsen and Susan Finsen, Trutt's case is considered either the most damning example of animal rights terrorism to date or a sinister attempt to discredit the movement, depending on whose testimony one chooses to believe.

On 11 February 1988 Fran Trutt was arrested in Norwalk, Connecticut, and charged with placing a 12-inch radio-controlled pipe bomb near the parking space of Leon Hirsch, chairman of U.S. Surgical Corporation. Hirsch had won the longtime enmity of animal rights activists for extensive use of dogs in training company salespeople to implant surgical staples, even though the technique could be shown as well without living animals. . . .

Marc Mead, the man who drove Trutt and the bomb to the scene of the crime, was upset by publicity that appeared to suggest he was an accomplice. In early January 1988 Mead delivered a press release to the *Westport News* explaining that he was really a hero, since he and the authorities had carefully staged the entire episode, assuring that no damage or injury would occur. The ensuing investigation

Geza Teleki, an ethologist and global expert in primatology; Dr Michael Fox, a writer, veterinarian and ethologist; Dr Ronnie Hawkins, a physician who had worked with laboratory primates; Dr John McArdle, a primate anatomist and former primate researcher; and Donald Barnes, a lay psychologist who

revealed that Hirsch had employed a man named Jan Reber of Perceptions International to arrange the entire event. Reber had in turn hired Mary Lou Sapone as an agent provocateur to incite Trutt to obtain and plant the bomb.

According to Trutt, Sapone told her shortly after they met that Hirsch ought to be "blown from here to kingdom come" and offered to pay for the bomb. That Sapone also attempted to enlist Merritt Clifton of *The Animal's Agenda* in the U.S. Surgical bombing lends credence to Trutt's story. Clifton apparently told her that this was a "half-assed, stupid idea," and the matter ended there. Sapone apparently also infiltrated Earth First!, as she was listed as its Connecticut representative when founder Dave Foreman was arrested in May 1989 at the culmination of an 18-month FBI investigation.

On 17 April 1990 Trutt accepted a plea bargain, pleading "no contest" to charges she tried to murder Hirsch. . . . Reber continues to profit from the backlash against the movement, publishing the *Animal Rights Reporter,* a magazine designed to give information about the movement to those intent on fighting it (at a hefty subscription price that puts it out of range of most within the movement). The *Animal Rights Reporter* denies any connection with Perceptions International, though they do seem to share office space.

Lawrence Finsen and Susan Finsen, *The Animal Rights Movement in America.* New York: Twayne, 1994, pp. 173–74.

had radiated monkeys for seventeen years in the military before rejecting such practices. These people accompanied me through the laboratory at night, signing affidavits afterwards. I was grateful for their support because their professional assessments of the state of the animals and the laboratory would lend credence to my testimony in any future legal proceedings.

THE RAID

On 8 September I took my affidavit and those of the five expert witnesses, as well as my notes and photographs, to the Silver Spring, Maryland, police. After their preliminary investigations Detective Sergeant Rick Swain obtained the precedent-setting search and seizure warrant from Circuit Court Judge John McAuliffe. The first raid of a research facility in the United States took place at IBR on 11 September. Swain and a search team of six confiscated the monkeys and the files.

We had considered carefully the problem of where we could house seventeen traumatized, fragile monkeys. The National Zoo, the facility most capable of assisting, refused to help. Local animal shelters, although sympathetic, were not equipped. We were finally forced to adapt the basement of a local activist's home. After the installation of drains in the floor, new windows, a ventilation system, insulation, etc., their refuge was ready.

A devoted PETA volunteer built new cages that were more than twice the size of those at IBR. For the first time since their capture in the jungle, our refugees had something to sit on comfortably and enough room to extend their cramped and pitiful limbs. They even had food containers and objects to handle and explore. Our delight at seeing them relish even these minor improvements was shadowed by our anxiety about what might follow. We were on an uncharted course, and the future of the animals was to be tested as their case passed through the courts.

The events of the next few days did not augur well. Taub's attorneys swung into action, demanding the return of their client's property. We were shocked to hear them introduce two recent US Department of Agriculture reports of inspections of IBR, marked 'Minor deficiencies' and 'No deficiencies noted'. Judge David Cahoon listened to the assurances of improvements given by a veterinarian who had worked earlier for Taub, yet refused to hear from our experts, who were prepared to swear that a return to IBR would jeopardize the monkeys' safety and well-being. Taub's motion to have the monkeys returned was granted. The abused were to be returned to their abuser the next day.

That night the monkeys disappeared. Bench warrants were issued for the arrest of Ingrid, Jean Goldenberg, director of the Washington Humane Society/SPCA, and Lori Lehner, whose home had been the monkeys' temporary resting place. Lori spent a night in jail before it was decided that there was insufficient evidence against any of the women.

Taub then held a press conference, demanding the return of the monkeys, which he now valued at between $60 and $90,000 each (a total value, according to Taub's arithmetic, of between $1,020,000 and $1,530,000 for an experiment costing a total of $221,000). Taub then offered only a $200 reward for their return.

The problem now was that without the monkeys there could be no criminal prosecution of Taub. Yet to return the monkeys would most likely mean their further suffering and death at Taub's hands. Negotiations began between the police and the monkeys' new guardians, through an intermediary. Secret conditions were agreed upon—mainly that if the monkeys were returned, they would not be returned to IBR. But the guardians' trust was betrayed, not by the police but by the court. No sooner were the monkeys back in Maryland than Judge Cahoon cancelled a full hearing without ever allowing any of the State's witnesses to testify. He immediately ordered the monkeys back to IBR. A crowd gathered at Lori's home, and people stood in the street and cried as the monkeys were loaded into Taub's rented truck. Wellwishers and those who had come to love the monkeys then stood vigil outside IBR, hoping for new developments to save the monkeys.

Taub on Trial

Taub was now charged with seventeen counts of cruelty to animals: one count for each monkey. Meanwhile the National Institutes of Health (NIH) announced its suspension of Taub's grant after conducting its own investigation and set a date for Taub to account for his expenditures and research results. At later hearings of the US House Subcommittee on Science, Research, and Technology, at which I testified on the conditions at IBR, the NIH admitted that in the IBR case, their system had failed.

Five days after the monkeys were sent to IBR, one of them was injured and another, Charlie, died of what Taub described as a 'heart attack'. These two wild male macaques had been placed together in a cage just 17 inches wide, while a commercial steam cleaner was operated in the room—resulting in a fight, as even a novice could have predicted. The police demanded Charlie's body, which was sent to Cornell University for a necropsy. The examiner reported back that the cause of death could not be determined because some important parts were missing, namely Charlie's heart, lungs, kidneys, a testicle and several glands. Judge Cahoon, finally realizing his mistake, reversed his earlier order and shipped the monkeys out of IBR and into safekeeping at NIH's Poolesville, Maryland, primate quarantine centre. There they joined almost 1,000 other unfortunate primates. The NIH was ordered not to take any 'extraordinary measures' unless authorized by the court. Nonetheless, Hard Times had to be destroyed after being in great pain and paralysed from the waist down for two days. Taub's surgery had caught up with Hard Times. Taub fought to deny this monkey even his final release, arguing that he wanted to keep Hard Times alive to complete his experiments. Next Nero's arm had to be amputated when a chronic bone infection that had originated months earlier in Taub's laboratory threatened his life. Again Taub fought the action. Today Nero is in much better shape, without his mutilated arm.

As for the criminal trials, the first one lasted a week, during which time Taub was defended by two of Washington's most prestigious law firms, Arnold and Porter, and Miller, Miller, and Steinberg.

The animal experimentation community didn't know what to do; it could take the risky step of ostracizing one of its own, or clutch Taub to its bosom and blame the whole incident on 'lay ignorance'. For the most part it chose the latter course. We had cogent testimony from experts, but clearly we presented a threat to others in the animal experimentation industry. Taub's defence fund grew. He sat flanked by six attorneys, his public relations representatives behind him, while Roger Galvin, the Assistant State's Attorney, stood alone, presenting the case for the State of Maryland.

Taub was vociferous in his own defence, even appearing to frustrate his counsel by his loquaciousness. The *Washington Post* viewed his stance as that of 'a professor lecturing a class full of students'. He had nothing but contempt for our concerns and went so far as to charge that photographs introduced by the prosecution were 'staged' and to insinuate that someone had bribed the caretakers into doing a sloppy job.

It soon became clear that psychological suffering, a lack of cage space and critical sanitation problems would not be considered violations of the law by the courts. We knew we were in for an uphill fight.

THE VERDICT

On 23 November 1981 Taub was found guilty of six counts of cruelty for failing to provide proper veterinary care to six of the monkeys. It is hard to describe our feelings when the verdict was announced, but at last now, whatever might happen to the monkeys as we continued to fight for their safety, the public would know that something was definitely wrong with the way in which some segments of the scientific community operated. The criminal conviction had chipped a hole in the wall that protects animal experimenters from public scrutiny.

As we had expected, Taub appealed his conviction. The second trial was even more difficult. This time the new judge required that the prosecution present only evidence relating to the six monkeys who had figured in the conviction—no matter what the other monkeys had been through, the jury would not be allowed to know. The twelve jurors were instructed that they must find Taub not guilty if they could not unanimously determine that the monkeys had suffered physical pain extending beyond their deafferant limbs. . . .

Two researchers, friends of Taub from the University of Pennsylvania, testified that monkeys were nothing more than 'defecating machines', that it was acceptable not to administer veterinary care for a broken arm and that an infestation of cockroaches provided a 'good source of ambient protein' for laboratory primates. To testimony by one of Taub's expert witnesses that there were 'no data' to suggest that heavy accumulations of excrement were a health hazard, Mr Galvin rebutted that if this were true, the American public had been fooled into thinking they needed sewage systems.

AFTERMATH OF THE SILVER SPRING MONKEYS CASE

Unfortunately, there were many things that the jury was never allowed to consider in making its decision, things it was never allowed to hear, know about, or see. For example, the jury was not permitted to hear about the discovery of two 55-gallon barrels filled with the corpses of monkeys and weighted down with used auto parts and wood. The jury could not ask, 'What became of them? How did they die?' The jury was never allowed to hear that Taub was denied a grant application because between 80 and 90 per cent of his animal subjects died before the end of his experiments. It could not see the 1979 US Department of Agriculture inspection report that read: 'Floors were dirty with blood stains all over them.' It was never allowed to know that Taub operated illegally, in violation of federal law, for seven years, while receiving hundreds of thousands of federal tax dollars. The jury did not know that Caligula suffered from gangrene and mutilated his own chest cavity, that blood splattered the wall and ceiling of the converted refrigerator chamber, that the NIH had investigated Taub and found him in violation of its own guidelines, that Charlie had died of an unexplained 'heart attack'. It was never allowed to see or hear of the surgically severed monkey hand or the skull that Taub used as paperweights in his office. And, perhaps most unfortunately, the jury was never allowed to see the living evidence, the monkeys themselves.

With all the new restrictions and limitations, four of the jury members felt there was insufficient evidence left to convict Taub without doubt, while eight of the jurors wanted a guilty verdict on all six counts. The verdict, of course, had to be unanimous. After two and a half days of deliberation the jurors reached agreement. The jurors unanimously found Taub guilty on one count. Later conversations with members of the jury showed how hopelessly restricted they had felt. A local newspaper report described the jurors' 'unprecedented' interest in following through on the case and their concern for the fate of the monkeys.

Taub was not to be stopped. He appealed this conviction to the Maryland Court of Appeals in Baltimore and this time succeeded. The court, after months of waiting, ruled that animal experimenters who receive federal tax funding do not have to obey the State anti-cruelty laws. No matter how heinous the deeds committed by an animal experimenter in Maryland, the court held that the experimenter could no be prosecuted. Sadly, the court did not consider whether or not Taub had treated the monkeys cruelly. The court made it clear that it was not interested in resolving this question. Rather, as stated in its decision, 'The issue in this case is whether the animal cruelty statute . . . is applicable to research pursuant to a federal program . . . we do not believe the legislature intended [the cruelty statute] to apply to this type of research activity under a federal program. We shall, therefore, reverse Dr Taub's conviction. . .' (*Taub v. State,* 296 Md 439 (1983)). The court's opinion enraged not only the Maryland State's Attorneys Office but also the many scientists and supporters who saw Taub slip through a crack in the criminal justice system.

At the time of writing, the fate of the monkeys is undetermined. Taub, encouraged by the reversal of his conviction, appealed against the NIH's decision to terminate his grant. If this application is successful, he has pledged to continue his experiment, which involves surgically crippling the monkeys' remaining normal arms and, ten days later, 'sacrificing' them. This would probably take place at the University of Pennsylvania, where some of his closest colleagues are employed. We have vowed never to let this happen.

The Taub case has been an intense, consuming battle, accompanied by many small battles. It devoured our time and resources, taught us some new values and confirmed some old ones. It renewed our resolve to research our targets carefully and thoroughly before 'going public'. It made us understand how valuable persistence is.

The ALF and the "Unnecessary Fuss" Video

LAWRENCE FINSEN AND SUSAN FINSEN

In 1984, four years after the Silver Spring monkey trial made national headlines, PETA (People for the Ethical Treatment of Animals) was once again at the heart of a controversy which led to an extended, high-pitched battle between researchers and activists. The cause of the outcry was a series of videotapes stolen from a head injury research laboratory at the University of Pennsylvania by the Animal Liberation Front (ALF) which showed experiments being conducted on baboons by Dr. Thomas Gennarelli. The ALF delivered the tapes to PETA, whose edited thirty-minute documentary taken from footage of the tapes, ironically titled "Unnecessary Fuss," was considered so damning that even those who had helped fund Gennarelli's study were moved to abandon his defense once they saw his methods in practice. The story of the video and the controversy is here told by Lawrence Finsen and Susan Finsen. Lawrence Finsen is professor of philosophy at the University of Redlands in California. Susan Finsen is also the author of the article "Obstacles to Legal Rights for Animals: Can We Get There from Here?" Both are cofounders of a grassroots animal rights group, Californians for the Ethical Treatment of Animals.

P ETA [People for the Ethical Treatment of Animals] has served on a number of occasions as liaison between the Animal Liberation Front (ALF) and the media, as the ALF could not present their own results and case to the press very readily, given the illegal, underground nature of many of their

Excerpted from *The Animal Rights Movement in America: From Compassion to Respect,* by Lawrence Finsen and Susan Finsen (New York: Twayne Publishers, 1994). Copyright © 1994 by Twayne Publishers. Reprinted with permission.

actions. On 28 May 1984 such a raid was made on the laboratory of Thomas Gennarelli at the University of Pennsylvania. Gennarelli had been receiving approximately $1 million per year in federal grants for 13 years to study head injuries of the type received in sports and automobile accidents. For many years the grants had gone into the development of a device that could deliver precisely measured blows to the heads of baboons, so that subsequent investigations could differentiate between severity of blows in an objective, reliable manner. After the device was ready, the research involved cementing the device onto the heads of baboons, and then delivering blows of different force to the baboons. Learning of the experiments, a local group, the Pennsylvania Animal Rights Coalition (PARC), and the national group, Fund for Animals, denounced them. Gennarelli met with the groups but refused to let them inspect the laboratory.

The ALF raiders were greeted with a surprise when they entered the lab: the researchers had maintained a record of their research on videotape. Rather than disturbing the laboratory or liberating any animals, the raiders simply removed some 60 hours of videotapes, recognizing their value to the movement. And in fact, that value was immense. The ALF's press release called the tapes the "Watergate tapes of the animal rights movement." PETA (to which the ALF had delivered the tapes) offered the Department of Health and Human Services (HHS), the branch of government that has oversight of the National Institutes of Health (NIH), the opportunity to view the entire 60 hours of tapes, but HHS officials declined. Despite NIH Director Dr. James Wyngaarden's public assurances that Gennarelli's lab was "one of the best in the world," an inspection at this time revealed 74 violations of the Laboratory Animal Welfare Act.

By September, PETA had produced and made public a documentary based on 30 minutes excerpted from the tapes. Gennarelli had been quoted in a newspaper interview in 1983 as saying he did not want his work publicized because it could "stir up all sorts of unnecessary fuss among those who are sensitive to these sorts of things," so the documentary was ironically titled *Unnecessary Fuss*. And indeed it did stir up quite a bit of fuss. The tape showed a brutal experiment, and the impact on most viewers on seeing the baboons receiving numerous intense blows, as well as their subsequent stupors and inability to stand or even hold their heads up certainly accounts for the tremendous power of the tape to move audiences. The tapes not only packed this tremendous emotive force but also revealed numerous violations of the Federal Animal Welfare Act (e.g., surgeries that were not aseptic, animals left unattended on the operating table, researchers smoked while performing surgery), and a cavalier attitude of the researchers toward the intense suffering that the baboons must surely have undergone. One of the most damning aspects of the excruciating 30 minutes was a scene in which researchers were shown removing the device from a number of the baboons' heads. After spending millions of taxpayers' dollars to develop a device that would deliver precisely measured blows to the head, and after imposing severe suffering on dozens of baboons, the researchers confounded their own results by using hammer and chisel to remove the cemented devices from the heads of the baboons. Any precise measure was now meaningless in light of the additional, unmeasured blows from screwdriver and hammer. The words of "Sonya," a spokesperson for the ALF, expressed the widespread feeling: the videotapes revealed "the callousness, wastefulness, inhumanity, and arrogance of the animal experimentation industry."

"NORMAL, LEGAL CHANNELS"

Throughout the year following the break-in, efforts were made by animal rights activists and organizations to shut down Gennarelli's lab from a variety of directions. In November 1984 law professors from the University of Pennsylvania (led by Professor Gary Francione, a longtime animal rights activist) attempted to initiate a dialogue with the research committee of the university but were not allowed to show the committee *Unnecessary Fuss* or to bring an independent scientific advisor to the meeting. In January 1985 it was revealed that the head of the research committee, Dr. Jacob Abel, had previously worked with Gennarelli on a head injury project. In April 1985 a mass demonstration drew 1,500 people to the university campus. In June the university appointed a "blue-ribbon" committee to investigate allegations against the lab. The report, issued in August, maintained that there were no problems, no wrongdoing at the lab. It was later discovered that one of Gennarelli's grant applications mentioned the chair of the blue-ribbon committee, Truman Schnabel, as having been instrumental in the "planning and implementation of the Head Injury Clinical Research Center."

Having tried unsuccessfully to get HHS officials to view the tapes in their entirety, PETA took their case to Congress, which was soon to be considering an appropriations bill for the NIH. They succeeded in securing two showings of *Unnecessary Fuss* on Capitol Hill, and in May 1985 some 60 members of Congress petitioned HHS Director Margaret Heckler to stop funding for Gennarelli's lab, still without success. A number of animal rights organizations joined the cause, with the International Society for Animal Rights (ISAR), the National Antivivisection Society (NAVS), and the American Antivivisection Society (AAVS) all helping to fund a series of newspaper advertisements in the home districts of the 13 members of Congress on the Health and Human Services subcommittee of the House Appropriations Committee, which had the power to amend the appropriations bill and thereby deny funding to Gennarelli's lab. All these efforts failed, and, despite the heat, Gennarelli's lab was continuing with its research.

In fact, throughout this period local law-enforcement agencies in Pennsylvania were turning up the heat on the animal rights activists, rather than the laboratory. [PETA's Alex] Pacheco and members of the Pennsylvania Animal Rights Coalition who had held a joint PARC/PETA press conference in October 1985 were served with subpoenas to appear before a grand jury investigating the break-in and theft of the tapes. Activists maintained that the investigation involved numerous violations of their civil rights.

It was clear that "normal, legal channels" were not succeeding in bringing about any relief for the baboons. By July 1985 the laboratory had been exposed, protests had occurred, and members of Congress had even petitioned HHS Director Heckler to interrupt funding of the lab—but all to no avail. PETA turned to civil disobedience. The 100 protesters had been through a day-long training session, involving coaching by veterans of civil disobedience protests, attorneys from the Animal Legal Defense Fund (ALDF), and PETA leaders.

SUCCESS THROUGH DISSENT

Initially, the activists' plan was to occupy NIH offices and present their demands of the NIH: to halt funding of Gennarelli's lab, to stop using baboons in the lab, and to include an animal advocate on the NIH grant committee. On 15 July 101 activists went into the eighth-floor offices of Murray Goldstein, director of the NIH division that funded the lab, and sat down, intending to remain until arrested and removed by police for trespassing. They expected to be there a few hours at most. After a few hours NIH personnel had abandoned the surrounding suite of offices, and the protesters now occupied these as well. All contact with the activists was cut off.

Apparently, the NIH had decided to wait out the protesters, who they figured would certainly give up after a day or so without food or contacts. The activists were not to be defeated so easily: they hauled food up the eight stories in a basket tied to a rope. Then a congressman's wife ended the food and telephone embargo with a well-placed phone call of her own. Banners hung from the windows of the NIH building, and outside a candlelight vigil was maintained by supporters each night. Alex Hershaft of the Farm Animal Reform Movement (FARM) initiated a hunger strike on the third day to increase the pressure on the NIH. On the fourth day, HHS Director Heckler announced she was suspending delivery of funds to Gennarelli's lab until an NIH investigation was complete. Her action, she claimed, was based on a preliminary report of the investigating team, which stated that there were indications that the laboratory had failed "to comply with the Public Health Service Policy for the care and use of laboratory animals." (Later, activists who were part of the protest were to cite a different account of Heckler's acquiescence, stating that Heckler finally viewed *Unnecessary Fuss* as a result of the sit-in, and before the 30-minute film was over she had called to cancel Gennarelli's funding.) At any rate, the activists emerged victorious from the building on July 18.

A few days after the sit-in James Kilpatrick viewed *Unnecessary Fuss* and was moved to write a passionate piece in his nationally syndicated column entitled "Brutal Research Techniques Unacceptable." The conservative columnist wrote: "though I am no antivivisectionist, I found [the film] appalling. . . . [I]t was high time for someone to rescue these baboons from the hands of their tormentors." Kilpatrick's column was followed by editorials expressing support for the activists and concern about controls on research in major media sources such as the *Washington Post* and the *New York Times*, the latter advocating passage of the Dole-Brown bill to impose tighter controls on laboratories, currently under consideration by Congress. NBC's "Nightly News" and "Today Show," Cable Network News, and other broadcasters showed portions of *Unnecessary Fuss,* giving many viewers a glimpse of the horrible suffering wrought by Gennarelli's research.

The campaign had lasted over a year, but the persistence and careful planning had paid off. The campaign had a specific, limited focus, although media coverage appropriately related the issues in question to larger questions about control of animal research. Numerous channels were pursued to close the lab, civil disobedience being employed only when it was clear that other avenues were blocked. Despite the Philadelphia district attorney's (unsuccessful) attempt to discover who had conducted the raid, little criticism of the ALF's break-in has been raised. In fact, the break-in became a classic example in the argument for the underground activities of the ALF—after all, had they not entered illegally and stolen the tapes, the movement would never have had the crucially damning information that ultimately closed the lab down.

Thus the modern animal rights movement was launched by a number of successes that dramatized what the new philosophies were pointing out: that the plight of animals was not the aberrant behavior of occasional acts of cruelty but exploitation at the hands of respected, government-sanctioned institutions as business as usual. Additionally, these early actions dramatized just how far we have come from the early days of the ASPCA, when prosecution of individual wrongdoers (once anti-cruelty statutes were on the books) and public education seemed the promising routes.

CHRONOLOGY

1641
Nathanial Ward of the Massachusetts Bay Colony composes the "Body of Liberties," which forbids "tyranny or cruelty towards any brute creature."

1822
Dick Martin's Act, an act prohibiting bullbaiting and other cruelties, is proposed and becomes law on June 10.

1828
A bill similar to Dick Martin's passes in New York.

1835
Anticruelty statutes become law in Massachusetts.

1838
Connecticut and Wisconsin adopt anticruelty statutes.

1866
The American Society for the Prevention of Cruelty to Animals (ASPCA), an organization dedicated to "promoting humane principles, preventing cruelty, and alleviating pain, fear, and suffering in all animals," is founded by Henry Bergh in April.

1868
The Massachusetts Society for the Prevention of Cruelty to Animals (MSPCA), an organization modeled after Bergh's, is founded by George Angell.

1870
A Washington chapter (WHSPCA) is founded.

1877

The American Humane Association (AHA), the first national organization promoting the welfare of animals and children, is founded.

1883

The American Anti-Vivisection Society (AAVS) is founded by Caroline Earle White to lobby against animal research in America.

1885

French scientist Louis Pasteur develops a rabies vaccine through his experiments with rabbits and dogs.

1899

The Animal Rescue League of Boston, which is "committed to the rescue and relief of suffering homeless animals," is founded by Anna Harris Smith; the Anti-Cruelty Society, "dedicated to helping companion animals and their guardians forge closer relationships," is founded in Chicago.

1907

Every state in the union has an anticruelty statute.

1910

A law passes in Massachusetts allowing the MSPCA to inspect slaughterhouses; vigorous efforts to repeal the law are quashed.

1920

An antivivisection measure placed on the California ballot is defeated by a two-to-one vote.

1949

The Metcalf-Hatch Act, which permits researchers to seize unclaimed animals from shelters, is passed in Minnesota, followed by Baltimore and Los Angeles.

1951

Christine Stevens founds the Animal Welfare Institute, a U.S. organization that monitors the treatment of research animals.

1958

The Humane Slaughter Act is passed: "No method of slaughter or handling in connection with slaughtering shall be deemed to comply with public policy of the United States unless it is humane."

1959

British researchers William Russell and Rex Burch publish the *Principles of Humane Experimental Technique,* which leads to the search for alternatives to animal testing.

1964

English writer Ruth Harrison's book *Animal Machines* stimulates concern for animals and leads to the development of animal welfare policies and regulations in several western European countries.

1966

The Animal Welfare Act is passed, regulating transportation, sale, and handling of cats, dogs, and certain other animals for use in research and experimentation.

1972

The Marine Mammal Protection Act is passed, which prohibits the killing, capturing, or harassment of marine mammals without a permit; Ronnie Lee and Cliff Goodman found the militant group Band of Mercy, which will later become the Animal Liberation Front (ALF).

1973

The Endangered Species Act is passed, which designates critical habitats for species ruled endangered by the secretary of the interior and develops programs for conservation.

1975

Activist Henry Spira coerces the New York Museum of Natural History to cease its experiments on castrated cats.

1976

Amendments to the Animal Welfare Act are passed, granting slightly better protection for animals in transit and banning animal fighting venues.

1979

Spira leads a successful coalition to repeal the Metcalf-Hatch Act.

1980

Revlon, caving in to Spira's prodding, desists its Draize tests, which involve the use of inflammatory substances in the eyes of albino rabbits.

1981

Alex Pacheco, founder of People for the Ethical Treatment of Animals (PETA) infiltrates the Institute of Behavioral Research in Silver Spring, Maryland, where he discovers monkeys suffering from neglect and abuse; the head researcher, Edward Taub, is found guilty of six of seventeen counts for cruelty to animals, but the conviction is later reversed.

1984

ALF steals six years' worth of research data from the lab of Thomas Gennarelli at the University of Pennsylvania Head Injury Laboratory, showing footage of researchers delivering severe blows to the heads of baboons; ALF delivers it to PETA, and ferocious legal battles ensue.

1985

The Health Research Extension Act of 1985 is passed, which establishes the formation of state-sponsored animal care committees and the development of plans to reduce use and suffering; the Food Security Act is passed, allowing the secretary of agriculture to "set standards governing the humane care of animals by dealers, research facilities, and exhibitors."

1987
Revlon agrees to stop all animal testing and to contribute millions of dollars to alternate research.

1989
The Mice for Biomedical Research Law is passed, enabling facilities to provide a continued supply of mice for research.

1990
Las Vegas nightclub entertainer Bobby Berosini sues PETA for defamation of character after PETA videotaped Berosini and accused him of abusing the orangutans used in his act; PETA countersues, but the judge rules in Berosini's favor.

1994
The Nevada Supreme Court reverses the earlier decision against PETA after seeing the Berosini videotape.

2001
After seesawing, Congress decides against including rats and mice under the revised Animal Welfare Protection Act.

FOR FURTHER RESEARCH

Ted Benton, *Natural Relations: Ecology, Animal Rights, and Social Justice.* New York: Verso, 1993.

Lawrence Finsen and Susan Finsen, *The Animal Rights Movement in America: From Compassion to Respect.* New York: Twayne, 1994.

Michael Allen Fox, *The Case for Animal Experimentation.* Berkeley: University of California Press, 1986.

Michael W. Fox, *Farm Animals: Husbandry, Behavior, and Veterinary Practice.* Baltimore: University Park, 1984.

Stanley Godlovitch, Rosalind Godlovitch, and John Harris, eds., *Animals, Men, and Morals.* New York: Grove, 1974.

Harold D. Guither, *Animal Rights: History and Scope of a Radical Social Movement.* Carbondale: Southern Illinois University Press, 1998.

Ruth Harrison, *Animal Machines.* London: Vincent Stuart, 1964.

James M. Jasper and Dorothy Nelkin, *The Animal Rights Crusade: The Growth of a Moral Protest.* New York: Macmillan, 1992.

Jim Mason and Peter Singer, *Animal Factories.* New York: Crown, 1980.

Mary Midgeley, *Animals and Why They Matter.* Athens: University of Georgia Press, 1983.

Ingrid Newkirk, *Free the Animals!* Chicago: Noble, 1992.

James Rachels, *Created from Animals: The Moral Implications of Darwinism.* Oxford: Oxford University Press, 1990.

Tom Regan, *The Case for Animal Rights*. Berkeley: University of California Press, 1983.

Tom Regan and Peter Singer, *Animal Rights and Human Obligations*. Englewood Cliffs, NJ: Prentice-Hall, 1989.

Bernard Rollin, *Animal Rights and Human Morality*. Buffalo, NY: Prometheus Books, 1981.

———, *The Unheeded Cry: Animal Consciousness, Pain, and Science*. Oxford: Oxford University Press, 1990.

Andrew Rowan, *Of Mice, Models, and Men: A Critical Evaluation of Animal Research*. Albany: State University of New York Press, 1984.

Hans Ruesch, *Slaughter of the Innocent*. New York: Bantam Books, 1978.

Richard D. Ryder, *Animal Revolution: Changing Attitudes Toward Speciesism*. Oxford: Blackwell, 1989.

Henry Salt, *Animals' Rights Considered in Relation to Social Progress*. 1892. Reprint, Clarks Summit, PA: Centaur/State Mutual Book, 1985.

Peter Singer, *Animal Liberation*. Rev. ed. New York: Avon Books, 1990.

Peter Singer, ed., *In Defense of Animals*. New York: Basil Blackwell, 1985.

Marjorie Spiegel, *The Dreaded Comparison: Human and Animal Slavery*. New York: Mirror Books, 1988.

E.S. Turner, *All Heaven in a Rage*. London: Michael Joseph, 1964.

John Vyvyan, *In Pity and in Anger: A Study of the Use of Animals in Science*. Marblehead, MA: Micah Publications, 1988.

INDEX

Abel, James, 206
"Act to Prevent the Cruel and Improper Treatment of Cattle, An" (Martin), 12–13
Adams, Carol, 151
Agassiz, Louis, 77
agribusiness
post-WWII growth of, 18
American Animal Welfare Federation, 155
American Antivivisection Society (AAVS), 16, 41
animal rights vs. welfare position of, 151
founding of, 41–45
as woman's movement, 44–45
American Association for the Spread of Knowledge of the Extent and Existing Methods of Vivisection, 48
American Humane Association (AHA), 15
antivivisection movement and, 17
American Medical Association (AMA), 16
American Museum of Natural History
animal experimentation by, 85–86
Henry Spira's campaign against, 22, 86, 88–93
American Society for the Prevention of Cruelty to Animals (ASPCA)

anti-Draize test campaign and, 179
antivivisection movement and, 17, 43–44
criticism of, 80
Henry Bergh and founding of, 13–15, 70–81
roots of, 71–72
Amory, Cleveland, 20, 55
Black Beauty Ranch and, 108–14
Angell, George T., 14–16
animal experimentation
activists' argument against, 146–47
ALF raids against, 66–67, 204
alternatives to, 147
defense of, 49–50
is necessary for scientific progress, 139–40
Kewalo dolphin case, 164–73
regulation of, 53–54
vs. abolition of, AAVS position on, 43–44
Silver Spring monkeys case, 187–202
Animal Liberation (Singer), 21, 23, 82, 141
Animal Liberation Front (ALF), 22–24, 62, 64–65
goals of, 67
tactics of, 66–67, 68
Unnecessary Fuss video and, 203–209
animal rights
activists

dangers posed by, 147–49
demographics of, 87
vs. animal welfare, 19–20,
141–42, 152–54
influence of Charles Darwin
on, 34–40
infringement of, and human
accountability, 121–22
movement
growth of, in 1980s, 62–68
has sold out to "new
welfarists," 150–62
Henry Spira and grassroots
activism in, 82–97
is dangerous to scientific
progress, 139–40
media coverage of, 92–93
radicalization in, 55–56
*Animal Rights and Human
Morality* (Rollin), 129
*Animal Rights and Human
Obligations* (Regan), 116
*Animal Rights Crusade: The
Growth of a Moral Protest, The*
(Jasper and Nelkin), 52
*Animal Rights Movement in
America: From Compassion to
Respect, The* (Finsen and
Finsen), 62, 195, 203
Animal Rights Reporter
(magazine), 195
animals, moral status of, 116,
129, 131–34
contractarianism and, 118–19
cruelty-kindness views on,
119–20
Darwinism and, 130
inherent value and rights
view of, 125–28
and rationality of animal
behavior, 135–36

utilitarianism and, 120–25
Animals' Agenda (magazine),
56, 161
animal sanctuaries, 60
Animal Welfare Act of 1966,
54, 141, 148
amendments to, 153–54
"new welfarism" and, 156–58
*Animal Welfare and Human
Values* (Preece and
Chamberlain), 34
Animal Welfare Institute,
52–53
anthropocentrism
as justification for animal
research, 102
anticruelty societies
antivivisection movement
and, 42
wealth of, 55–57
antivivisection movement,
15–18
decline of, 50–51
early opposition to, 49
in late-nineteenth-century
U.S., 41–51
Appleton, Emily, 14
a priori knowledge
Kant's theory of reason and,
133–34
Arcadian, The (journal), 79
Aronson, Lester, 86, 93
Aspen Hill sanctuary
PETA and, 158–61
Association for the Assessment
and Accreditation of
Laboratory Animal Care
International (AAALAC),
148
Astor, Jacob, Jr., 14
Avon

position of, 152, 153
anti-Draize test campaign
and, 179
Hume, David J., 133, 137
Humphrey, Hubert, 18
Hunt Saboteurs Association, 65
Hutcheson, Francis, 30

Institute for Behavioral
Research, 23
conditions of animals at,
189–90, 191–92
raid on, 196–97
see also Silver Spring monkeys
case
International Society for
Animal Rights, 19–20

Jasper, James M., 52
Johnson, Frank, 177, 178, 182
Johnson, Samuel, 30, 32
Jones, Helen, 19
Journal of Zoophily, 45

Kant, Immanuel, 129
Keen, 49
Kewalo dolphin case, 164–71
legacy of, 172–73
Keynes, Milton, 65
Kilpatrick, James, 208
Kingsley, Charles, 39
Koch, Ed, 22, 91, 92
Kunz, John, 193

Laboratory Animal Welfare
Act of 1966, 20, 156, 204
Lamarck, Jean de, 35, 37
language
moral status of animals and,
131–32
Lawrence, John, 30

LD50 test, 22
Lectures on Ethics (Kant), 129,
134
Lederberg, Joshua, 185
Lee, Ronnie, 23, 65
Leffingwell, Albert, 44
legislative campaigns
antivivisection, 47–49
Lehner, Lori, 197
LeVasseur, Kenneth W.,
164–73
Life (magazine), 20, 53
Lincoln, Abraham, 13, 73
lithium, research on, 144
Lovell, George S., 43
Lovell, Mary F., 41, 42–44, 45
Lyell, Charles, 36

Malthus, Thomas, 36
*Man and the Natural World: A
History of the Modern
Sensibility* (Thomas), 27
Mandeville, Bernard de, 32
*Man Kind? Our Incredible War
on Wildlife* (Amory), 110
Marine Mammal Protection
Act of 1967, 20
Martin, Richard, 12
McArdle, John, 195
McAuliffe, John, 196
McGreal, Shirley, 107
McMillan, James, 16
Mead, Marc, 194
meat-eating
defense of, 30–31
mechanism
in animal psychology studies,
39–40
media
coverage of animal rights
movement, 92–93